THE ART *of* ARRANGING FLOWERS

THE

ART

of

ARRANGING
FLOWERS

·LYNNE BRANARD·

BERKLEY BOOKS, NEW YORK

THE BERKLEY PUBLISHING GROUP
Published by the Penguin Group
Penguin Group (USA) LLC
375 Hudson Street, New York, New York 10014

USA • Canada • UK • Ireland • Australia • New Zealand • India • South Africa • China

penguin.com

A Penguin Random House Company

This book is an original publication of The Berkley Publishing Group.

Library of Congress Cataloging-in-Publication Data

Branard, Lynne.
The art of arranging flowers / Lynne Branard.
p. cm.
ISBN 978-0-425-27271-8 (pbk.)
1. Florists—Fiction. 2. Single women—Fiction. 3. Flower arrangement—Fiction.
4. Flower language—Fiction. 5. Community life—Fiction. 6. Psychological fiction.
7. Washington (State)—Fiction. I. Title.
PS3602.R34485A37 2014
813'.6—dc23
2014001466

PUBLISHING HISTORY
Berkley trade paperback edition / June 2014

PRINTED IN THE UNITED STATES OF AMERICA

10 9 8 7 6 5 4 3 2 1

Cover photo by Thinkstock.
Cover design by Lesley Worrell.
Interior text design by Kristin del Rosario.

To Sally McMillan,
midwife of all my stories, for the calm, easy way you deliver bad news
and the joyful, delighted way you share the good.
For standing with me, for encouraging me,
for always caring about what happens to me,
to my loved ones, and to my work.
You are a brave and beautiful woman
and I am deeply, deeply honored to call you my friend.

I want to unfold. I don't want to stay folded anywhere,
because where I am folded, there I am a lie.

—RILKE

·PROLOGUE·

DAISY was not crazy. At least not like they said. She wasn't unstable or paranoid. She wasn't dissociative or delusional, nor did she ever display homicidal tendencies. She didn't impose some means of self-mutilation or harbor a borderline personality. She did not require restraints or group therapy and she never intended harm. She took her meds and she was fine. She was not crazy.

The day she died, that cold gray day when I withdrew into myself, that day I cleaned the house from top to bottom, wiped down every wall, emptied every trash can and discarded most of my clothes, that day when I scrubbed and mopped and threw away the things of no matter, closed the curtains in the front room, unplugged all the clocks and disconnected my phone, put on my grandmother's only black suit, changed the sheets, and lay down on the bed, I was the one who was crazy. I was the one who should have caused everyone worry. I was the one who should have been locked up and tended to. I was the one who should have been restrained and drugged and analyzed, because unlike my beautiful and gentle sister, I meant harm to everything alive and breathing.

I meant harm to my colleagues and to my neighbors, to the doctor who could not bring himself to say she was dead but rather mumbled to me about some deleterious psychosis and charted in his notes the date and time that she "expired." I meant harm to the chaplain who spoke of death as if it were merely waking up from a troublesome night of sleep, the librarian who wanted to fill my arms with books about grief and loss, the church lady who left loaves of bread and tins of cookies at my door, the mailman who kept bringing bills and cards and form letters from magazines for trial subscriptions, the children laughing as they passed by on the street, the birds that would not stop singing, the nurse who called to tell me I left my coat in the waiting room, and all the people watching as I entered and exited her room without saying a single word, shedding a single tear, asking a single question. I hated them all, and I meant harm to every one of them.

But of course, they never knew they were in danger. They never perceived that I could manage such evil, was capable of such heinous, horrible desires. They never asked. And if they had, they would have discovered that the harm I meant for everyone else was secondary to the harm I meant for myself. Mostly, I just wanted to die with Daisy. I wanted to be done with this life of come-and-go mothers and missing fathers. I wanted out of this homeless existence. I wanted to be dead just like my sister. And for a long time I was. It was just that no one knew. I took a leave of absence from law school, stayed in bed, ate only what was left in kitchen cabinets and at the door of my apartment.

I was crazy. I was broken. I was dead.

And then, one day I wasn't. It took months and it took grace and it took some unexpected slight shift of sadness that slipped just enough, just barely enough to make room for beauty. And once it happened, once I saw it happen, I got up from bed and I went out to the corner market for milk and chocolate bars and I decided to live.

Now I am alive and breathing and mostly back together, damaged but still "strong in the broken places," as Hemingway would say.

When people first asked me about my business venture, about why I do what I do, how I switched from being a student of law to a florist, I used to shake my head, look around at where I was standing, where they were asking, and I would say, "The flowers saved me."

Of course, that is never the answer anyone expects to hear. It's an explanation that's not deemed acceptable. Most people don't understand a relationship with plants, a love of stalks and blooms, the art of arranging flowers, and most people never heard about my sister's death and my coming back to life.

I cannot fully tell the story of being pulled out of bed one dawn in early spring by the sight of sharp, verdant leaves of ivy: sharp, verdant leaves that were alive and somehow creeping out of a small pot, motioning me to the window. I cannot explain the burst of color, the brightest blue of the hydrangea bush, so bright it hurt my eyes, the tip of the tiniest pink crocus shadowed by slender blades of grass. I can't articulate how I felt about the yellow monkey-flower, the sweet pea and the hollyhock, or how I was saved by the soft petals of the orange rose, the color so elegant, so masterful, it literally forced breath back into my body.

I used to try to explain about my death and resurrection when I was asked in innocence or passing why I became a florist, but I soon learned it is too much of a story. It is too intimate a portrait of loss, and most folks don't want to hear of deep longings, of grief being soothed by beauty. So I never tell that story even when I'm asked how I survived Daisy's death. I never say that I owe flowers my life and that I am simply giving back to the source of my salvation. I never say that I grow, select, arrange, and sell flowers because

I now belong to them and because it is my way to honor them. They snatched me from the jaws of death and set me back on the path of life.

I just mention the community college courses in floral arrangements and the chance meeting of the former owner of the florist shop in the small Washington town near my mother's home place. I just explain about the little bit of money I had to invest and that flowers are easier to understand than people. I just say that as odd as it sounds, at the age of twenty-five, I discovered, suddenly and miraculously, that I have a gift for creating bouquets.

And of course, with that, they smile and nod and show a measure of appreciation and then ask if the price quoted online includes delivery. That's really all they want to know of a life like mine anyway, and really, that's all I should be willing to share.

And so, every morning for twenty years, I have risen and taken my place behind a counter, near a large refrigerated storage room known as the cooler, the smells of life and death mingled and waiting in every molecule of space, the deep and bright blooms from gardens near and far flashing all around, and I take in the deepest breath, holding it, closing my eyes, opening them at the moment I exhale, and I think of the magic of it all, the serendipitous magic of how a thing like grief can crack a heart wide open and how color and light, stemmed and covered in leaves, can knit it back together.

That is the real truth of who I am and what I do, but most people here in Creekside don't know anything about that. All they know is that I arrived and occupied Sam Jenkins's place just before they put in the stoplight at the intersection of Main and Fifth streets. They know I keep a file on everyone, remembering dates and favorite flowers.

They know my bouquets last longer and are cheaper than the flowers they order off the Internet. They know I have some knowledge of herbs and remedies and that I can take what they tell me and satisfy their desire of expression.

They know I live alone with my dog, Clementine, ride my bike or walk to work, have a van for deliveries.

They know my name is Ruby Jewell, that I'm Peaches Johnson Jewell's oldest child, Claudette and Wynon's only living grand-daughter, and that I own the Flower Shoppe.

·ONE·

R UBY, I can't believe I forgot again! Happy New Year, Clementine."

The wind chime on the front door sounds, and Clementine raises her head, yawns, and then settles back down; she is sleeping beneath the table, and I come around the corner. I am carrying a short clear glass vase filled with a bouquet of roses, yellow ones from Lubbock, six of them surrounded by thin stems of baby's breath with a few slender reeds of eucalyptus and bear grass.

"They are spectacular," Stan Marcus says, shaking his head. "Exactly what she likes. You are omnipotent."

"Stan, I keep a database. I knew it was your anniversary. It's not really omnipotence when the computer sends up a flag on the calendar page." I place the vase of roses next to the cash register. Stan is always one of my first customers of the New Year. His anniversary is the fifteenth day of January. It's typically very slow the week after the holidays and I get his bouquet made early.

"I should get one of those things," he replies.

"You don't have a calendar page on your computer?" I ask, ringing up the sale.

"No, I don't have a computer." He reaches in his back pocket for his wallet.

"Oh." I punch in the buttons: medium bouquet, no delivery, store pickup. "Stan, you're an accountant, how is it possible for you not to have a computer?"

He hands me his credit card. "I have Marcy. She does all the data entry, prints up those fancy forms. I keep up to date on the laws from journals and sort through boxes of receipts. I didn't start with a computer in 1962 and I just never found I needed one." He puts his wallet on the counter. "Yellow pads," he adds. "A carton of those and a calculator is all the computing I need."

"It's thirty-seven dollars," I say, running his card on the machine. "Well, maybe if you had one you'd remember your anniversary every year." I smile.

Stan Marcus was my very first customer in Creekside. I have made a floral arrangement for every anniversary, Valentine's Day, and his wife's birthday. Lucky for Stan and for me, Viola likes flowers. He rarely modifies his gift purchases.

"Oh, I don't know," he replies. "I guess I like finding out it's my anniversary with a phone call. Sort of gives me a rush, like it did forty-five years ago when I asked Viola to be my wife and she said yes. When you call to remind me, it just feels like the same surprise all over again, to remember I got to meet and marry the love of my life. I like hearing it from you. It's better than a flag on a screen."

"Okay," I say. "But one day Viola might like to know you went shopping for her, you know, ahead of time." I hand him back his card and the receipt.

"Viola likes flowers. She buys herself whatever she wants, but flowers, she says, should come from love."

"And it's a marvelous thing that you know that. It may be the reason you're still married after forty-five years," I note. I'm smiling again.

"Well, that and I take her over to Seattle a couple of times a year to stay at the Four Seasons. She does love a day in the city, a massage in the evening, and a glass of wine on the wharf at sunset."

"Yes, I can see why she loves you. She's a lucky woman, Stan."

"Always and forever, I am the lucky one." He winks at me and puts the Visa and receipt in his wallet and sticks it in his pocket. "And that is something I never forget."

"Do you need a card?" I ask, already knowing the answer.

"That has been purchased and signed."

I know that Stan picks out Viola's cards months in advance. He has a folder of them at his office. He told me of a particular stationery shop he visits when he goes to Post Falls to visit his mother in the nursing home. He often buys her flowers too, although she likes the dish gardens, African violets, succulents. I always pick her out something that lasts. She doesn't have a garden anymore, so she likes to take care of houseplants. Stan says that it gives her a sense of responsibility.

"Thank you, Ruby." He reaches for the vase. He lowers his face into the clump of flowers, takes in a deep breath, and grins. "Yellow roses for my girl from Texas. Some things never change."

"Viola has always made it clear what she likes." I close the register and rest my hands on my hips.

"See you in a couple of weeks," he says, remembering that it will be his wife's birthday soon.

I nod too. I know it well.

"She'll be sixty-five this year, you know? Doesn't look a day over forty," he adds.

"Then I'll order something special from the warehouse," I say.

He turns for the door. "You'll find just the right thing," he replies, "You always do. Good-bye, Ruby; good-bye, Clem." He speaks again to my dog, who is still sleeping soundly beneath the table behind me and does not reply.

I watch the sway of the chime as the breeze slides in through the door when he leaves. I turn to Clementine, my yellow lab, and she winks. I glance back to the street and notice the boy peeking in the window only after Stan has stepped away from the sidewalk and moved across the street.

· Two ·

THE Flower Shoppe," I say, answering the phone on the second ring, tugging my sweater around me. It's a bit chilly today.

"Ruby, it's Madeline from over at the church."

She doesn't have to tell me which church because I know Madeline and I know she's been the secretary at the Creekside Lutheran Congregation for as long as I've been the florist just up the street from where she works.

Ruth Jane is the secretary at St. Bede's Catholic and Miss Bertie is over at Harbor Light Baptist. There's a Foursquare Gospel and a Free Methodist Church in Creekside as well as a few other Christian meeting groups, but they don't have secretaries to order their flowers. Mostly I hear from pastors' wives and presidents of the women's councils of the other congregations, but Madeline and Ruth Jane and Miss Bertie are my best church contacts.

"Palms," I say, noting the date on the calendar. Madeline always calls in January, a few weeks before Ash Wednesday, to order fronds for the Palm Sunday church service. A small group of women on the altar guild dry and fold them into crosses to hand out the Sunday before Easter. It takes them at least a month to do all the work.

The Catholics just give out the stems, so Ruth Jane doesn't call and order until a week before the event, and the Baptists don't order any flowers for the spring season except the lilies. They don't care a thing about pomp and liturgy, but they do want their Easter lilies to line the stage and fill the windowsills at the sunrise service, and they do want them full and blooming when they pick them up after the eleven o'clock hour to take them home.

"We'll have the usual," she says, meaning she's ordering the stripped double palms with the split leaf fronds that I get from Plant City, Florida.

About five years ago Madeline saw a special offer listed in some church supplies catalog for palm fronds and just ordered direct when she was getting bulletins and communion wafers and qualified for free shipping. When the palms arrived—date palm fronds, stems of short, curved, green tender blades—the palm frond cross committee called an emergency meeting with the pastor and Madeline almost lost her job.

Stripped double palms are what the members of the altar guild want, and stripped double palms are all I order. Madeline doesn't try to pinch a penny when it comes to Palm Sunday anymore. She just tells me how many stems to order and who will be picking them up. She doesn't even ask me if the price went up; she just confirms the number and tells me the name of which altar guild member will be stopping by when they arrive and stays out of it.

"Sixty?" I ask, flipping through the Lutheran church notebook that I pulled off the shelf from beneath the register.

I use the computer calendar, but I also like to keep handwritten notes about my customers. All the regulars have their own notebooks: small spiral-bound notebooks, red, yellow, and blue ones that I buy in bulk and keep for five years before moving them to boxes in a back closet and starting over.

"Sounds right," she answers. "We never have more than forty in worship, but you know how the altar guild feels about running out of palm crosses. I tried to tell them one time that we could collect the crosses we didn't use, keep them in a good dry storage place, and save them for the next year, but you would have thought I suggested that we give the organist a raise."

I hear her take a breath.

"That is not how we do things, Madeline Margaret Marks."

And I know she's imitating Clarise Witherspoon. Her voice is high and pinched.

She sighs. "And that was the last time I made a suggestion to the altar guild."

"Probably for the best," I say.

"Daphne will pick them up," she adds, knowing I have her number. "I also need to order two arrangements for Sunday's service. It's Lila's birthday." That is all the information I need.

Lila Masterson was the matriarch of Creekside Lutheran Congregation and died about six years ago. Every spring her daughter from California calls, asking to have two vases of flowers placed in the sanctuary on the Sunday closest to her mother's birthday. She also asks that after the service Madeline takes one arrangement and places it on Lila's grave and that the other one gets delivered to the nursing home where Lila died.

It's a lot of work for a church secretary who only makes eight dollars an hour and lives thirty miles out of town. I started delivering the flowers on Saturday evening and picking them up after church and fulfilling the requests of the bereaved daughter three years ago when Madeline had a breakdown placing the order. She cried and explained that if she had one more thing to do for that church, she was pretty sure that she would be putting the flowers on her own grave. That's when I stepped in.

"Has it already been a year?" I ask. I glance over at my calendar. My Sunday was empty but I knew I had been considering a drive to Waits Lake this weekend. I like to see it in the winter, the thin sheets of ice forming along the shore.

"I hate to ask you to do this again." Madeline apologizes when I don't say anything else.

"It's fine," I reply. "I don't mind."

"Put something tropical in the arrangement," she says. "That costs more, doesn't it? Birds of paradise, aren't they expensive? Or better yet, Ruby, charge extra for your services since you have to make more than one delivery. She won't miss the money. Lila left her a fortune."

I smile. "I need to go to the nursing home anyway," I say. "They have a box of vases ready for me to pick up."

"Then charge her at least for the stop at the cemetery."

"I will, Madeline," I reply, knowing I won't. The cemetery is just behind the church. I can't really justify adding charges even if it is another stop and even if it means I can't get to the lake. "But just to ask, how come nobody in the church won't just pick it up and take the arrangement to her grave after the service?"

"Phhhhh . . ." She makes a noise as if she's waving the thought away. "Everybody in this church is too old to walk out to the cemetery with a vase of flowers. There ain't room on anybody's walker for a floral arrangement. It would take the entire ladies' Sunday school class to get out there and put it on the grave, and even then somebody would fall and twist an ankle or break a hip. I tell you, Ruby, this place is nothing but a funeral parlor just marking one death after another."

I shake my head. She's been saying the same thing for ten years. Still, it's true. Lila was eighty when she died and they all said she was the youngest soprano in the choir.

"I'll order the palms and I'll make sure the flowers are on the altar table Saturday evening. And I'll stop by before supper on Sunday and take them out."

"You're a good egg, Ruby Jewell, everybody says so."

"You're one of my best customers, Madeline. Got to keep those Lutherans happy even if everybody has to stick their noses in the arrangement to be able to tell what flowers I actually put in there."

I hear a laugh.

"I'll leave you a little something on your desk."

"Oh, Ruby, I must say I do like that part of Lila's birthday week."

I smile. She knows that I always take a small vase and make an arrangement for her before delivering the flowers to the cemetery and the nursing home. I figure that's the least I can do for a woman who takes care of so many and who always makes sure the church treasurer pays my bill first. "Tell Reverend Frederic I said hello."

"If I see him, I'll tell him. He hasn't been in all week. He was off Monday and Tuesday for his sister's surgery in Colville, had a golf game on Wednesday, a pastor's meeting in Spokane on Thursday. I had to do the bulletin without any help. I just hope he likes the hymns I picked and the opening prayer I wrote for him. If he hadn't called this morning, I was going to make him up a sermon title."

I laugh again. "I'll see you, Madeline," I say.

"See you, too."

And we hang up.

I glance out the window, and the boy I saw before the phone rang is gone.

·THREE·

I HEAR the sounding of the bell on the back door. Cooper has arrived.

"Ruby!" He sings out my name. "Ruby Jewell!"

And I smile. I love how Cooper thinks of me as a musical number. He walks through the rear of the shop and into the front part of the store. His face is hidden behind an armful of gladiolas. White ones and pink ones, they are beautiful even if they are out of season and grown down in California in a greenhouse.

"Gladiolus," he says, his face still shrouded. "Diminutive of *gladius*, which of course means 'sword.' Sometimes called the sword lily." And he tilts his head around the blooms. *"En garde!"*

"They are lovely, Cooper." I reach out and take the handful of long stalks to smell. The fragrance is slight, easy. "Do you just have the pink and white?"

He shakes his head and walks over to the glass candy jar that is sitting by the cash register on the counter. He reaches in and takes out a cinnamon fireball. He unwraps it and tosses it in his mouth.

"We have lavender with the white markings, creamy orange, and red."

"Perfect." It is the week of the Ladies' Auxiliary Annual Luncheon and they always love the long, thin flowers, iris and glads. They say the tall ones improve their posture, make them sit up in their chairs.

I take the stalks he has given me and walk back to the cooler. I open the door and place them in the large black plastic bucket.

"O my darling, O my darling, O my darling Clementine." He sings the lyrics while he bends down and scratches Clem's head. He stands up as I walk around the corner, and he takes a seat on the stool next to the arranging table.

"Will you marry me, Ruby Jewell?"

And I laugh. I pop him with the stem of myrtle I just picked off the floor. "You were married once before, Cooper," I remind him. "It didn't go so well."

"Yes, but that was because she didn't understand me. She knew nothing of beauty, nothing of queen cups and bluebells. You know my heart."

I study him for a minute and I almost take him seriously, and then I remember that it's Cooper saying these things. I swat him again.

"You cheated on her with the florist from Spokane Valley," I say. "And when you were engaged to her, you slept with the florist in Moscow. You're a rogue, Cooper Easterling, and I know better than to believe anything you have to say."

He shrugs. "It's the flowers," he says with a sigh. "They intoxicate me, make me do things I shouldn't do."

I walk over and straighten the green tissue that is stacked on the edge of the table. "I somehow think you'd be the same guy even if you sold cuts of meat."

He shakes his head. "Have you ever seen a butcher?" he asks. "I seriously doubt I'd have the same reputation if I were hauling slabs of elk and sides of pork across the state. I don't think that cargo lends itself to romance."

"True."

He holds his hands in front of him, interlocks his fingers, stretches out his arms, and raises them above his head. His shirt rises and I see the gray hairs covering his belly. I turn away. The sight of his exposed abdomen makes me nervous. It's too naked. He's too vulnerable.

"So, who are you working on this week?" he asks as he drops his hands on his knees. His lips are starting to turn red from the cinnamon candy.

"I've still got more to do on Conrad and Vivian," I answer.

"I thought you finished with those two. I thought the winter arrangement of the thin green holly leaves and the roses, the large ones, all swirling with red and white, the tiny stems of anemones, I thought they did the job. I honestly thought you were done with those two."

I shake my head. "She's not convinced."

"Did you use the light red ribbon?"

"Twisted it with the gold," I reply.

"Clear or painted vase?"

"White porcelain, one of those you brought from Oregon."

He nods, remembering the shipment.

"Medium or tall?"

I sigh. I had thought of everything. "Tall."

He makes a *tsk*ing noise with his tongue against the roof of his mouth. "*Tsk . . . tsk . . . tsk.*" He doesn't say anything for a couple of minutes and I tap at the edge of the stack of tissue.

"Maybe it's just not meant to be," he finally says.

"No, I just have to try harder," I answer him.

"I have belladonnas," he informs me. "Fifty stems. I have three boxes of ginger and at least a hundred stalks of September flowers. Freesia, alstromeria, orange and yellow, purple iris, orchids."

"Which ones?" I ask.

"Arandas and Mokaras. Purple and yellow. I sold all my pink in Spokane."

I shake my head. "It's too early for orchids," I say, mostly to myself, but Cooper is listening.

"A stem of cymbidium," he suggests.

"White or pink?" I ask.

He smiles. "White with that little narrow lip of purple."

"A stem of cymbidium." I'm thinking. "Elegant," I note.

"Slid into a nest of purple dendrobiums."

"Thai," I recall the orchid.

"Sexy," he responds.

"I don't know, Cooper." I hesitate. "Vivian scares easily. She hasn't gone out on a date since her brother took her to the spring fling."

"I don't think that qualifies as a date," Cooper notes. "Not even in this town."

I'm still thinking. "Conrad is just as nervous. He lives with his mother on the other side of the mountain. He only comes to town to work and go to church and bowl on Thursday nights. He doesn't even grocery shop here. It might be too much, too fast."

"How long have you been working on the two of them?" Cooper asks.

I add up the months in my head. "Six years," I answer.

"And Conrad and Vivian are at what age?"

I shrug. "Forties," I say, sounding a bit unsure.

"It's time, Ruby. They've had long enough to try this thing on their own. Give her the orchids."

I pause. It is a big decision.

"You're right," I agree. "I've been cautious long enough." I take in a breath. "What is life if not rising to a challenge?"

He claps his hands together.

"Bring me the dendrobiums," I say with confidence.

Cooper jumps off the stool, landing on both feet. He puts his hands on his hips. "It's for the best, Ruby," he says, and bends down once more, giving Clementine a good rub. He rises up, gives me a big nod, and heads out the back door. "You'll see."

I roll my eyes and shake my head. Cooper Easterling will be the death of me.

·Four·

CLEMENTINE and I have a brief walk around the block and it is after lunch before I have a chance to check the e-mails and see if I have any online orders. There are six. Valentine's Day is just a few weeks away and the new website that Frank Goodrich designed for the shop has been featuring holiday specials. I've already gotten ten requests for the Chocolate, Bear, and Roses Arrangement. That was Frank's idea; he claims he's a marketing genius.

There's actually really very little floral work involved in this seasonal gift. He found out that I could order a box of stuffed bears from a toy warehouse wholesale and that I could get a supply of chocolates at very little cost from Denny at the drugstore. Denny's employee, a high school student with math deficiencies, ordered twelve dozen mini boxes of Valentine candy instead of just one dozen and when the mistake was realized, the supplier wouldn't take them back and Denny was desperate for a buyer. I'm not sure how Frank found out.

Denny promised to sell the candy to me at a really great discount, which Frank said I could use as a promotion with a stuffed animal and one long-stemmed rose. I thought it was not a bad idea, ordered the bears, bought the chocolates, but then felt bad later when I had to decline Denny after he begged me to hire the employee who had made the mistake. I told him I already had Jimmy to deliver and Nora to help at the counter and clean up. I didn't need a high school student who couldn't do basic addition and subtraction. "Besides," I told him when he phoned, "she's your daughter. I suggest you get her a math tutor. She's going to be with you a long time."

People assume that florists love Valentine's Day, that it's our bread and butter, our greatest money-making holiday on the calendar. And they'd be right that it's busy; and they'd be right that we make a fair amount of our income on that one day of celebration. But I don't know a florist who loves Valentine's Day. It's hard work and most of the orders are too constrictive. Most everyone only wants the red roses. Traditional. Long-stemmed. A dozen. A little baby's breath or bear grass. A tall clear vase, thick red ribbon. No imagination. No room for personal preference or creative imagination. A dozen long-stemmed red roses in a tall vase with a red ribbon. No deviation.

I used to try to make people see, try to show them what they really needed, what their loved one really wanted, tried to explain that violets were actually the true Valentine flower, but I got tired of the hassle and the disappointment and the long stares that came from minds already made up. So I just tell Cooper how many buckets of red roses I want, and I collect the tall clear vases from everyone throughout the year and I make thirty-five or forty traditional arrangements.

Over the years I have, of course, proven myself with the regulars. And they rarely disappoint. "You know best, Ruby," my old-timers will say. "Just put a little of your magic in it and I don't care what flowers you stick in that vase." I do get a fair number of those requests on Valentine's, and that's what keeps me from closing down the shop during the second week in February. That and the fact that Jimmy and Nora need the work.

"You still open?"

I glance up. Jenny Seal is standing at the door.

"Yes, yes," I say, waving her in.

"How are you, Jenny?" I ask. I remember that Justin, her fiancé, had ordered a small bouquet for her, to be delivered last month. She was in the hospital, on the sixth floor. Oncology.

She turns slowly, closes the door, and walks over to the counter. She keeps her head down. "I got home from the hospital a couple of weeks ago," she says.

I nod. "I'm so glad."

"I have cancer," she announces, and her candor surprises me.

I nod again.

"I had my breast removed," and she reaches up and touches the left side of her chest. She keeps her hand there and she looks like somebody getting ready to say the Pledge of Allegiance. After a bit, she lowers it.

"How are you feeling?"

"A little sick, like when I had my tonsils out," she answers. "Weak, you know, like I haven't eaten."

"Have you eaten?" I'm not sure why I asked, but it seemed like the right question at the time.

She nods. "Soup, mostly," she replies. "I threw up a lot after the operation."

"Is your mom staying with you?"

Jenny's mother, Jean or Jennifer, I'm not sure of her name, lives on the West Coast of Washington State. She got a job over there a couple of years ago and Jenny stayed in town with a friend to finish high school. I'm not sure of the relationship between the mother and daughter, only that she did make it back for graduation last year and that she called when she found out her daughter was engaged.

I'm doing the flowers for the wedding. Gerberas. Standards and minis. Loveliness, Bella Vistas, whispers, a few flamingoes. Jenny likes pink. I got Cooper to order me a bunch of the Bella Vistas to put in the arrangement I made for her a couple of weeks ago. I wanted it to look like the wedding bouquet we discussed with just a few stems of orange fabios.

I added the orange to her hospital arrangement because I know that the color is a gentle energizer, boosting a weak pulse rate and lifting exhaustion. It helps to strengthen the immune system.

She shakes her head. "She came to the hospital. I told her to go home. I didn't want her to come back here with me."

I don't respond.

"She's very anxious," Jenny adds.

And I recall the phone conversation I had with her last month. She asked me what Jenny had wanted and spent a lot of time sighing as I explained the kind of flower arrangements Jenny preferred. She wanted pictures and a detailed price list and asked if I planned to be in attendance at the wedding in case the flowers needing tending. She wanted to know how long the blooms would last and if the mother of the bride had any say about the wedding décor. I expect "anxious" is a polite way to describe Jenny's mother. I smile sympathetically.

"I came because I thought maybe you might help me."

I wait.

Jenny drops her head. "Justin's been so good to me," she announces.

"Yes," I agree.

"He buys me flowers every birthday and every year on the anniversary of our first date."

I nod.

"It's been five years," she adds.

I smile. I know because it's in the customer notebook I made for Justin.

"And that was a lovely bouquet he gave me at the hospital. I wanted to tell you thank you for that."

I wait for her request.

"He hasn't seen me since the surgery," she says haltingly. "He hasn't seen what I look like." She lowers her gaze.

And suddenly, I start to understand why she's here.

"I'm crooked and scarred. I look like a boy." She won't face me.

I walk around the counter to her. "Jenny, Justin loves you."

She doesn't respond.

"I will never forget the first time he came in here wanting to get you flowers. He paid me all in single dollar bills he saved from mowing lawns. He wanted to propose to you on your first date."

Jenny smiles. "He did."

I laugh.

"Come sit behind the counter." I motion her to the stool that I keep in the back of the shop. Clementine gets up and walks over to her, dropping her big head on Jenny's knee. Jenny smiles, gives her a rub, and I lean against the table in front of her.

"He doesn't care about what you look like. He just wants you to be okay," I tell her. "He has never cared about what you looked like. He fell in love with your heart. He would think you are the most beautiful woman in the world no matter what body part is missing from you. He's in this for the real reasons. He loves you."

"I don't want him to feel sorry for me." She shakes her head. "I don't want him to stay with me, to go through with the wedding because he feels sorry for me."

Clementine returns to her spot beneath the table.

"Jenny, it doesn't matter if you have breasts or not. Justin Dexter loves you and I know these things. His affection for you is real."

She nods but doesn't appear convinced.

"Okay." I sigh.

She raises her face. "Do you have anything?"

I don't reply. I know why she's here. She was in the shop when I was making the arrangement for Tonya Lipton when her sister called and claimed Tonya was depressed. She watched me put in several stems of white flowers, lilies, orientals and long narrow callas. She asked me a lot of questions about the choices I made, and I had explained that the color white promotes healing of spirit, that white light is a natural pain reliever, increasing and maintaining energy levels and relieving depression and inertia. White dispels negativity from the body's energy field. Ever since Jenny watched me that afternoon, talking with Tonya's sister and arranging white flowers, she's asked me about the healing and stimulating properties of flowers. She is learning my work.

"You don't need anything," I explain, studying her.

She is so frail, so thin, and she doesn't believe me.

I sigh. "Okay, jasmine will help. It's good for bringing love, increasing sexual desire, and promoting optimism; it alleviates doubts. Justin does not need it, but you do."

I head over to the storage room and take out a few stems of jasmine. I walk back, wrap them in tissue, and hand them to her. "Just put them in a tall, narrow vase near your bed."

She takes them from me and smells. "It's nice," she says.

"Don't worry about Justin," I tell her. "There is not a thing wrong with his mind or heart. I saw him when he came in and placed the order. He's only concerned about you. He's not having second thoughts about your wedding. You just concentrate on getting better. You just get better."

She nods. "How much do I owe you?" she asks.

I shake my head. "Just bring me some mint from your garden when you feel better."

She nods. "Okay."

And she slides off the stool gingerly, walks around the counter, and stops at the door. She turns to me. "We haven't changed the date," she announces. "Not yet anyway. I may have to have treatments. That means I may lose my hair too. But for now, we've kept everything like we planned."

"September twenty-third," I say, recalling the wedding day and not saying anything about the consequences of chemotherapy. "It's the anniversary of your first date," I add. "You'll have your gerberas. I have already talked to the supplier. The church will be filled with pink daisies. It will be beautiful, just like you."

She nods slowly, puts the jasmine under her nose, and heads out the door.

I watch her walk to the corner, turn right, and move in the direction of the small duplex she shares with her best friend, Louise Tate. It's not more than half a mile away, but I worry she shouldn't have walked so far so soon after her surgery, and I decide I should telephone her just to make sure she made it okay.

·FIVE·

I T's after five o'clock when I walk over to the door and turn the sign from *Open* to *Closed*. I glance out the window and see the boy again, the one from earlier in the day, the one I do not recognize. He's leaned his bicycle against the brick wall of the building across the street, and it seems as if he's looking for something in the tall grass around his feet. I watch him for a second and am suddenly surprised when Henry Phillips is standing right in front of me on the other side of the door.

"Am I t-t-too late?"

I read his lips, even the repeated letters, his stutter, shake my head, and open the door. "Hi, Henry," I say, and make room for him to enter past me. "You're early."

Henry is the barber across the street. He buys a small bouquet of flowers every week and places them on his mother's grave. He likes roses, the spray variety, any color, or the tall stems of Marianas and green tea, cool water and whites. He told me his mother always had a small vase of roses on her kitchen table, flowers she picked from the bushes she grew when they lived in Colorado. I always have them ready for him on Thursdays. He only works half a day on Fridays, closes at lunch, and drives over to the cemetery to change out the arrangements, so he usually comes by on Thursday evenings to pick up the flowers. I typically never see him except then.

"I-I want to buy flowers for-for . . . someone." He walks in and stands at the counter.

Henry has stuttered for as long as I have known him. He's a very intelligent man, an excellent barber, and extremely shy. The men say he doesn't talk much when he cuts hair, hums to the music on the radio, is pleasant to all of his customers but rarely engages in conversation. Everyone is used to his introverted ways, and most of the men seem to like to go to a place where they get to do all the talking. He has kept a steady business for as long as I have known him.

"Great," I reply, walking around him to the other side of the counter.

He doesn't respond.

I wait.

We stare at each other for a few seconds.

"Do you know what kind of flowers you want?" I finally ask, not trying to hurry him along, but just trying to be clear about what I'm arranging.

"I-I . . . think she likes yellow," he says quietly. "Sh-sh-she wears a lot of yellow."

I smile. "Then yellow it is," I respond, and I walk back to the holding area and pick some of the best stems of yellow flowers I have. I come back with my arms full. "I have daffodils," I tell him. "Just got a fresh bunch over the weekend. It's early, but Cooper can find anything."

I lay them all on the table behind the counter where I am standing. "The freesia is nice too, and I have a few stems of golden alstroemeria. How do these look?" I hold up the flowers and wait for his approval.

"Ye-yes." He nods, and I get to work.

I am cutting and sorting and arranging when I notice Henry is humming. I don't look at him, but I smile. I like it. I go back to the cooler and pull out a few stems of greenery. While I'm there I see the leftover blazing stars I picked a week or so ago. I was surprised to find them so early in the season, and I picked a few. The blooms are still vibrant and strong. I take what's left, deciding to add them to Henry's yellow bouquet. When I return to the front, the boy from outside, the boy with the bike, the one I hadn't seen before today, is standing just inside the door. I had not heard the chime ring.

"Oh," I say, surprised to see another customer. "Hello."

He lowers his gaze, and I notice his hands are behind his back.

"I'll be right with you," I say, and return to the task at hand. "Henry, would you like a vase or leave these long-stemmed?"

He appears confused. "I-I don't know." He slides his fingers through his hair as if the question has troubled him. "Which is be-best?"

If I knew the person receiving the flowers I could tell him, but I have a policy of not asking a customer who is getting the flowers. I figure if they want me to have that information, they will tell me. To ask such a thing feels like an invasion of privacy, and discretion is a professional and personal courtesy I always extend.

"Long-stemmed is not as formal," I tell him. "It's more of a gift of the moment. It's like the roses your mom picked from her bushes," I explain. "To give long-stemmed flowers is to say, 'I saw these and just picked them for you, to brighten your day, to tell you

I was thinking of you.' It's a random act of kindness with just a hint of intimacy."

He blushes but then nods as if he understands.

"To give flowers in a vase," I continue, "is to demonstrate that more thought went into the gift. This kind of arrangement says, 'I was thinking of doing this for you because I remember that it's your birthday or our anniversary.'"

Henry looks away.

"Or I want to acknowledge a special occasion or honor an important achievement, and having given this much thought, flowers seem most suitable."

He chews on his lip, runs his fingers through his hair again. He's thinking, thinking. I turn once more and glance at the boy waiting behind him. He is very patient.

"No vase," he finally decides, and I nod in approval.

"Will these be given right away or should I put them in little tubes of water to help them last longer?"

"R-ri-right away," he answers.

I smile, take in a deep breath, pull out three sheets of green tissue, smooth them down on the table in front of me, and begin placing the flowers. The daffodils are central, their long golden heads still tight in the thin band of skin wrapped around them. I put in a branch of emerald palm behind them and a few freesia, two medium daisies, and even up the ends of the stems. I add the alstroemeria, the blazing stars, and one long, full branch of bright yellow snapdragons. I push and pull at the blooms, add a few sprigs of narrow grass, shape and mold, exhale, and then step back for my last inspection.

I pick up the bouquet and carefully wrap the tissue around and around, securing it at the back with a tiny straight pin. Then I fluff up the top of the green edges and place it once more on the table.

I look behind me and pull a long piece of wide grosgrain ribbon, purple to make the flowers pop, cut it, and tie it around the bottom of the bouquet. I walk over, handing my work to Henry.

He doesn't speak for a moment and I think the silence is particularly golden. He is admiring my work.

"I-i-it's like sunshine," he finally says.

"Thank you, Henry," I respond, thinking it's the most beautiful compliment I could receive.

He reaches for his wallet.

"Why don't I just add it to your bill?" I ask him. "The end of the month is next week and you can just pay for them when you pay for the others."

"Th-th-thank you, Ruby," he responds, cradling the bouquet in his arms, like a baby.

"Not a problem," I say. "I'll see you Thursday."

He nods, turns, and walks around the boy and out the door.

I wait until he's on the sidewalk, and then I turn my gaze to my next customer.

"He's giving those to Miss Peterson, the librarian," the boy announces, and we watch Henry head across the street to his barbershop.

The news surprises me. He turns back to face me.

"I've seen him there on Saturday mornings," he explains. "I go to the library on Saturdays because that's when Grandma comes to town and gets her hair done and she thinks that's the best place for me to wait for her."

I nod. I still don't know who this boy is.

"He has a crush on Miss Peterson. He checks out a stack of books every weekend. Is that a dog?"

"Maybe he just likes to read," I say, and move the mouse on the computer pad, waking up my computer so that I can get to my files and add the arrangement to Henry's bill. "And yes, that's Clementine."

Clem stays where she is, but her tail wags.

"Nah, nobody likes to read that much," he surmises. He's still watching the dog. "You can bring her to work?"

I type in the numbers and close the files. I study my newest customer. "One of the perks of owning your own business: You can bring your pets to work." I smile at the boy. "Is there something I can help you with?" I ask.

He nods, faces me. "I need a job," he says. "I know a lot about flowers."

"Aren't you supposed to be in school?"

"I can work afternoons."

"Why aren't you in school today?"

"Teachers' workday."

I pause. I got nothing else.

"Okay," I reply, not quite knowing how to respond. I was not really in need of another employee.

"I could pick flowers for you. I found some real pretty ones over near where I live with my grandmother." And then he pulls his hands around to the front, holding out a bunch of paperwhites. "I know where a lot of these grow." He places them on the counter in front of me. "I figure I can find a lot more when spring comes."

I smile. "You know that you're not supposed to take flowers from other people's property, right?"

"Oh, these are from my grandparents' farm," he says. "Grandma said I can pick all I want." He pauses. "She plants a lot of flowers every year."

"And just who is your grandmother?" I ask.

"Juanita Norris," he answers.

And then I place him. He is the son of Diane Norris, who died a couple of months ago. She lived somewhere over in Montana but was buried here in Creekside. I did several flower arrangements for her funeral. I recall some of the sentiments written on the cards that accompanied the two peace lilies and the small basket of winter flowers. *We will miss her so much*, and the customer had requested that it be signed, *Everybody at Bill's Barbecue and Bourbon*. Another had only wanted to leave the message, *I'm so sorry*. No name given. A small white card pinned to the white ribbon at the base of the plant.

Jimmy had delivered all of the arrangements and had said that he knew the girl when she was small. He remembered her from school, where he worked as a bus driver for thirty years. He said that she had starting hanging out with the wrong crowd before she got to high school, was pregnant at fifteen. Her mother and daddy had raised her son, the boy standing in front of me, until he was five or six. Diane completed a stint in rehab and spent a few years in prison, but when she got out she wanted custody of her child.

Jimmy said it almost broke her parents' hearts and they fought her in court, but the judge sided with the mom, and the boy and Diane left town and moved to Billings. That had been about four years ago. She died from an overdose and her son was returned to Creekside and to his grandparents.

I did a spray of white and pink carnations for her coffin and a large basket of pink sweetheart roses to stay at the grave. I added a sprig of lavender in the bottom of the basket since I know it helps with grief and guilt. I'm never sure what flowers do for the dead but I figure even a spirit, especially a sad one, is still able to gain something from beauty.

"What's your name?" I ask.

"William," he answers. "I like Will best."·

"Then Will it shall be."

He stands, waiting, and suddenly I remember his request for employment.

I sigh.

"I learned about flowers from my mom," he says, as if the information will somehow influence my decision.

And, oddly enough, it does.

"Okay, Will," I acquiesce. "You can sweep up in the afternoons, carry out the trash, wash out vases, and just help me around the shop." I think about what I'm doing. "I can only pay you three dollars an hour, and you can't work more than five hours a week."

"Can I walk your dog? Can I find flowers for you?"

I see the hunger in his eyes, the grief, the desperate way he is trying to stay connected to his dead mother.

"Yes, to both," I answer, and he pumps his fist in the air.

"But . . ." I interrupt the celebration. "Clementine likes to chase cats, so you have to be careful when you have her on the leash. She's very strong."

He watches Clem as she comes out from under the table. Hearing her name and the word *walk* has captured the dog's attention.

"Okay," he says in agreement. "I will hang on tight."

"And you can only bring me flowers that come from your grandparents' farm. You can't pick flowers from other people's property."

He nods.

"I'll pay you only for the ones I can use. So don't pick a lot, because we need to see how I'll be able to add them to arrangements. I want to make sure we don't waste them."

He nods again.

"Have your grandmother call me if she wants to talk to me about our agreement, okay?"

"Thank you, miss."

"Ruby," I say, since I hadn't told him my name.

He seems surprised.

"Miss Ruby," I repeat, and he smiles.

"Thank you, Miss Ruby." And he turns and heads for the door.

He stops just before walking out. "I really like Clementine, and your name is as pretty as a flower."

And I watch him jump on his bike and head in the direction of his grandparents' farm. I shake my head. I don't know what I have just gotten myself in for.

·Six·

I walk inside my house and right away I feel her. Or I feel the absence of her. Sometimes one hurts as much as the other and I can't even tell whether it is grief or longing that overtakes me. Daisy always filled up a room coming and going. In life and death she is simply bigger than anything else.

Clementine ambles past me, heading to her water bowl. I take in a breath, shake off the memories and thoughts of my dead sister, place my keys on the table in the foyer, hang my bike helmet on the wall hook, shed my jacket and gloves, slide off my shoes, arranging them by the door, and walk to the kitchen. I pour myself a tall glass of water and drink most of it, leaving a little, which I pour in the small pots of African violets resting on the windowsill.

"What shall we have for dinner?" I ask my dog, and she lifts her head from where she has found a spot to rest in front of the stove and then glances toward the refrigerator. I follow her gaze. "Chicken?" I ask, and she stands up. "You're so predictable, Clementine. Wouldn't you like a hot dog or sausage? Why is it always and only chicken?"

Clementine shrugs and I pick up her food bowl, pour in two cups of dry food and get the container of canned chicken from the fridge. I sprinkle a little meat on top and place the bowl back on the floor. She immediately goes over and eats. I watch her for a few seconds. She has become very dear to me, my best friend even, although I know that sounds like a cliché.

Jimmy gave me Clementine. He had picked her up when he was making a delivery out on the old farm road. Alisa Rogers had just given birth to her first child and Lester, her husband, had ordered her a tall vase of Asiatic lilies, yellow carnations, lavender cushion spray chrysanthemums, and pink roses. It was a summer special; I called it my Pastel Ever Pretty Arrangement and I sold it for twenty-five dollars including delivery.

When he called, he asked about blue flowers—Alisa had given birth to a boy—but all I had on hand were a few bluebells and one or two light purple irises, so he finally agreed the special was best. I put it together and Jimmy took it out just a couple of hours after he called. They were coming home from the hospital and Lester wanted flowers awaiting them, and he told Jimmy where to find the house key and exactly where to place the arrangement so that it would appear that Lester had bought the flowers and put them on the kitchen table before he left for the hospital to bring her and the baby home.

Jimmy was walking back to the van when he spotted the puppy out in the ditch near the house. She was huddled near the bank and when Jimmy walked over, she hardly moved. He picked her up and could see she was hungry and frightened and had probably been left out there on the country road by somebody who didn't want a puppy. He called Lester at the hospital since he had his cell number, and Lester said he didn't know anything about the dog and certainly couldn't take her.

"A baby is about all we can manage right now," he told him. "I can drop her off at the shelter later if you want." But Jimmy said no and brought the puppy back to the shop and by the end of the day, after a bowl of milk and a visit to the vet, and a warm towel where she took a long nap, Clementine had made her home with us; and since Jimmy lived in senior housing where dogs were not allowed and Nora preferred cats, I became a pet owner. That was ten years ago. Clementine has been at my side ever since.

I blow out a long breath and think about my dinner. My tastes are simple too, but I want a little something more than canned chicken so I look in the cabinets and pull out a can of soup. It seems like a perfect night for a grilled cheese sandwich and a bowl of tomato soup. I'll even have a big glass of milk. Comfort food never seemed so comforting.

After dinner I turn on a little music, soft jazz, a station from Spokane that is mostly news and interviews in the mornings, classical in the afternoons, and local bands, jazz and blues in the evenings. Tonight there's a feature on a new album by Norman Brown, a guitarist from Missouri, a favorite of mine, his music always light and easy, his sounds compared to his contemporary George Benson. It's a nice way to settle into darkness.

I pour a glass of wine, sit on the sofa, lean back, close my eyes, and think about the day. I think about Jenny and worry about how frail she looked, the dark circles beneath her eyes, the pale color of her skin, the loose way her clothes hung on her body. Without family around to tend to her, I can only hope her roommate is watching out for her. I remember that Louise Tate is studying to be a nurse at the community college, so maybe she sees this as an opportunity to practice her skills and that in a few weeks we will all be able to confirm to her that she is going into the right profession.

I hope Justin is up for what is ahead of them, that he manages to show just enough concern without hovering, that he is patient and easy with Jenny, that he somehow understands that a young woman with breast cancer has very specific needs and very unpredictable emotions. I hope that together they can weather this storm.

I think about Cooper and his advice on the orchids. I consider Conrad and Vivian and still I am unsure they are ready for such a passionate exchange. I remember Stan, delivering the yellow roses to his wife, the celebration of another anniversary, and I recall the year she left him for three months, and the ragged way he was until she returned. I never learned the reason for her departure or return, but I knew it the moment she was back.

It was in spring and Stan had met me at the door before I opened the shop and wanted to know what flowers I had that could celebrate a homecoming and make it so a person would never want to leave. I worked all morning on the presentation, so clear I was on Stan's desperation. I used arching callas, long stems reaching from the vase, hands welcoming her home, white hydrangea, and bright green cymbidium orchids, deep verdant aralia leaves surrounding all the flowers. I called it Grace and Romance, knowing Stan would need a little of both to keep Viola happy, to keep his wife at home.

I think of how there were tears standing in his eyes when he came back to pick up the arrangement later that day, how he couldn't speak, but how much I knew he liked it. He tipped me a hundred dollars that day and even though I tried to make him take it back, he refused me. "It's the only way I know how to thank you," he said, the words muffled and choked. So I kept the money and bought exotics with it: bird of paradise, pincushion protea, red ti leaves, and dark pink sweet williams. I put them in all the arrangements I made for the next week, never charging what I paid but enjoying the simple luxury of doing something so extravagant.

I think of Henry and wonder if what the boy said is true and that he has a crush on Lou Ann Peterson, the librarian. I think that she must be ten years older than Henry and I consider how the thought of the two of them together had never crossed my mind. I cannot see how he will ever have the nerve to speak to her and wonder how he presented her with the bouquet of long-stemmed yellows.

"Maybe the library is a safe place for him. He doesn't stutter when he reads, you know," I say out loud, and Clementine nudges me with her nose. She is lying on the sofa next to me and I know she'll not be happy having to go outside to pee before we go to bed. It's cold tonight and this winter has seemed especially hard on her. She lags behind on my bicycle rides to and from the store. She doesn't seem to care too much about a walk at lunch. A big dog at age ten moves like an old person, and I think her hips have arthritis in them and I should probably start giving her those glucosamine-chondroitin sulfate pills that Ruth Jane told me about.

Then suddenly I find myself thinking about Will, the little boy standing at my window all day, playing across the street from the shop, and who finally got the nerve to come in and ask for a job today. I wonder if his grandmother knew where he was, and it dawns on me that he's probably about the same age as Clem, ten, and I think of the lives they have both lived in one decade. She, abandoned as a baby, growing up in a flower shop, he, abandoned by his mother in death and returned to grandparents he likely no longer remembers.

"Maybe you'll have more to offer the boy than I do," I say, and Clementine sleeps and I place my arm across her neck, take a swallow of wine, lean back, and close my eyes. This day, I realize, is done.

·SEVEN·

THE phone is ringing and I am dreaming of windows and doors, of turning knobs and twisting locks, using keys, of trying to get in or out; I can't tell. I just move from one place to another, pushing and pulling, twisting and turning, trying to find the way. The sound of the phone is also in my dream and I stop what I am doing to see who is calling me. Clementine sits up and I feel her breath on the back of my neck. I awake, realize where I am, and reach for the phone.

"Ruby, it's Jimmy. I'm sorry to wake you up."

I blink and cough and shake my head. I try to focus. "Jimmy?" I manage to say as I lean over and turn on the lamp beside me. Light fills the room.

"Yeah, so I came over to Spokane last night and I got a busted radiator. I don't think I'll make it back to do the deliveries today."

I hear him breathe.

"I'm real sorry about this."

"It's okay. What time is it?" It feels really early.

"Six fifteen," he replies.

It seems earlier than that.

"Okay, all right," I mutter.

"Ah, you know what? It's five fifteen. I read my watch wrong. Geez, I'm sorry, Ruby. Will you be able to get back to sleep?"

I clear my throat. "Jimmy, is something wrong?" I sit up and Clementine leans over, resting her head on my leg.

"No, no, I'm just . . ."

"Where are you?"

"Spokane," he answers, but doesn't sound very confident.

"Where in Spokane?" I ask.

"Your time's up, buddy." I hear a voice in the background.

"I gotta go, Ruby. I'm sorry."

He hasn't hung up yet, and suddenly I know what has happened. Jimmy's been picked up by the police again. Jimmy fell off the wagon.

"Do you want me to come get you?" I ask. I've done it before. I know the way to the city jail. I know how to do this.

"No," he answers. "I just need to sleep it off and, well, I don't want you to see me like this. I'll be back soon. I'm sorry," he says again.

"Jimmy."

I hear the click of the phone and the line goes dead.

I hang up the receiver and slide under the blankets, and Clementine drops down from her spot on her bed to the floor beside me. I'm not sure I can go back to sleep now. I'm not sure I want to go back to sleep, dreaming of trying to open doors and windows, dreaming of trying to get away from wherever I am. I'm not sure sleep will bring me any measure of peace.

I close my eyes and think about Jimmy.

He told me when I hired him that he had a history of alcoholism. It was the first thing out of his mouth after introducing himself. I guess the AA greeting had been instilled in him. "My name is Jimmy and I'm an alcoholic." Only he didn't say it exactly like that. Close, though.

He told me he'd lost his bus driver's license and that was why he needed work. He brought a reference from his supervisor, a couple of letters from friends. When I explained that delivering flowers required a driver's license to operate the van, he said he didn't lose his regular license, just the one for driving a school bus. At the time, I found his story illogical and difficult to believe, but it turns out it was the truth. The judge who handled the court case was an old army buddy of his, told him he couldn't drive for the school system any more but he wouldn't punish him by taking away his personal driving privileges. He got in AA and stayed sober for a couple of years. I hired him when he showed me his eighteen-month token.

The last time he was arrested he got in a fight in a bar; he wasn't out in the streets so his license wasn't an issue, and the time after that, he was just ticketed for being a public nuisance, asleep on the park bench in town on Easter Sunday. As far as I know he's been sober ever since and never had a problem with his driver's license. But this time, this time it sounds like he was driving. This time it sounds like he left town, drove to Spokane; and I doubt his buddy the county judge can do anything for him. He'll lose his license for sure. And once that happens, I'm not sure how much help a delivery-man who can't make deliveries can give.

I don't know what makes Jimmy fall off the wagon. I can't understand how he can go for so long without a drink and then suddenly find himself in a liquor store or at a bar or in jail. Of course, if anybody knew what made a sober recovering drunk start drinking again, they could make a ton of money. I figure a lot of family members would pay big bucks to have that kind of information, secure that kind of knowledge. After all, with that bit of wisdom, they'd know when to pick up the children early from school and drive them out of town or when not to invite friends over for dinner, when to stay away from social gatherings and church outings, maybe even know when to lock the alcoholic in their room or out of the house. I think of my dream and wonder if it has any bearing on these thoughts. I guess not and I go back to my line of thinking.

If Daddy had known which days Mama could manage to work the program and which days she couldn't make it past the corner market without ducking in for a bottle of wine, I guess things would have been a lot more comfortable in our house. As it was, the three of us could never tell which day she would be the attentive wife and mother and which day she would be a mean, sloppy drunk.

Daisy was better than Daddy or me at predicting when Mama was going to drink. She wasn't always right but she was right a lot of the time. "Don't tell her about the new teacher," she'd say. And I couldn't understand why hearing about a personnel change at school would cause Mama to reach for the bottle. Or Daisy would catch me in the cafeteria at lunch and remind me, "Make sure you tell her about the dance next week." And she'd be right. For Mama to find out there was a new teacher would make her nervous and anxious, and those were definitely triggers for drinking. And somehow, knowing there was some event upcoming for one of her daughters, an event that she thought was important whether we did or not, could keep her sober for a couple of weeks.

I never figured it out and neither did Daddy, but somehow, Daisy knew.

Not always, of course. Even she couldn't predict the three-day binge that started on a Wednesday in August when there was nothing out of the ordinary coming or going in our lives. Even Daisy didn't know how violent Mama could be after drinking all that time at the casino and coming home to find her daughters watching cartoons alone, their father gone to work.

I reach up and feel the scar on the top of my head, remember the pool of blood, the sharp crack of the belt before the buckle hit. I remember the doctor pulling Daisy away, the sound of the curtain sliding between us, closing me off in the cubicle in the emergency room, the needle in my scalp, and the nurse holding me down, trying to say things to keep me still. I remember us packing our bags, going to a foster home for a few days, and then coming to Creekside, moving in with Grandmother, the horrible way I ached. If we had known about that binge, well, there would be lots of things different for me right now. There would be lots of things different for all of us.

I rub the scar on the top of my head, letting the memories slide away, and hope Jimmy is safe in his jail cell. I hope no one hurts him. I decide to think about all this later and I roll over, reach for the lamp, and turn it off. It is dark again and I think I'll be able to go back to sleep after all.

·EIGHT·

I DON'T understand." Nora is on the phone. I check the clock. She's early and I wonder if Jimmy called her too. I know they are friends and I wonder sometimes if their relationship isn't something more.

I smile at her and she lifts her hand as a greeting. Clementine pushes me along and takes her place under the table.

"So, you want the Valentine special but you don't want it delivered on Valentine's?" She rolls her eyes at me.

I walk over and put my lunch in the fridge and take a cup and pour myself some coffee. Nora has made a fresh pot. I fix it the way I like it, with a little milk, head back to the cooler, just to check on the flowers, see what needs to be thrown out, what must be used in arrangements today, and then make my return to the counter. Nora is still on the call.

"Let me ask Ruby." And she drops the receiver beneath her chin and blows out a breath. "It's Steven Peters." I don't know who that is, and the expression on my face gives me away. "Stevie, Maude's youngest," she clarifies.

I know now. Stevie is in his second semester at a college in Idaho; he's a good kid.

"He'd like to order the special for next week, the bear and the chocolates, but he doesn't want it to be delivered on the fourteenth. He wants it delivered on the seventeenth."

"But that's not Valentine's Day," I say.

Nora rolls her eyes again. "I know! That's what I've been trying to explain."

"But the candy has *Happy Valentine's Day* written on the top of the box, and the bear has a heart on its chest that says the same thing. It won't make sense to send it on the seventeenth."

She's staring at me as if to say she's already gone through all of that reasoning with Stevie.

There is a pause. I'm not sure what is being asked of me.

"If he wants it delivered on the seventeenth, that's fine. We can deliver it on the seventeenth." I take a sip of coffee. "Who is he sending it to?" I ask before she has the chance to pass along what I've said.

"Jessica Roberts," she answers.

"Is it some kind of joke?"

She shrugs.

I reach out for the phone. She hands it to me.

"Stevie, it's Ruby," I say.

"Hello, Ms. Jewell." Steven is always very polite and respectful.

"So, you want a Valentine's Day special but don't want it sent on Valentine's Day, is that your order?"

He stalls a bit and I can see he hates that he ever made this call. "It's a joke," he finally explains.

I guessed right. "It's not a very funny one," I say. "Haven't you and Jessica been dating a while?" I recall the high school prom from last spring. He ordered a lovely wrist corsage, tiny red sweetheart roses, and a matching boutonniere. She wore a red strapless dress. He wore a red bow tie. Maude brought pictures.

"About a year," he says. "But this is our first Valentine's Day together and I always get dates for special occasions wrong." He hesitates. "It's like a private joke. I thought Thanksgiving was a week earlier. I missed her birthday by a day. I wanted to be a few days late for this holiday too. She thinks it's funny."

"Steven, she really doesn't," I reply.

He doesn't respond, so I explain.

"She's acting like she thinks it's funny because that's what girls do for the first year they're dating somebody, they act like stuff their boyfriend does is funny, but trust me, nobody likes to think their significant other forgets important dates. See, it'll be February fourteenth and all of Jessica's friends will have gotten something—cards, flowers, candy, jewelry, something—and even though she might remember your little private joke, for three days she has to be hiding from her friends so as not to have to say you didn't get her anything or she has to lie or she's forced to try and explain this private but not very funny joke the two of you have. And Steven—" I wait to make sure he's listening.

"Yes, ma'am." He is.

"Missing Valentine's Day really isn't funny."

"Could I send it the twelfth?"

I sigh. "Well, it's better than the seventeenth," I say.

"Can you deliver it to the school on the twelfth?"

Nora is still standing next to me. She has folded her arms across her chest.

"Yes, Steven, we can," I answer.

"Okay, that's what I'll do then. I'll send it early."

"Okay."

He sounds so confident, so sure of his decision, I don't try to change his mind. I just take the credit card number, what he wants to say on the card—*Happy Valentine's Day, Jessica*, not very original—and confirm once more his order. When I hang up the phone, Nora is shaking her head.

"I thought he was the one boy in that household with some sense. I guess all Maude's sons are missing a little something upstairs." She taps her forehead.

I know she's referring to Maude Peters's oldest child, who's in prison for breaking into a church, and her middle son, who dropped out of high school to join a group of hippies who came through town last summer. I have to agree with her because I thought Steven was a smart boy, but now, I'm not sure he's any brighter than the other two, just in college.

"He's sending it early then?" she wants to know.

I nod. "But I'm going to add another delivery for Jessica on the fourteenth. We'll be going to the high school anyway and I like Stevie, even if he lacks a sense of humor."

"But aren't you creating a false sense of security for the girl, making her think her boyfriend knows more than he does?"

I give her a look. "Richard Dell, Kevin Watson, Stan Marcus . . ."

She interrupts. "Okay, okay, I get your point."

I was naming the men whose wives and girlfriends have gotten flower arrangements before an order was made. The men count on me to remember what they so often forget.

"You know that you spoil the men in this town," she notes. "There isn't another florist in this state who can be given credit for keeping marriages intact. You're better than Dr. Phil."

"Yeah, well, it's a shame I don't make his money." I add Steven's order to my Valentine list. I think about Jimmy and how I'm going to make all these deliveries next week.

Nora reads my mind. "I can drive the van," she says.

I take a sip of my coffee and turn to her.

"He phoned me after he talked to you. They let him make two calls."

I raise my chin. I can't think of what to say.

"We don't usually talk about these things, but you should probably know," she says. "I'm Jimmy's sponsor."

So that's it, I think; that's why the two of them seem so close. I knew Nora was an alcoholic too, but I had never considered that she was his sponsor. It does make perfect sense now, though, because as I recall, when I was thinking about hiring Jimmy, she had mentioned that she thought it was a good idea. I guess she figured it would help her keep an eye on him. And yet, thinking about the way things turned out, I'm not so sure it all worked out exactly as she had hoped.

"Do you know what happened?"

She shakes her head, walks over and picks up the broom, starts sweeping. "What always happens, I imagine."

I wait and I lean in. I realize I've waited for this answer all my life.

"He got thirsty."

I feel my eyebrows knit together. "That's it? That's what always happens?"

She shrugs. "That's what happens to me," she answers.

I'm about to ask her something else, something more, when the chime on the front door rings and we both turn to see who's coming in so early.

·NINE·

"RUBY, I need some plants to take to an open house."

Kathy Shepherd walks in the door. I feel my backbone straighten. Kathy Shepherd is a real estate agent. She was the one who sold me the shop. She's also my yoga instructor and she is always reminding me a string is pulling on the top of my head. "Up, up," she says, lifting my posture every Saturday. She's a little bossy in class but she's all we've got in Creekside. There's a gentle stretching class for seniors, but they're real strict about the age limit because too many people were signing up and the old people complained. Kathy's yoga class is the only one that those of us under fifty can join.

"Nothing too exotic," she says. "It's the Buckley place."

I know which house she means. It's a traditional Colonial Revival style and sits on a large lot on the west side of town. Wade Buckley was the town veterinarian until he sold his practice and moved out to Waits Lake at the end of last year. He got ordained on the Internet and does weddings and pet funerals.

"Somebody's looking to buy Wade's house?" Nora asks, and I wait for the answer.

"The new guy who bought his practice. John Cash is his name and I hope he's got a lot of it."

"A lot of what?" Nora asks. She's not always quick on her feet.

"Cash," I say.

"Oh. His name is John Cash, like Johnny Cash?"

Kathy shrugs. "He's from the southern part of the state, near the Oregon border," she tells us. "Recently divorced, I heard."

Nora glances over at me, giving me that hopeful look.

"Has a lot of dogs," Kathy adds.

"Well, he is a vet," I respond. "They're supposed to like dogs." I turn to glance down at Clementine. She looks up and winks.

"Anyway, I need to borrow four or five," Kathy says.

I have a deal with the real estate agents. They can rent my plants for ten dollars a day. I know all the agents in the county and I've never had a problem with this business arrangement. It's a good use of my plants and they usually buy one of the spathiphyllum or schefflera arboricolas when they make a sale. For the most part, they're all good customers, although Kathy isn't one of my best. She rents a lot of my plants, never damages any of them, but she prefers to give baked goods to her clients. I suppose she has some kind of arrangement with the Mennonite baker up the street. Kathy is real skinny; she does a lot of yoga, but Kathy also likes pie.

"You want me to give them to you now or deliver them later?"

"Do you mind taking them out there around lunchtime?" She turns to look out the window and I see she's driving her Cadillac and not the SUV. It's parked right in front of the shop. "I hate to ruin my seats."

"Sure, I can do that," I answer. I don't recall having any deliveries for today. I was mostly going to make the arrangements that go out later in the week. "You want to pick out the ones you want?" I ask.

She shakes her head. "Just get me four and put two on stands by the front door, one on the dining room table, and one upstairs in the master bedroom. Wade left a lot of his good stuff in the house since that lake cabin doesn't have as much room. He wanted to sell everything before he moved, but I told him it shows better to have a little furniture in the rooms, gives it more of a homey feeling, and that house needs all the homey feelings it can get. It's very spacious."

I think about the Buckley house. It is very spacious. Wade's wife liked to entertain. She died last summer and I suspect that's why he's made such a huge life change.

Kathy reaches into her purse and pulls out a couple of twenty-dollar bills. "Can you leave them for tomorrow too?" she asks. "I want to take a few pictures and I don't have time today."

I think about the request. I know there are a few deliveries scheduled for tomorrow. It's Jane Clinton's birthday and I need to get arrangements to the community center for a luncheon. I've got a lot to do today, but I shrug off those thoughts for now. I can pick the plants up after I make the deliveries. "Sure," I answer. "How do I get in?"

She rifles through her purse and pulls out a small plastic bag. There are four keys inside it and she takes one out. "It opens all the doors," she explains, handing it over. "I'll come by and pick it up later in the week. I also need to buy some flowers for my parents' anniversary party this weekend. I need a big centerpiece and a couple of small arrangements to place around the room. It's their fiftieth. That's gold, right?"

I nod.

"What kind of flowers go with gold?" she asks, and then waves her hand in front of her face before I can answer. "Just make them look like that arrangement you did for Cora and Ralph's fiftieth anniversary party."

I recall the event she means. It was in November, held in the fellowship hall at the Baptist church. I called the arrangement A Bit of Gold and it had white roses, white spray roses, white alstroemeria, and white lilies, accented with greenery in a golden ribbed Jardinière vase. Kathy attended the party because she sold Cora and Ralph's house when they moved into a condo on the golf course, and she had mentioned then how much she liked the flowers.

"I think that was perfect with the gold decorations." She pauses to consider what she wants. "Let's see. I'll need a little one for the table when you walk in the door to sign the guest book, the large one for the head table where my parents will sit, and another couple of small ones for where people place the gifts." She taps her finger on her chin. "Do you have four gold vases?"

My mind is reeling because I have to call Cooper right away. I'm going to need to order white roses. "Um, yes," I reply, recalling the box of silver and gold vases I bought from a floral show last year.

"Great! Let's put all of the arrangements in gold vases. That should satisfy my sister. She said for me to spend about two hundred on flowers. Oh, and a corsage for Mom and a small rose for Dad, something that matches all the others. Let's go with white, I guess. Will that be about two hundred dollars?"

Nora is punching numbers on the calculator. She does my bookkeeping in addition to helping me clean and work the counter. "Two hundred twelve," she answers, and I'm impressed that she knows enough about the arrangements to know how much to charge. I give her a big grin.

"Perfect," Kathy responds. "You have my credit card on file, right?" And she takes back the twenty-dollar bills she had placed on the counter to cover the plant rental. "Just put everything on that."

I nod. I'm pretty sure she has a Visa card for the real estate company on file with me, but I'm not one to ask about business and personal charges. I let the customers sort that stuff out. I take out my pad and write down the order so I won't forget this conversation.

"So, just get the plants at the Buckley house by two this afternoon. My appointment with Mr. Cash is at three. And then you can pick them back up any time after lunch tomorrow. I'm going to try and take my pictures in the morning. And I'll come by Friday before you close to pick up the anniversary flowers. The party is Saturday evening at the Silver Bear Lodge. We can put those in a box or something so they won't spill, right?"

I nod. I'm making all the notes I need to have for myself about plants and golden vases and white roses. "Thank you, Kathy." I finish writing and glance up from the counter.

She studies me. "Posture," she says, and I snap up tall. "And don't forget to breathe."

I inhale.

"Perfect," she responds with her teacher's voice. "I'll see you on Friday," she adds. And she turns to walk out the door.

We watch as she opens the driver's door and gets into her Cadillac.

"I never liked her," Nora says, and her comment makes me laugh.

·Ten·

I AM making a list of supplies I will need for the rest of the week when Captain Miller walks in the door. Nora has gone to pick up Jimmy. He only had to stay in jail overnight. She is going to stop by the wholesale shop in Spokane and pick up some red ribbon, extra greenery, and little hearts on sticks to add to the bouquets being ordered for next week.

"Ruby, I find myself in a quandary."

Captain Miller was an astronaut. He's the most famous man in Creekside, the smartest too, I imagine. He has four PhDs but he retired from the military as an officer and prefers Captain to Doctor, so that's how he's addressed by most of us around here.

He flew four missions to the moon in the 1970s. He claims he had an epiphany on the second trip, suddenly understood the notion that everything in the universe is connected, that we are all made of stardust. He came home, sold everything he owned, studied paleontology and ancient mysticism at a college in Texas, and became immersed in the fields of quantum physics and the nature

of mind over matter. He started a foundation and has written lots
of books, gets asked to speak all over the world. He's a brilliant man
but most everyone in Creekside hasn't a clue about what he does or
how he thinks.

"Captain Miller," I say. The smile comes naturally; I think the
former astronaut is one of the most kind and lovely men I know. I
see him at the park on Sundays; we occasionally run into each other
at the grocery store and we are often at the library checking out
books or returning them at the same time, but he rarely comes to
my shop. I have no idea what kind of quandary he is in to come to
a florist to ask for assistance. "How can I help you?"

He sighs and scratches the top of his head. He looks like a science professor: wire-rimmed glasses, the navy blue bow tie perfectly tied. He wears a tailored tweed jacket and thick corduroy
pants. "Good morning," he says, as if he is correcting himself and
is offering a proper greeting. He bows slightly.

I keep the same smile intact.

"I have been invited to attend a gala with the president of the
United States next month."

I'm impressed. "How wonderful!" I have heard he has met many
statesmen over the years. Even though the space program has fallen
on hard times, astronauts are still heroes to most people in our
country.

He nods and lowers his eyes, a small show of humility.

I wait. I still am not sure of what I will be able to do to assist
him. I wonder if he wants to take flowers to the president's wife, but
that just seems silly.

"My quandary is that the invitation is for two persons."

I still don't understand.

"I was planning to take my sister. She lives in Boca Raton and
is a big supporter of this president."

"It sounds as if she would love to join you."

He shakes his head. "She's taken a fall and is not able to travel comfortably."

"Oh, I'm sorry about that." And I wait.

He clears his throat. "Ruby, I know we don't know each other all that well. Our conversations have been limited to the books we find at the library and the state of the grounds at the town park, and I also know that I am more than a few decades your senior, but I feel as if we would be excellent companions at this event."

I'm so startled I must appear afraid.

"I'm so sorry," he apologizes, waving his hand in front of his face, shaking his head, and turning to walk away.

"No, no," I plead. "I'm just surprised, is all." I'm afraid I have hurt his feelings.

He turns back to face me.

"I . . . I've never been asked to go to a gala with the president," I explain. "I'm just surprised." I also have the thought that I haven't been asked out by a man in a very long time. James Harvey, the high school principal, asked me to go to the prom last spring, but he was just in need of another chaperone since the English teacher was out on maternity leave.

He smiles, but it's easy to see he is still worried he should not have asked me.

"When is it?" I ask, not at all knowing how to respond. I like Captain Miller, always have. I enjoy the eccentricities of interesting people. I find the former astronaut fascinating. In fact, I never told him but I read his book about his space travel, about his epiphany. I always wanted to ask him about it all but just never had the nerve to approach him. Still, I had never thought of going on a date with him. And that is what this is, right?

"It's not so much a date," he says, as if he has read my mind, "as it is a social event that two friends attend together."

"Oh, okay," I say, glad to have that cleared up. I'm still waiting for him to tell me when it is, and then I need to know where. I'm not really interested in flying to Washington, D.C. Who would watch Clem?

"It's March fifteenth, the day of the ides," he adds.

I nod. I know a little Shakespeare.

"It's in Seattle. I would fly the Cessna. We'd only be gone for a few hours."

I had heard he had a private plane that he kept at the hangar at the small airport up the hill. I think it was Bernie Wilson, the lawyer, who told me it was a real expensive one, twin engines, six seats. He said it was the nicest private aircraft he had ever seen.

March fifteenth, I think. It's just slightly more than a month away. I check the calendar by the cash register and can see that it's on a Saturday, so I wouldn't have to open the shop the next day. Clementine will be fine at home for that long, and I'll just have Jimmy drop by to check on her if I'm running late.

"Captain Miller," I say, surprising even myself. "I would love to accompany you to Seattle to the gala." I can't imagine why I am doing this, and I glance over at the orchids I was arranging for Vivian Jerome.

After Cooper brought them, I just couldn't do it; I chickened out and put them away. And then, this morning, seeing them in the cooler, I changed my mind again. I was starting on the arrangement right after Nora left. I intend to call Conrad to come pick it up this afternoon. Maybe it is already working some of its magic.

He is smiling and nodding and bowing. I wonder how long it has been since he's asked a woman out, and I think he must have put the bow tie on just for this occasion.

"I am the guest speaker at the Rotary gathering in Deer Park this morning," he says, and that's when I realize that the bow tie wasn't meant for me. "So I guess I should be heading in that direction."

I nod. I know the group meets at eleven o'clock. They meet at the steak house in town and they have lunch to follow. Sometimes they buy tulips for a centerpiece or give carnations to the speaker.

"Thank you, Ruby. I am honored that you will accompany me." There is a slight rose color added to his cheeks.

"I am honored, Captain Miller, that you have asked."

"Dan," he says, calling out his first name. "Please, call me Dan."

I feel my own cheeks warm and I look away. "Okay, Dan."

And he turns to walk out. I wait until the door closes and he has passed by the shop windows. I glance down at Clementine, who has watched the entire exchange. There is an inquisitive look on her face.

"I really can't say," I tell her, knowing that she is hoping for a reason to explain what has just happened. I shake my head and pick up the long stem of cymbidium. I hold it to my nose and close my eyes. Vivian will not know what hit her.

·Eleven·

I CHECK the clock on the wall and see that it is already fifteen
minutes after one and I still haven't gotten the plants in the van
to take out to the Buckley house for Kathy. I was hoping that Nora
would have made it back by now. She's been gone for more than
four hours and I wonder if there is some problem with getting
Jimmy out of jail. I'm surprised she hasn't called.

When I haven't been thinking about my morning proposal and
what happened to make me say yes to Captain Miller, I have been
making the arrangements for the week, looking over my orders,
and thinking about the Buckley place and what plants would work
best for today's showing.

For the stands that will be placed on both sides of the front
door, I have decided on two dwarf umbrella trees, schefflera arbor-
icola, that are equal in height. I have had them for months and
they need a little fresh air, a change of environment, so I bring
them in from the corners where they've been, wipe off the tan
plastic planters, and pinch off a couple of the dead leaves. I test the

soil and add a little water, tell them they are beautiful, and place them on the table behind the counter.

I then pull out the good-luck bamboo from a shelf in the rear of the shop; it will work nicely in the master bedroom. I remove the river rocks inside the plastic cube planter and wash and dry them, returning them to anchor the plant. I tie a bright purple ribbon around the stems because purple is especially potent for banishing what lies in the past. It seems to me that if the new veterinarian is trying to start a new life, he'll need all the positive energy he can get to help rid himself of what he is leaving behind. Finally, I decide on a cyclamen for the dining room table. Simple, elegant, the upswept pink petals and the jewel green leaves add a splash of color without overwhelming Kathy's potential customer. It is a friendly plant and easy to move from place to place.

I look over the four plants I have placed on the table, the four plants chosen to fill up an empty house, and I find their tall green bodies full of life and eager to please. "You are doing important work today," I tell them, as if they are employees heading out to serve the public. "And I will make sure I pick you up tomorrow afternoon in time for your evening dinner and bath."

Clementine sighs and stretches. She is used to my one-sided conversations with plants, with the mail, and with her.

"I am so sorry I'm late!" Nora bursts in the front door, startling me and the dog and maybe even the four potted plants. I think I see a stem of bamboo tremble.

"No worries," I reply, turning to the door and to Nora, who is trying to catch her breath. She has one hand on her chest and the other clutching the set of car keys. Her face is bright red. "They hadn't released him yet," she explains. "So I had to wait for them to process all the paperwork and for him to meet with the arresting officer. It took a lot longer than we thought."

I smile. I certainly had enough to do to keep me busy, and I hadn't even thought about having to leave for the showing of the real estate property until just a few minutes before.

"I took Jimmy home," she adds, and moves inside the shop. She drops her keys in her coat pocket and then joins me behind the counter. She shakes her head. "Oh, the cyclamen looks nice; is it a new one?" She has just noticed the plants on the design table.

"No," I answer. "Just hidden in the back. I think the trip will be good for her and the others. It must get terribly boring to have to stay in the same place all the time."

Nora nods. She knows the way I think of the plants, how I treat them like humans, how I move them from week to week, giving them a new view out the window, a spin on the shelf, how I spray them down in the evenings and add a little fertilizer to their soil on Fridays. She knows all of my tricks and peculiarities when it comes to the plants and flowers at my shop, and she has never let on that she finds it odd or unreasonable. This is just one of the reasons I keep Nora on the payroll even though I barely have enough money to cover the bills.

"Is he okay?" I ask, referring to Jimmy.

She picks up a river rock from the bamboo, then replaces it in the planter, blows out a long breath, walks behind the table, takes off her coat, and hangs it on the hook by the back door. "He got beat up," she replies. "He doesn't remember what happened. Some guy at a bar is all he knows."

"Did they take him to the hospital?"

She shakes her head. "He told them he didn't want to go, so they just bandaged him up in the jail. He's got a big lump on the back of his head, a few scrapes, a busted lip. I think a rib is broken but he wouldn't let me take him to the emergency room either. And even if I did, I doubt they would be able to fix what's most battered."

She waits, and I don't respond. I'm not sure I'm following her.

"His pride," she explains. "His bruised and battered pride, not to mention his sobriety record."

I nod, turn away. I feel sorry for Jimmy, sad for him. I'm not an alcoholic, but I understand a daily struggle. I understand the work it takes to keep a monkey off your back or at least to be able to keep going day after day even while it weighs you down. Jimmy is a good man, but even goodness can't push away darkness.

"You want me to help you put these in the van?" Nora asks, and I nod. It would take me at least four trips if I try to do it myself. I reach for one of the dwarf umbrellas, careful not to bend a stem.

"The stands are already in there. I put them in right after you left because I always forget to load the props."

"What is it about the accessories that we can never remember to take them with the deliveries?" she asks.

"We're flower people, Nora, not decorators. Flower people." I'm heading to the door.

"*You're* flower people," she responds. "I'm not sure what I am."

And there is something about the way she says this, the resignation in her voice, the self-loathing, that causes me to stop and turn to her and when I do, I see what she is thinking, the slumped way she is standing, the drop of her chin, the building up of tears. I walk back, put down the plant I had just picked up, and take her by the arms. She will not meet my eyes.

"Nora Dell, you listen to me."

She does not raise her face.

I continue. "You are one of the finest people I know. You are kind and funny and honest. You can add numbers in your head that take me a pad of paper and a calculator to even put them in correct order. You are never late to work and you are always there when I need you. You understand how I run my business and how I like my coffee, and Clementine loves you like you're family. You are not responsible for Jimmy's mistakes. You are not responsible for this event. I know that you are a good sponsor, and you are the best friend I have."

Her shoulders are drooped and her eyes stay lowered.

"Hey," I say, making her look at me. I wait until she does.

"You couldn't have stopped this from happening. There is nothing you could have done to change Jimmy's mind or keep him from going to Spokane and going to that bar and getting in a fight and landing in jail. Jimmy makes his own decisions, and if he decides he wants to drink, there is nothing you can do about it."

She nods slightly.

"You know this stuff," I add. "You're the one who told me this stuff," I remind her. "My mother's choices were my mother's choices. You remember that little speech?"

It is hardly noticeable but there is a tiny movement of her lips. It is barely a smile, but it counts as far as I'm concerned. I have said everything I know to say about this matter.

"Now, I have to deliver these plants to a dead woman's house, a dead woman who will jump out of her grave and wrestle me to the ground if I don't place them in just the right spot before company arrives. Are you going to be okay?"

She nods, and I pull away.

"You get any lunch?" I ask.

She shakes her head.

"All right, I brought some yogurt and fruit and a half a chicken salad sandwich with me this morning. You eat it. I'll stop by the Happy Fortune and pick something up after I'm done at the Buckleys'."

"No, I can't eat your—"

I interrupt her. "I'd rather have an egg roll anyway. Please, eat the lunch." I study her. "Did you check your blood sugar?" I ask. Nora is diabetic.

"It's a little high," she reports.

"Well, do what you need to do and eat the lunch. You can organize the Valentine's delivery schedule and cut some red ribbon if you need a project."

She nods.

I watch her closely.

"You're a good friend, Nora," I say again. "To me and to Jimmy, a very good friend."

She sniffs and picks up the cyclamen, following me out the door.

·Twelve·

This is one fine house," I say to the plants resting in the tubs in the back of the van. I turn off the engine and take in the view. I recall that the architecture of the Colonial Revival style sought to follow the American colonial architecture of the period around the Revolutionary War. The houses, like Dr. Buckley's, are usually two stories in height with the ridge pole running parallel to the street, a symmetrical front façade with an accented doorway and evenly spaced windows on either side of it.

There is an elaborate front door, complete with decorative crown pediments and an overhead fanlight. The window openings, though symmetrically located on either side of the front entrance, are hung in an adjacent pair rather than as single windows.

It appears as if someone has either painted or power-washed the outside of the place because the white wood glistens in the afternoon winter sun. The shutters, turquoise blue, stand bright and clean, opening to let the light pour through the windows. The yard has been weeded and mowed, and the narrow flower bed that sweeps around the house and along the sides is marked with new red bricks and filled with fresh soil. The front steps gleam and there are two plant stands, empty but already placed by the door.

Somebody has been getting this house in good condition to sell, and for a moment I wonder if Dr. Buckley hasn't moved back from the lake to do the work. But I don't really think that he has. I haven't seen him in town in months. It's probably Kathy's pushing and prodding and the work of Timothy Barr's painting company and Jerry Dexter's landscaping crew completing all the labor. More than likely, Wade Buckley just gets the bill.

The house hasn't been on the market that long, a few months, but I know there isn't much real estate action in this small town and I know Kathy wants a commission. This is probably her most lucrative property, and I'm sure she'd love nothing better than to get the new veterinarian's name on a contract for this house rather than on one of the cheaper places on her list. If she landed this sale, she would likely take the rest of the winter off.

I dig in my pocket for the house key she gave me and get out of the van. I head to the back and take out the two umbrella trees to put on the porch stands. Once there I realize ferns would have been more traditional, their long leafy stems dropping over the sides, their full pushy bodies filling up the space around the front door, but I still like the schefflera arboricolas and I remain confident with my decision. They're regal in their guard positions, tall and thin, but still up to the task of greeting and welcoming those who enter. I stand back to admire them.

Next I open the door and check out the interior. Kathy was right; there is furniture throughout, sparse but well placed. A sofa in the living room; two small tables with lamps; a couple of chairs, a wingback and an overstuffed one, carefully placed, one under the window and another along the wall. There are white sheer curtains and a few paintings, a large oriental rug in the center of the room and a coffee table set with an open book and two small candleholders, tiny silver birds, their faces set toward the light coming through the door.

There is a dining table and chairs, a china cabinet bearing a few saucers and cups, dinner plates, and a knickknack here and there to give a little color and fill up the shelves. There is the slightest scent of furniture polish, lemon I think, and I assume Kathy has also acquired the services of Linda Brown's cleaning company because everything appears recently swept, mopped, and wiped down. It is obvious that Kathy has spared no expense with this showing, and like her, I am hopeful she will be rewarded for her careful attention.

I return to the van to get the other two plants, walk back in, and place the bamboo in the center of the dining table, thinking its bright purple ribbon is just the right touch. I judge and approve it and then head upstairs to the master bedroom to set the cyclamen somewhere to provide a little life. I find the perfect spot right away.

There is a small empty table beside a queen-sized bed that is covered by a quilt in a jewel box pattern, probably one that Janice Buckley bought at the craft show that they have every fall at the community center. She was a big supporter of local artisans, and we have some wonderful quilters in Creekside. I put the cyclamen on the table, spin it around to find its best side, and rub a leaf gently between my fingers the way Clementine likes me to fondle her ears. The pink petals stand at attention, the bright color rich and opulent, bringing out the same shade found in the delicate stitches of the quilt.

I look over at the bed and can't help myself, but I wonder if this was Wade and Janice's bed, wonder if this was the room where she died, wonder if he left it like it was, the dresser against the wall, a full-length mirror in the corner, a tall armoire near the window, all of the wood dark and rich, cherry or mahogany, I can't say for sure. The bed, a sleigh frame, covered with eight or ten decorative pillows, thrown easily near the headboard, the light green bedskirt matching the quilt perfectly. I wonder if Wade just packed his bags and walked away, letting Kathy deal with the dust and the memories, the clothes and the jewelry Janice wore and the things the bereaved husband couldn't stand to sell or handle or give away. I wonder if this was the way their bedroom was when she was alive and he was more than half himself.

I lean over and smooth down the quilt and think about Janice, how bright and cheerful she always was, how fond she was of this town, this house, the people she entertained. I think about her petite body, how she walked every morning, waving as she passed my shop, a big smile on her face, how she always had a vase of fresh flowers delivered to her on Mondays, how she truly wanted my business to thrive.

I realize that I hadn't thought much about it in a while, but I miss Janice. She was a fine human being, a good citizen, an attentive friend. And even though Wade wasn't ever a real sentimental man, never really talked about their marriage, or spoke of his undying love for his wife, or participated in public shows of affection, it is clear her death has paralyzed him. In the same way that cancer tortured and wracked Janice's little body, grief has spoiled and smashed Wade's.

I sit down for a second and then slide back and lean against the pillows. The mattress is soft and I take in a breath and close my eyes. Janice and Wade slept here; I'm sure of it. I sense the ordinariness of this space, the unspectacular nightly routine of two people who know each other, love each other, are accustomed to each other, crawling under these covers and lying together, the simple but splendid way couples sleep, back to back or spooned around each other, the light touch of fingers around fingers while turned face to face.

I realize, lying here in the Buckleys' bed, that I have only known this intimacy, this easy way to end a day and fall into my dreams, with my sister. I have only known what it is to share such sacred, holy space with Daisy, mostly when we were children but a final time just before she died. I have never wrapped myself around anyone else and I somehow suspect I never will.

I sense the lived-in nature of this room, this bed, but I also know too well the sorrow. I turn over to my side, pulling my knees to my chest, and do not even hear the sound of the car driving up the driveway or the opening and closing of the front door. I do not know that I am no longer alone until I hear the voice calling from below.

"Hello. Am I at the right place?"

I jump up, smooth down my shirt, my slacks, check my hair in the mirror, and hurry downstairs.

·THIRTEEN·

H ELLO." I enter the kitchen and find a man standing at the kitchen sink, peering out the back window.

There are chickadees at a feeder. Kathy even made sure to set out bird food, obviously hoping to fill the yard with animal life, knowing this might be a nice touch for showing a house to a veterinarian. I'm surprised she didn't ask to borrow Clementine. Having a big dog by the fireplace might have been the clincher.

He turns to me and I think he looks disappointed, or maybe confused. I'm not sure which emotion it is that has caused the deep crease in his brow and his lips to press together, forming such a tight line.

"You're not Kathy," he says.

I'm still not sure if it's disappointment or confusion.

"No," I answer. "I'm not."

I pause and then realize I should probably introduce myself, since I'm the one who isn't supposed to be here.

"Ruby Jewell." I move closer to him and hold out my hand. "I'm the florist," I say, and then decide that isn't really the right introduction, but for some reason I keep going. "I brought some . . . I work with . . ." Suddenly, everything I say sounds inappropriate or is somehow doing away with the portrait Kathy was trying to paint.

I know, of course, that everyone understands that real estate agents want the best light shined on a property and that they'll do what they can to create and direct that best light, but everyone also understands that in order for that proposition to work, the best light needs to be in place, shining on things in as natural a way as possible when a potential buyer arrives. If not, it suddenly appears as if everything might just be some tactic or ploy and a person begins to question the sincerity of their agent and the genuine good nature of the house.

My presence at the Buckley house when the customer arrives, my arranging the plants that are being rented to the real estate agent for the purpose of staging a pleasant presentation, is sort of like members of an audience walking in while the unhidden puppeteers practice, the puppets nothing more than plastic faces and pieces of cloth merely stuck and moving on human hands. You may stay and watch the show, but somehow some of the magic is now missing.

"I need to be going." I drop this stranger's hand, clear my throat, nod a good-bye, and start to hurry out of the room. Maybe he won't tell Kathy I was here. Maybe I can get out before she drives up.

"It's okay," he responds, folding his arms across his chest. "I think this house is too big for me anyway."

I turn back to face him.

"Kathy seems bent on giving me Dr. Buckley's entire life here in Creekside. The office is great, but this house . . ." He looks around. "It's clearly more Dr. and Mrs. Buckley than me." He waits. "I'm John," he adds.

I nod as if I know, because the truth is I do know.

"How many children did they raise here anyway?"

"None," I answer. "It was just the two of them and their pets."

"Did they stable horses in here?"

I can't help myself; I laugh. "No, just a few dogs."

He is shaking his head. "I wouldn't know what to do with this much space," he confesses.

"Mrs. Buckley entertained a lot," I explain. "There were many socials and get-togethers in this house."

"Ah," he replies, drawing out the word, nodding for emphasis. "Well, I figure the only get-together I will be hosting will be Super Bowl parties, and my socials will likely be poker games."

"I see." I glance around the kitchen. "Well, still, for a decent Super Bowl party you need good counter space, and you do have a lot of that here."

He was grinning when he caught my eye. "Yeah, I see what you're saying. Now that you mention it, even to host a respectable poker game you need a big fridge and a good table area."

"Maybe extra bedrooms if the game goes too late and your guests need accommodations," I add.

"Nah, I'll let 'em come and play cards, buy the beer and pretzels, but I don't want my poker partners staying over. I need my personal boundaries; it doesn't matter how big my house is."

I smile as I study John Cash, Kathy's client. He is tall, lanky: a man, it is easy to see, who used to hunch as a boy, trying to hide his height, trying not to stand out or over his classmates, trying to fit in. He has long hands and beautiful blue eyes. His hair is thick and messy and he is wearing a long-sleeved flannel shirt, red and blue stripes, and a pair of tan cargo pants. He has on hiking boots, and the back of his pants on his right leg is caught on the top of his boot. He has a warm smile, broad shoulders, and I believe he is right: This is much too much house for him. It's clear to see that he is a log cabin kind of guy, a farmhouse guy, maybe, but definitely not a Colonial Revivalist.

I hesitate. I know I need to leave, but I am clearly delaying my departure.

"You'd have room for your family to visit." Now I'm fishing.

"My parents don't travel, and my sister prefers hotels," is his answer.

"Children?" I ask.

Now he knows I'm fishing. He shakes his head, and I see that this is a sore subject.

"Horses?"

He smiles, shaking his head. "Just a rowdy pack of shelter mutts and a parakeet."

I nod and glance away.

"You?"

It's only fair that he asks.

"No children, no family, no horses. One shelter mutt, no parakeet."

"And just how big is your house?"

I look around. "About the size of that living room."

We're staring at each other and suddenly I am really, strangely, completely uncomfortable in this moment.

"So, I'm going to go now," I say as I back up. "Ask Kathy about the Chatham place. It's on Flowery Trail, has its own creek and a tree house." I turn to walk out. "Oh, and there's a great room in it, perfect for a Super Bowl party."

I make it to the front door, and then with my hand on the doorknob, I look back. He is watching me.

"The bamboo is a nice touch," he says. "Almost makes me want to buy this place."

I can't help myself but I'm grinning. "Then maybe you should make an offer," I suggest. "And if you mention how much you like the plant, I bet she'll let you keep it." And before he has the chance to respond, I turn around, open the door, and head down the front steps.

I am in my van and pulling out of the driveway, and I am extremely pleased that I have gotten all the way down the street before seeing Kathy's Cadillac making the turn in my direction.

She's talking on her cell phone and I sigh in relief; she doesn't even notice me.

·Fourteen·

W HAT'S wrong with you, and what is Captain Miller talking about in this message he left that the invitation states 'cocktail attire'? And who is this little boy and why does he want to put a leash on Clementine?" Nora met me at the back door.

It's about three questions too many, and I walk in without answering any of them. Will is sitting on the floor near the table petting my dog. I had forgotten about the boy. It took a little time to get things straightened out with his grandmother for him to have the job. I never said anything to Nora about him joining the staff and now I'm surprised he's actually here. He clearly thinks of this as his first day of work.

"Don't take her near the cats," I tell him. "Clementine doesn't like cats."

"Where are the cats?" Will asks.

It's an appropriate question, and I'm impressed that he's thinking about his task. "They hang out at the garage on the corner and the empty lot by the railroad tracks."

He considers the aforementioned locations. It appears this was the direction he intended to go.

"Take her across the street, go over the tracks, and walk down past the old Mexican restaurant and out to the creek behind the Lutheran church. She likes it out there and there aren't any cats."

Will nods, hooks Clementine to the leash he had in his lap, and she stands and seems happy to have a place to go and someone to take her. I walk around the counter and open the front door. The two of them walk out to the sidewalk. Will stops. Clem sits. They both look up and down Main Street and then cross together. I can't tell who is walking who, but I think they'll be fine. Clementine is an easy companion. Unless there are cats. Then she's somebody I don't recognize.

"Who is that kid?" Nora is standing right behind me, watching.

I turn around and almost run right into her, she's so close. She backs up and moves into the store. I follow.

"Will Norris," I answer.

She shakes her head. The name isn't ringing a bell.

"Juanita's grandson," I explain.

"That's Diane's boy?" she asks, peering over my shoulder, still able to see Will and Clementine until they finally disappear behind the old house on the corner of the street.

I nod.

"He looks nothing like her," she comments.

"What did she look like?"

"Short, chubby, purple hair, piercings in her nose and lip and eyebrows, a tattoo of a feather across one side of her face." She continues watching out the window.

I don't say a thing. I just follow her gaze.

"Of course . . ." She turns around to face me when I move behind the counter. "If you take away the hair color and the tattoo and the piercings, it's possible that they bear a resemblance."

I roll my eyes. "You think?"

She waves her hand in front of her. "Never mind about him. Why did you seem so funny when you came in?"

I pick up the orders by the cash register that must have been placed while I was gone and glance over the tickets. "I don't know what you mean," I reply.

She walks over to me and gets real close to my face. She starts to sniff me and pulls away.

"You met Kathy's customer. You met that veterinarian."

I stare at Nora. I do not know how she can pick up on things so quickly. I swear she's psychic, and I wonder what she would know if she hadn't damaged herself so much in her drinking days. I figure she'd be working for the government or writing an astrology column for the paper at the very least.

She's right, of course, but I'm not letting on. "I just ran into him on my way out the door," I lie.

She gets real close again, leans in, and tilts her head from side to side like she can see better out of one eye, hear better out of one ear.

I back away and move around the counter to the other side of the design table. "What is this order from Kyle Bridges?" I glance down at the ticket she filled out.

She is studying me; I can feel her staring but I don't look up.

"He wants twelve long-stemmed roses for Nancy," she answers, referring to Kyle's wife.

"He work an extra shift again?" I ask.

Kyle buys twelve long-stemmed roses when Nancy gets mad, and she usually only gets mad when he takes an extra shift at the fire station. Creekside firemen work four days on, three days off, ten-hour shifts, but Kyle has a reputation for filling in for his buddies. Sometimes he works twenty hours straight. Nancy doesn't think Kyle is as much kind and generous to his colleagues as he is invested in the late-night domino games that take place at the fire station after hours. Kyle has explained this little hiccup in his marriage to me before.

"She changed the locks," Nora replies.

"Again?"

"Did it and then went to work. Kyle still can't get in. He had to go back to the station to take a shower and get his meals. I guess he's hoping the roses will at least help him make it through the front door, if for no other reason than to pack a suitcase for the rest of the week."

I make a kind of humming noise that I like to make when I've heard hard news, and Nora appears as if she's not going to make any other inquiries about John.

"Is he coming by to get them?" I ask, heading to the rear of the shop.

"He should be here any time."

Glad to have a task so that I don't have to get the third degree about John Cash or about a message from Captain Miller, I go into the cooler and pull out twelve of the healthiest red roses I have. I examine them closely and snap off a few of the leaves still attached to the bottom of the stems. I pick out about ten branches of seeded eucalyptus and a handful of variegated pittosporum. I also grab one full-bodied stem of snapdragons, tiny white flowers, that I can delicately place somewhere in the bouquet.

Snapdragons are a natural reducer of anger, and I figure Nancy could use a little anger reduction even though I'm pretty sure that the newlyweds are going to have to find some way of compromise regarding Kyle's work schedule. The flowers help, but eventually the fireman is going to have to make a choice: the buddies at the station or his lonesome wife.

I suspect he's not far off from figuring it out, and I think maybe I should add a few white chestnut leaves in the bottom of the vase. Maybe the herb can help Kyle decide to settle in more at home.

I walk the flowers out to the front of the shop, drop them on the table, go through the other door to the closet near the back door, and find my jar of white chestnut leaves on the third shelf. I open the container, shake out a few leaves into my hand, and put the jar back where I found it. When I return to the design table behind the counter, Will is back and Clementine is helping herself to some water in her bowl by the sink.

"We didn't see no cats," Will reports. "And Clementine peed a bunch of times. We went all the way down the creek to the liquor store, back around the diner, and down Second Street by the church." He pauses. "She's a good dog."

Clementine glances over from the bowl. She raises her head in my direction as if to say, *He's a good boy.*

I nod at them both.

"You want to empty the buckets in the cooler and pour in some fresh water?" I ask.

He shrugs, and I turn to Nora.

She immediately understands that I'm asking her to show him how and waves Will around the counter and toward the cooler. "It's hard," I hear her explain. "You can't touch the tops of the flowers, have to pick them up only by the stems very carefully, and then you walk the buckets all the way out past the back steps to empty them."

I smile, find my scissors, and start snipping the ends off Kyle's roses.

FIFTEEN

I GLANCE at the clock above the door. Cooper is already six hours late delivering the Valentine's flowers. I had planned to spend the morning getting a good start on the specials: one single rose, a bud vase tied with a red bow, and just a bit of greenery, stems of dagger fern or emerald palm. Nora had already secured the little boxes of candy to the stuffed animals and there was a line of teddy bears standing beside empty vases, covering the entire design table.

Without the shipment of roses, however, that activity, along with assembling the standard dozen long-stemmed bouquets, was sidelined and I had to work on the other arrangements. Those included the funeral spray for John Clover's service over at the Baptist church, red and white and blue carnations, the American flag made out of flowers, a special for the veterans; a birthday bouquet of pink and yellow gerberas for Nancy Wilkerson to be delivered this afternoon just before she leaves from work at the hardware store; and a dieffenbachia with three tiny butterfly ornaments and two helium balloons to be picked up after three for a housewarming gift for a friend of Maude Peters in Colville. I certainly had enough to keep me busy, but on the day before Valentine's I needed my red roses as early as possible.

"Do you want me to try to call him again?" Nora asks. She is sweeping up the leaves and stems from the floor. She is clearly aware of how many times I have looked at the clock.

I shake my head. "I still have other things to do," I answer. "He's always late for Valentine's," I remind both of us. "He'll get here before five."

She walks over to the front window and glances up at the sky. She turns back to me and doesn't say what I know she is thinking. The weatherman is calling for snow later tonight, and that can mean real trouble for florists trying to make deliveries. Jimmy is still employed at the shop, printing out the tiny gift cards and pinning them to the ribbons, keeping the storage room clean and the van tidy, carving out bricks of green foam. He's in the back room now, washing and cleaning out the vases; there are plenty of chores to be done, but without a license, he can't make deliveries. Nora doesn't drive so well in snow, so that means if we wake up in the morning to more than a couple of inches, I'll have to make the runs.

I prefer to stay in the shop on Valentine's Day because I'm usually swamped from morning to evening creating all those last-minute bouquets. It doesn't matter how many Hallmark commercials there are or how early in the month retail owners hang their red holiday banners, there are always four or five frantic customers running in wanting something beautiful to take home to their sweethearts. Without Jimmy to make deliveries and with Nora uneasy about winter driving, I know I'll be out for most of tomorrow, so I need to make some extra arrangements to stick in the fridge before I leave today.

Since I've already used all the red roses I had, those last-minute shoppers are going to have to do with the white ones left over from

Kathy's anniversary bouquets and the pink spray roses I always have on hand. I walk back to the cooler to see what else I can use. And when I return about fifteen minutes later, my arms full of freesia and bells of Ireland, daffodils and the flamingo mini gerberas, John Cash is standing at the counter. Nora, I can easily see, is charmed by the new veterinarian, as is Clementine, who has been roused from her sleep and is standing by his side.

"Oh," I say, wishing I had checked myself in the mirror, wishing I had not put on the old green smock I was wearing that was covered in spots and stains, and wondering why I was suddenly wishing for things I never remember wishing for before.

He smiles. Clementine turns to me but then quickly looks back up at Cash, presses her nose against his leg. She is so transparent.

"Dr. Cash bought a house," Nora announces.

"Oh," I say again. *Maybe we could opt for another word*, I think. I glance around, trying to find a place for all the flowers I have in my arms, since the table is stacked with Nora's work.

"You were right. The place on Flowery Trail is perfect."

I feel the "oh" about to surface again and I tighten my lips around it, and instead I simply nod.

"Looks like you got a busy day ahead of you tomorrow." He eyes the overflowing design table, the bud vases, the bunch of blooms in my embrace. "I always wondered how florists manage to get all those orders filled for Valentine's Day. I never imagined enlisting the help of an army of bears."

I follow his glance ahead of him, behind Nora, and I understand his reference. The stuffed bears are standing at attention, ordered in a perfectly straight line. They are soldiers armed and ready for duty.

Suddenly, Nora laughs. It is way too exaggerated and John catches my eye. I smile and shrug and Nora stops, realizing she's the only one laughing. She clears her throat.

"I'm just going to go to the back and see if Jimmy needs any help." She peers over her glasses and gives me a wink. It's as big a gesture as her laughter and it embarrasses me. I see that John has glanced away. He is scratching Clementine, which is, at the moment, greatly appreciated by us both.

I lay the flowers on the edge of the counter and wipe away the tiny leaves clinging to my smock. "So, the house is good?" I should probably move over and stand across from him, but I feel more comfortable with a little distance between us. I prefer a bit more space than apparently does my dog. I glance down and see how she is leaning into his legs.

He rises and I realize I had forgotten the blue of his eyes.

"It's just like you said," he replies. "I love the little creek, and the great room is, well, great. And even though I must say the tree house is inviting, I'm not quite sure it was built for someone my size."

I smile.

"I made an offer last night and it was accepted this morning."

"Well, congratulations," I say. "Sounds like you're happy, and I know the Chathams are glad to have a buyer, and I'm sure Kathy is pleased to have made the sale."

"Truthfully, I'm not so sure about the real estate agent. I think she was holding out to the last minute with the hope that I might change my mind and take the Buckley house."

I had forgotten that she was counting on selling that property and suddenly wonder if she knows it was my suggestion that he see the other house.

"Oh, don't worry," he quickly adds, apparently reading my expression. "I never asked specifically about the place. She doesn't know you gave me the idea. I just described my ideal home, which happens to have a creek and a tree house, and she took me right to the address. She's beating herself up, actually, because she thinks it was entirely her idea."

I nod with relief. I don't really want to lose Kathy's business. Her parents' anniversary party helped pay for some necessary repairs on the van. She's a good customer, not to mention the only yoga instructor in Creekside. If I make her mad I'll be back doing my fitness routine in my living room using borrowed videotapes from the library. And I know my posture would suffer. I suddenly feel myself straighten at the thought of Kathy's Saturday morning class.

"I came by to get the bamboo."

I'm not sure what he means. "Oh." There, I said it again. I shake my head and I realize he means the plant that I used at the Buckley house. I suppose he wants to buy it.

"I'm hoping that it will look just as good in this house as it did in the other."

"I can't think of a reason that it shouldn't work just as well."

"And it does bring luck, right?"

"Peace, actually," I answer. "It's called a good-luck bamboo, but it's really considered lucky because of its peaceful vitality and sturdiness." Suddenly, I'm sounding like an encyclopedia. Clementine glances in my direction; she notices the same thing.

"Well, one certainly can't go wrong with that growing in a corner of his house."

I'm just about to respond when I hear the back door swing open and Cooper's loud and booming voice. I smile at John, and I'm not sure whether I'm relieved or disappointed that my Valentine shipment has finally arrived.

·Sixteen·

W ELL, we survived another year," I announce to Clementine
as I lock the front door and flip the sign from *Open* to
Closed.

She has risen from her resting spot under the table and is watching me. When she sees me grab the stool and put it by the counter,
she heads back to where she was, realizing we're not leaving at our
usual time. I walk over to the cash register and blow out a big
breath, glad the busiest day of the year is done.

Jimmy and Nora just left and even though I'm tired, I still want
to tally the orders and check the cooler before heading out. I know
I can do this tomorrow, but I haven't added the numbers and I'm
curious about the day's total sales. I'm pretty sure the shop was
successful but I can't help myself, I want some confirmation that we
did in fact have a good day.

I glance around. All of the teddy bears and boxes of candy are
gone. I used most of the roses that Cooper delivered and from what

I can see, there are only two arrangements left in the refrigerator. The ribbon rolls are empty and I'm running low on green tissue.

I'm happy to see that my inventory is pretty much wiped out. And even though that could be dangerous for other types of businesses, for a florist, emptying the shop of supplies is actually the sign of a very good day. Luckily, I shouldn't need any red ribbon for a while; there are plenty of rolls of other colors, and even though I have used every one I had in stock, I don't usually get orders requiring bud vases during February and March, and with a few weeks before Easter I should have a little break before having to order another large shipment from Cooper. I am confident that there are still enough flowers left for the Sunday church services and birthday bouquets for the weekend, and I never run out of potted plants. I am not worried. I should be fine until next week.

I sit down on the stool and open up the accordion file by the cash register and pull out the tickets. First, I decide that I'll go through the early orders, some of them made weeks ago, making sure once more that I didn't forget or misplace one. I went through this process twice already, but I just need to be confident that I filled all the orders and made all the deliveries.

I am happy to report that after twenty years in this profession, I have never missed a delivery. From the very beginning of running this business I have understood that a florist forgetting to fill an order for Valentine's Day or any special occasion can never really be forgiven.

Most folks are gracious when mistakes are made. They'll overlook pricing problems or misspelled names; they'll not make too much fuss if you forget to add flowers that were suggested for a bouquet. But losing an order and missing the important delivery date, well, that's just a mistake that cannot be forgiven. There is no room in the florist profession for those glaring errors.

I look over the names and recall the reactions I received when I made the deliveries earlier: plenty of smiles, a few rounds of applause, pure delight and pleasure. I discovered I didn't mind so much having to leave the shop and make the deliveries after all. I know now why Jimmy likes this job so much better than driving a bus. Bringing flowers to people is a whole lot more fun than picking up children and dropping them off at school.

I think about the places I walked in with bouquets today, and one thing was the same everywhere I went. High school girls, blue-collar workers, and professionals: the jobs and titles don't matter, women do love their flowers.

I glance through the messages from their husbands and lovers, their fathers and sons. *With all my love. You are my everything. Please be mine. You're the best.* Every note is personal and prized, and as I read these short notes of adoration, I feel the tears gather in my eyes. It doesn't matter how long I do this work or how exhausted I get, every year I have the same reaction. I'm just a sucker for Valentine's Day.

Relieved that I didn't miss a preorder, I straighten the stack of papers and bind them together with a rubber band. Then I place them back in the folder so that Nora can log them on the computer later and then add them to the year's file box that we keep in the rear of the shop. I tally up those numbers. We definitely exceeded our sales from previous years. The teddy bear special worked out nicely.

Finally, I reach in and pull out the orders that came in today, the ones that were given and picked up while I was out making the deliveries. Nora writes down the names of the customers so I can make sure the purchases are added to their lists. She understands that I always like to know who stopped by or phoned in and what they bought.

Henry Phillips had come in sometime during the day and bought the large arrangement that I put together yesterday afternoon, the one I named Charmed and Romanced, created with light yellow roses, pink Asiatic lilies, yellow alstroemeria, and white waxflower, accented with leatherleaf fern. I suppose he was taking them to the library and hand-delivering them to Lou Ann. I wonder about their romance and if the flowers are helping it along.

Justin Dexter stopped by. I thought of him yesterday morning and figured with all that he's been doing to take care of Jenny, the day would just sneak up on him, and I had been right. I was glad to see that Nora had given him the arrangement I had made with them in mind.

I study the ticket and confirm that he bought the Yellow Spring Delight arrangement with stems of white freesia, fresh yellow tulips and calla lilies, white ones, mixed with stalks of green viburnum and graceful tendrils of ivy. The yellow would be good for Jenny, better than red, I had decided, so I'm glad he was happy with my choice, and I hope she felt well enough to enjoy his gift.

It appears as though the orchid did its magic for Conrad because it was Vivian who stopped by the shop after lunch. According to Nora's note, she bought the small but tightly arranged bouquet of hydrangeas, green and pink ones, lavender roses, tulips and green myrtle. It was a more feminine arrangement but still clearly a romantic one. I smile and think Conrad will be pleased.

There's a ticket for Will. I read over the order and it appears as if he came in the shop after school, walked Clementine, and bought flowers. The little boy must have spent all the money he made working last week to buy a small vase of belladonnas, vibrant blue delphiniums surrounding one red rose, and I assume the purchase was for his grandmother, Juanita. I see Nora didn't charge him the full price and I'm glad she knew to discount the boy's order.

I can see Will in my mind's eye sorting through the flowers in the storage room and picking the blue ones. Nora must have put the bouquet together and I'm sure she added a few sprigs of gypsophila, the tiny white buttons that accentuate the darker colors in arrangements. Juanita must have been pleased and surprised to receive her grandson's gift, and I feel the tears well again, thinking about a young boy's gift to his mother's mother, thinking of the tender ways children love.

With this second round of weepiness and knowing I still have one stop before going home, I decide I'm too tired to keep reading tickets. I'm stacking them together, putting them back in the file, confident I'll hear about the day's orders from Nora in the morning, when one slip of paper falls out of the stack and onto the floor. As I bend down to pick it up, I read the name and I suddenly feel an unfamiliar emotion. The tenderness is gone. This feeling is something akin to disappointment or envy; I can't say for sure. All I know is that when I see the line marked *Customer* and read the name *J. Cash*, I don't feel quite so in love with the day.

I stop to study the order. The veterinarian had also made a purchase today. He had obviously come by the shop, but not to see me, as I had imagined was the reason for his visit yesterday, but rather to buy flowers, to buy flowers for someone else. I feel a sudden twinge of that emotion again, or maybe it's more of a pang. I can't say, since everything about this feeling, this reaction, is new for me. But I read the ticket and know right away that he had someone special in mind when he placed the order. I glance over at Clementine.

"Did you know about this?" I ask.

She slides a bit farther under the table so that she doesn't meet my eyes.

He bought the Graceful Heart Bouquet, the last arrangement I made before going home last night, the one that used all the remaining roses, the one I put together so carefully, so deliberately, the one I created without knowing for sure who would buy or receive it. Bear grass pulled into the shape of a heart, tied with purple waxflower blossoms, velvety red roses with pittosporum, and all delicately placed in a ruby-red cube vase, the only one I had, the one Cooper gave me as a gift, the one I studied before filling it with blooms.

Dr. John Cash picked this arrangement to give to someone on Valentine's Day, and even though I am very clear I have absolutely no hold on the man, no ties to him—I barely know him, after all—the thought of him giving my delicate creation to another woman pinches a bit more than I think it should. And although I had not really given it any consideration, "pinched" is not at all the way I wanted to be feeling at the end of this day.

·Seventeen·

S orry I'm late," I say, brushing off the snow from the headstone and placing the tall gray cement vase back in its holder at the bottom of the stone. "I had to deliver today," I add, confident that my sister understands what that means.

"It'll be more than a couple of months before Jimmy gets his license back, and I can't afford another driver and he can't afford to lose this job." I reach around for the plastic stadium seat I had dropped and slide it closer, plopping down on it. I wrap the blanket around my shoulders and pull my wool cap down over my ears. Clementine is sniffing something at the base of the tree in front of us. She glances over at me and I nod, signaling that I see her and that she is fine.

"I ran out of the hot pink ones," I note, reaching up and clipping off a drooping leaf from the gerbera. "Hope you don't mind orange." I sit back and study the bouquet I made for Daisy. "All the red ones were spoken for."

Like most of the arrangements I keep at the cemetery, this one is filled with the brightest colors I could find. Today that means orange and yellow and bright gold. Daisy liked her flowers to pop.

"Cooper was late again and I was starting to think I would have to drive down to Spokane and pick up a couple of buckets of roses from the wholesale grower off Champion Street, but he finally showed up at two o'clock in the afternoon. That only left me four hours to get all the orders filled." I lean back on my elbows.

"Crazy guy. He claims it was traffic that made him late, but I know he was hitting on every florist from here to Moscow. He always thinks Valentine's Day is going to be his lucky day, even though every year I remind him that we are all too tired after this holiday to think about romance for ourselves. The last thing a florist wants on February fourteenth is for some horny salesman to try to get her in bed." I can hear my sister laugh. I figure she's heard this story before, but she always humors me by not interrupting.

"Did I tell you he kissed me once?" I know this will pique her interest.

I shake my head, remembering how he leaned in, smelling of mints and coffee, how I thought he was only going for a hug and how I leaned in as well, only to meet him lips to lips. I had known him for exactly one month.

"He had his tongue down my throat before I even realized what was happening."

Clementine suddenly joins me, drops down at my side. She remembers that day because she had to hear about it for weeks. When she knows the story I'm telling, I figure she'll get up again and walk away. Clementine hates to hear the same thing over and over. She doesn't leave, however; she just closes her eyes and sighs.

"I know you would have clocked him, but, well, I was just starting the business and he was giving me ninety days to pay instead of sixty and I needed the extra time, so I just pulled back and started trimming stems of aspidistra. You know me, I acted like nothing had happened even though I'm sure that he got the message loud and clear, and that's the last time he's tried anything with me." I glance up at the sky. It's getting dark and I count a few stars.

"I'd clock him today, though."

I think about John Cash and consider telling Daisy about the new veterinarian and the special order he placed sometime during the day while I was away, the tiny spark I thought I felt between us. I study the headstone and change my mind. She'd want to hear every detail and I don't even know them all to tell.

"It turns out Frank Goodrich didn't want any of his teddy bear arrangements. He ordered two bouquets of a dozen roses each again this year. One had red and the other had pink. I don't know who got the pink ones, since he picked them up himself, but I delivered the red roses to Verna Johnston over at the clinic. I think she's a little suspicious of Frank since she took a long time reading the card. I stood there a minute just to be polite, but when I got the feeling she might ask me questions about Frank and his flower orders, I headed out."

I remember how the young receptionist peeked over the card, her dark eyes casting a look of doubt, and how Jane Dryer, her coworker, walked over to the counter and stuck her face in the bouquet. "Someone must really love you," was the last thing I heard before clearing out.

There are things florists know that we must take to our graves. I glance up at where I'm sitting. "Or maybe to our sisters' graves," I say as a joke.

"Jenny isn't doing well." I change the subject and lean forward, pulling my legs under me. "I heard from Louise that she goes back to the hospital next week for more treatments."

I am disappointed that the narcissus didn't help with her insomnia. I recall Justin stopping by a few days ago saying she was still up every night after only a couple of hours of sleep. It worries me that none of the remedies I send are helping with her symptoms, alleviating none of her aches and pains. The only thing that seems to help any at all is the lavender. She seemed to like the little sachet I made for her to place under her pillow, and I send her sprigs in every bouquet Justin buys. I worry for them both that the cancer is more aggressive than they know.

"Stan remembered to get something for Viola this year, and Henry seems to be smitten with the librarian." I have a clear picture in my mind of the bouquet the barber bought and again find myself hopeful that Lou Ann is pleased by his affections.

"I think you're right about Jimmy and Nora," I report, recalling how Daisy once told me about her AA sponsor, how she had an affair with the man for two years before he left town, cutting it off. She said they are reminded over and over in meetings that sex is not to be considered by two recovering alcoholics bound by the twelve steps, but sometimes addicted people just can't help themselves. The shared stories of regret and disappointment, loss, and the day-in and day-out struggles create such intimacy between a pair that the only thing that keeps them from buying a bottle of booze is the wicked desire to be together.

"It's not supposed to happen," she told me one night in the hospital after I caught her in bed with the older man who she said had been her arresting officer, a policeman who had been the speaker at the meeting she had attended earlier that week. "But sometimes it just does. The sex doesn't last as long as a trip or a buzz, but it sure does take your mind off drugs for a minute or two." She had laughed when she said it, and for whatever reason I had laughed too. Daisy could find the humor in anything.

I see the longing in both Nora and Jimmy. I just don't know what it's for. Maybe redemption. Maybe to be connected to someone. Maybe it's just the desire to be lost in or to something other than addiction, other than despair. I don't know what the two of them do or even where they go when they leave the shop together, Nora driving them out past Main Street, heading north on Highway 311, the opposite direction from where both of them live. Since Jimmy's been back, I figured it was to an AA meeting in Colville or the evening one held at the nondenominational church in Valley, but I've never asked and they never tell. But I can't help but see how deeply they care for each other, how deeply they want for each other not to be broken.

I study the headstone in front of me, the vase of flowers, freezing now in the evening cold, and I think how we are all broken over one thing or another, how we all limp about, dragging our sorrows and troubles, our failures and disappointments, our perfect loneliness, and how it is when we suddenly open our eyes and see someone next to us dragging their own smashed bones. It seems only natural that we would want to crawl in their direction holding out our hands.

Daisy was an alcoholic and a heroin addict, but she always knew how to meet others, how to reach them, connect with them. I may not drink until I pass out or crave being high, but that certainly doesn't make me better than her because I could never do what my sister could do. People think I'm the smart one, the fortunate one, the unbroken member of the Jewell family, but they're wrong. Even Mama knew how to take a lover and squeeze life out of a roll in the hay. Daisy had so many friends that after she died they lined the walls of the funeral home, poured out the front door and stood under the windows. They all made sure they told me what Daisy meant to them. It was a little overwhelming.

Me? My heart can open to blooms and stalks, delicate petals and green leafy plants; I can love these creatures of beauty. But what I know of intimacy is wrapped too tightly in loss and misery and I cannot risk an unfolding. It is enough to fan the flames of adoration for others, sweeten the romance for someone else. It is enough to caress my flowers and cherish my dog. And without saying a word to my sister, I shake the thoughts of John Cash and a Graceful Heart betrayal out of my head. Daisy is bound to know I'm not telling her everything about Valentine's Day this year, but lucky for me, she can't force me to say anything more than what I have already said.

"I love you, Sis," I say as I place my hand on the headstone, spreading my fingers cold across her name. "It was a good day. I can pay the mortgage." And I stand up to leave.

I am almost by the gate when I catch a glimpse of the blue flowers as I'm throwing the beam from my flashlight from side to side. I recognize the bouquet right away from the description I read on the order slip, and I suddenly realize that I am not the only one who visited a grave that day. I walk over and read the name on the newest monument on the west side of the cemetery.

"Diane Norris," I say out loud, and quietly note the dates of her birth and death. "Beloved daughter and mother." The small delphinium blooms, blue stars, now wilted and drooped in the clear vase, were not given to Juanita after all. The bouquet that I imagined was lighting up a dinner table or a small bedroom desk, a grandson's token of love, had been bought and left at a grave.

"Happy Valentine's Day," I say to Will's mother. And I sense Clementine near me. I reach around, feel her warm breath on my hand, and turn to head home.

Do you have a dress?"
I have finally told Nora about my invitation from Captain
Miller. She keeps calling it a date. I keep calling it an outing. Nora
will look after Clementine while I'm gone.

"I have the one I wear to the weddings."

We are delivering flowers to the country club together. It's a
retirement party for the golf pro and the order was for twelve
arrangements of mums, footballs, yellow and white. The club manager placed the order and I didn't offer any alternative suggestions.
He sounded quite confident about his choice.

If it had been Carl Wyatt, the catering manager, the arrangements would have been a little more creative and a lot more color-
ful. He has great taste and I always love planning events with him.
Joe Maddox, the manager, has never ordered flowers from me
before. I didn't even recognize his name when he made the call. His
secretary, Nancy Beadle, usually orders flowers for his wife on her
birthday.

"The pink one?" Nora asks. "The one from 1988?"

I have to stop for a minute to remember what we were talking about. Oh right, my dress. "It was from the early nineties, but yes," I reply. "That's the one."

"Oh no, Ruby, you cannot wear that thing to meet the president. You shouldn't even be wearing it to the weddings anymore. It's old. It's too big for you. And there's a yellow stain on the right side, down at the hem. And if I know Captain Miller, he'll be in a tuxedo, a classic one, with a black silk bow tie and a perfectly creased cummerbund. His shoes will be polished to a mirror shine and he will be wearing a new pair of socks. No, no, no . . ." She shakes her head. "The pink dress will not be making an appearance on this date."

"It's not a date. And how do you know there's a yellow stain on the right side of my dress? And how come you never told me?"

"Darling Ruby, I know how little you care about what you wear, and when you're slogging baskets of flowers across a church sanctuary the age and fit of your dress doesn't really matter. To answer your question, I noticed the stain a year ago. I hoped you would discover it and get it cleaned. The fact that you haven't is even more of a reason you cannot be trusted with wardrobe details for your date with the astronaut."

We pull into the country club parking lot and I stop the van by the front door. I put the engine in park and turn to Nora. "When do I have time to go shopping?"

I realize I sound a little defensive. But now I have to wonder, does Nora talk to other people about what I wear to the weddings I attend? Has anyone complained about how I look? Does it matter what the florist wears?

I don't even want to know. I shut off the engine and pull out the key. We both get out of the van and I walk around to open the back door. I glance down at what I'm wearing. It's my favorite pair of army green Dockers. I have on hiking boots and a red flannel shirt, one I bought at a yard sale last year. I look over at Nora and she pretends she doesn't notice what I'm thinking.

"What are you doing tomorrow afternoon?" she asks.

I hand her two arrangements.

"I'm working on my taxes," I answer, pulling out two more and moving toward the front door.

"Well, you can work on them until noon. Then we're going to Nordstrom's." Together we head in the direction of the dining room and then she walks around me, leading the way.

We've both done numerous events at the country club. Nora and I know exactly where the dinner will be.

"Nordstrom's? Nora, I can't shop at Nordstrom's. The last time I went in there the only thing I could afford was a pair of panty hose, and they cost more than the shoes I was wearing them with."

She stops and turns around. We have just entered the main dining room. The tables are not yet set.

"You are going to a dinner with an astronaut. The man walked on the moon. You will be in the company of the president of the United States. We are going to Nordstrom's and we are buying you a suitable dress for the occasion and if I have to open up an account and pay for this dress for the rest of my life, we are making the purchase tomorrow."

"Yellow football mums?" Carl has joined us at the head table. He is clearly unhappy with the flower order.

"I know, Carl," I say sympathetically. "I tried to tell him you make great floral decisions, but he had his mind set on the mums."

"It's going to look like a high school booster club meeting," he responds, taking the arrangements from Nora. He moves around the table and we follow him as he places one of the bouquets at the center. He stands back and shakes his head.

"I have some yellow cushions, pink buttons," I tell him, naming the other flowers I have in stock that would go with the large mums. "But your boss seemed to think these would add the perfect touch."

"Oh please, Ruby, my boss thinks carnations are exotics. He hasn't a clue about the perfect touch." He spins the large vase around, searching for the best angle, which I can see is the one he just had.

"I knew leaving on vacation without going over the calendar with him was a mistake. His wife and I both know not to leave him in charge of decorative details." He spins the arrangement back around.

"Do you mind?" He faces me. "Maybe just a couple of medium to tall vases of the white cushions and green buttons?" He turns back to the football mums. "And how about asters, do you have any bunches of yellow and pink?"

I smile.

"I believe I do," I answer. I glance over at Nora and she's adding up the cost of the new bouquets in her head. I can tell that she's already figuring out how we'll pay for our shopping adventure.

"How many more of these did he order?" Carl asks.

"There's ten others just like these," Nora replies before I can.

"Oh, my." Carl hasn't stopped shaking his head since he's seen the flowers. "Well, just bring those in and I'll figure something out. Bring me four of the new arrangements. Ruby, you know what I like."

He reaches out and grabs me by the arms, and I lean down and put the bouquets I'm still holding on the table.

"Just charge the club whatever the cost," he continues. "Joe will never notice. Even if he does, I will talk to Velma. She will totally understand and make him pay for this disaster. She would be mortified if she finds out we hosted a party for members of the club with yellow and white football mums."

"You know, Carl, Ruby should charge you extra," Nora chimes in with her two cents. "She's been working all day."

Carl turns to Nora and then back to me. "A surcharge. I totally agree. I do the same thing if a customer changes his mind within twenty-four hours of an event. And believe me, it happens more times than I care to talk about." He raises an eyebrow. "Add ten percent to the bill." He turns to Nora, who is frowning.

"Ruby needs a new dress," my assistant responds. "She's got a date with an astronaut and the president."

I feel my face flush.

"Then make it twenty-five," Carl replies, clearly impressed. He touches his chest delicately. He has such a flair for conversation. "And for heaven's sake, let's go to Nordstrom's."

Nora looks at me and winks.

I can see there's no way out of this shopping trip now.

·Nineteen·

THE van is full. Jimmy put the seats back in so that the floral delivery vehicle is now transporting six people and one canine to Spokane to buy me a dress. This is not at all what I had in mind for my Sunday afternoon. Nora is riding up front with me. She told Jimmy about the shopping trip and he said he wanted to come and make amends for whatever happened at the bar when he was arrested. I have no idea how he's working that out except that he plans to spend his afternoon in the park across the street from the mall while we're shopping.

Carl decided Nora and I couldn't be trusted to pick out a special-occasion dress by ourselves, so he's in the seat behind us with his mother, Lucy Wyatt, who is visiting from Seattle and wanted to return a blouse. Will is the sixth person in the van. He's sitting in the back with Clementine. He came by the shop as we were getting ready to leave and asked if he could come along. His grandmother agreed, so he's the official dog walker, planning to stay in the park with Jimmy while the rest of us sort through racks of dresses and pants, shirts and jackets, sales and seasonal. I'd rather be in the park with Jimmy and Will and Clementine.

"So, Ruby, when did you start dating an astronaut?" It's Lucy Wyatt asking.

We've finally gotten everyone in the van and are heading south.

"I'm not dating Captain Miller," I answer, eyeing her in the rearview mirror. "It's just a special event that he invited me to attend with him."

"Well, when I was young, that was what we called a date," she replies.

Nora turns to me, her eyebrows lifted in a way to tell me she's not the only one who thinks what she thinks, her own unique way of saying *I told you so*. I've seen that look before.

"Will you be staying the night together?" she asks.

I can tell that everyone is waiting for my answer.

"Well, of course not," I say, trying not to sound offended even though I do feel a little affronted.

"You know, Mother, Captain Miller is the best-dressed man in Creekside," Carl chimes in, trying to change the subject, I presume.

"He is a sharp dresser," Nora adds.

"And he's not gay?" Lucy asks.

"Unfortunately, no," her son answers. "But he does order his shirts from Brooks Brothers and his silk ties from a designer in Paris. He has his suits made in San Francisco, where he goes twice a year to visit his brother. His shoes are custom made in Italy with a slightly padded footbed and a square toe. Oh, and his cuff links are created by a Cuban jeweler living in Miami."

The van is silent. We're all staring at Carl.

"What?" he asks, surprised to have all the attention drawn in his direction.

No one responds.

"He's a regular at the club and I asked him where he shops," he follows up. "He told me," he continues. "I'm not a stalker, if that's what you're thinking."

Nora has raised her eyebrows again. This time her look means something totally different from the *I told you so* one she gave me earlier.

"I think it's nice you're going on a date, Ruby." Jimmy has joined the conversation.

I had almost forgotten that he and Will were sitting back there.

"It's not a date," I reiterate to those riding in the van, but it's as if no one is listening.

"Why don't you date?" Lucy asks. "You're a good-looking woman, own your own business. Are there no eligible bachelors in Creekside?"

Before I can answer, she turns to her son. "We should fix her up with your cousin Stanley," she says.

"Mom, Stanley got married last summer."

"Oh, that's right," she responds. "They had the wedding in a barn."

"It was a stable," Carl notes. "Some new venue on the coast," he explains to the rest of us. "It was quaint."

"It was a barn," Lucy repeats.

"You'd have liked the flowers, Ruby," Carl says as he leans up closer. "They had long-stemmed oriental lilies, pink and white ones, purple iris, and a kind of tulip I'd never seen before. The petals curled in on themselves; the edges were almost like feathers."

"Parrots," I say. "Parrot tulips. They usually bloom later in the season. What color were they?" I ask.

"Yellow and pink," he replies. "And she had them everywhere." He sits back. "You'd have been pleased."

I smile. It's satisfying to be known for who I am, for my artistry to be honored, for Carl to know what I would think is tasteful.

"So, why don't you date?" It's Lucy again.

I was hoping that we had moved on from this topic.

Everyone is waiting.

She sits up now, shifts in her seat so she's very close to me and Nora. "You're not a lesbian, are you?" she whispers.

Carl answers for me. "Mom, no, Ruby is not a lesbian. As far as I know, I'm the only gay person in the van."

Lucy sits back. "It's a legitimate question," she responds. And I can feel her watching me from behind. "Well?" She is still waiting for an answer.

I shrug. "I haven't thought much about it," I answer. "I started my business, created my life, such as it is, and I just never have much time to socialize."

"Frank Goodrich tried to get you to go out with him when you first opened the shop." Nora remembers everything.

"Frank Goodrich tried to get *you* to go out with him when I first opened the shop," I say back.

She smiles. "We went out," she responds.

I see Jimmy glance up.

"You dated Frank Goodrich?" Carl wants to know.

"A couple of times," Nora answers. "He's interesting."

"He gets around, I'll give you that," Carl responds. "He brings someone different to the club every weekend."

"He does like the ladies," Nora adds.

"Is that why you don't date him anymore?" I ask.

"Oh, we still date," she replies.

Jimmy turns to look out the window.

"It doesn't bother you that he sees other women?" Lucy asks.

Nora waves away the question. "We're not engaged," she answers. "We just enjoy each other's company from time to time." She pulls down the visor and checks her makeup in the mirror. She slides her lips in and out and I see her catch a glimpse of Jimmy. I'm not sure of the meaning of this brief eye contact; it's not a look from Nora I know, but it is easy to see the spark between them.

"Well, I'm dating someone," Lucy announces, and it appears as if she has dropped a bomb in her son's lap.

"Who?" Carl asks. "Who are you dating?"

"Mr. Eldwin," she replies.

There is a pause.

"The plumber?" Clearly, Carl has placed the man.

"He's retired, but yes, he made his living as a plumber," his mother answers. "He owned his own business, too."

This, I believe, is for my benefit. I nod.

"Well, when did this happen?" her son wants to know.

"About a year ago," she says.

"Mother." Carl sits up and turns to face her. "You've been dating someone for a year and you didn't tell me?"

I can see them both from the rearview mirror. She is fingering the collar of her silk blouse and he is waiting for her answer.

"He moved in last month."

There is an awkward silence. Everyone suddenly seems uncomfortable.

"You're living with the plumber?" He is shaking his head. He blows out a long breath.

"Carl, I'm a grown woman. I have needs."

"Oh, I do not want to hear this," her son responds.

Nora pipes up. "I kind of do," she says.

"Are we there yet?" comes the little voice from the back. "I think Clementine has to pee." The rest of us sigh and smile, especially Lucy. I think we are all glad for the interruption.

"Almost," I answer, making the turn toward the park, and when I look in the back I can still see the surprise on Carl's face. No doubt Lucy will have a lot of explaining to do when they get home tonight.

·Twenty·

I BOUGHT a black cocktail dress, my first little black dress, which is apparently a rite of passage I missed in my twenties. It's a slim dark sheath with soft ruffles and a small peplum at the hips. It has cap sleeves with a triangle cutout that shows off just a bit of my back. It has a black narrow belt with thread loops at the waist, a hidden back zipper with a hook-and-eye closure, and it is fully lined in amethyst charmeuse with the silky side resting against my skin.

After trying on at least thirty dresses and narrowing my choices down to two, Nora cast her vote for the strapless faille with a structured corset bodice. However, once I modeled the two for what I declared was my final showing, she finally agreed with Carl that the sheath was more slimming. Besides, I told her I don't do strapless. I've never done strapless. I tried the dress on three different times and kept pulling my shoulders up to my ears, thinking that would somehow keep it from falling down. Lucy said I looked like I had been frozen in the middle of a shrug so Nora finally consented and I bought the one with the ruffles and peplum.

It turned out that the dress was the easy part. Once that was purchased, I was led downstairs to find appropriate outerwear, a long wool peacoat, then over to the shoe department for a pair of high heels, black patent leather, then to the jewelry counter for a faux pearl necklace and earrings, and then over to the accessories for a pair of black silk hose. Even with everyone chipping in, I spent as much money on this shopping trip as I did furnishing my house. I spent so much money that Nordstrom's wanted to assign me a personal shopper to assist me on future wardrobe purchases. After I explained to the department manager that this was just a onetime event and that I would likely never buy so many items in one trip again, Carl politely informed her that even though he was confident that Nordstrom's had great sales representatives, he was really the only personal shopper I needed. Still, when I opened the shoe box to show Jimmy the high heels, she had slipped a business card inside with a note saying Candi was available to assist me at any time.

By the time we left the store, everyone at Nordstrom's knew all of our names. They even knew where I was going to wear the little black dress, and, thanks to Nora, they knew that I was being accompanied by an astronaut. We were given champagne and free makeovers, which Carl especially seemed to enjoy. We were escorted by store personnel from one department to another, and when we had bought everything, everyone who had assisted me wanted to see the complete outfit. If it hadn't been for the booze, I'm pretty sure I would have turned down the request, but when I heard the cork pop on our third bottle, I knew I owed them a peek.

Dressed with assistance from the manager of the special occasions department, I walked out of the dressing room in the black dress and the high-heeled shoes, the coat thrown over my shoulder, the jewelry in place, the makeup fresh and my hair pinned up by Lucy, and you would have thought I was somebody. There were oohs and ahhs from the Nordstrom's folks, and I swear Nora even shed a tear or two. I felt like Julia Roberts in *Pretty Woman* when she came out dressed for the opera and Richard Gere couldn't take his eyes off her. Of course, most of my audience was drunk, and the ones who weren't, except Nora, were at least being paid to tell me I looked good, but it didn't really matter; I felt beautiful.

It's after ten o'clock and I walk into my house, place all my bags on the sofa, and fall into the chair next to it. I just sit for a second, trying to catch my breath. Clementine saunters in behind me, goes over to her water bowl, and then returns, dropping down beside me. I think she is worn out as well, Will having taken her on the river walk, going from end to end, at least three times while waiting for the adults.

I'm tired from the shopping excursion and I see now that I suffer from a bit of buyer's remorse, too. I'm sure I could have borrowed some jewelry from Kathy Shepherd or even found something in my own stash; I'm pretty sure I have a suitable coat, and I know I have an old pair of black panty hose. Still, I feel happy in a way I haven't in a very long time. Even with the fatigue and my concern over the amount of money I paid, I feel uniquely included in something that I haven't experienced in a long time, and an odd sense of belonging. I have spent the day intricately connected to members of a group. I feel like part of a family.

I don't remember feeling this way since I was I was kid, and as I consider this, I suddenly remember the strangest thing from when I was nine or ten years old.

I stand up, pull off my coat, throw it over the Nordstrom's bags, yank off my scarf, tug at my shoes until they fall, and sit back down.

Before my grandparents bought their farm and moved closer to town, they lived out in the country. Back then they still worked my great-grandfather's farm out past Quartz Mountain. I remember

Daisy and I staying at their house for about five months one of the early times we were taken from Mama, several years before she died. Their nearest neighbors were the Darbys, a large family who lived in a small log cabin about a half a mile behind us.

There were at least six kids, ranging in ages from a newborn to a teenager. We played with them all summer long. The father was a sharecropper, working the hayfields and tending the cattle that roamed the land all around their little house. He helped my grandfather and was able to stay for free in the cabin, eventually leaving in the fall when he got a job working in the apple orchards down at the Oregon border.

According to my grandmother, the Darbys were very poor, but as I think about them I remember that back then it didn't matter to me if they were wealthy or not. They were the happiest family I ever knew. I thought they had the best toys and the prettiest clothes, never realizing that everything they owned was made by hand or given to them from charity drives at local churches. They served the best dinners I ever ate, even though there was never much more than a pot of stew, glasses of fresh lemonade, and a plate of cold biscuits. And every time Daisy and I got to ride with the Darbys to the lake or to town in their old station wagon, every time we squeezed into the backseats with all six children, I always felt like I was a part of something big and delightful and even very, very rich.

On those rides I was shoved onto somebody's lap or pressed hard between two other children and we laughed as we fell into the pile, laughed as we slammed forward with every stop, Mr. Darby driving that way, speeding up and then putting on the brakes, just to watch us having fun, and we laughed as we got stepped on or pushed aside as everyone moved in and out of the car.

The trips that summer were always loud and rowdy. They were the best trips my sister and I ever had. Being in that station wagon was the only time I felt completely relaxed and completely at ease with being a child. I didn't worry about Mr. Darby getting drunk and crashing the car. I didn't worry that a police officer would stop us at the crossroads and we'd be taken to the station and have to wait on Granddaddy to pick us up. I didn't worry that I might have to drive home if Mama passed out, something I did at least twice before I turned thirteen, or whether she would pull out of the parking lot, forgetting me or Daisy and leaving us in the bar or at some store.

I squeezed myself between two other kids and laughed and sang and slid around in the car like everyone else in the back. I don't remember that much about where we were going, what we did when we got there; I mostly remember the rides themselves. The trip home was always, hands down, the best part of the day. That was, after all, when everyone fell silent, where we all found a place beside or near another and where most of us, the children anyway, exhausted from the day's adventure, eventually fell asleep.

We piled up on each other, some lying on the car floor, others stretched out in the back, and it didn't matter where I landed. I could always find a small view out the window and watch the stars. And even with the breeze blowing through the car, if I listened very closely I could hear Mr. and Mrs. Darby talking quietly to each other.

Sometimes their conversations were romantic, Mrs. Darby snuggled beneath her husband's arm, their whispers to each other marked by quick kisses and soft laughter; sometimes they spoke of more serious concerns, bills and unforeseen costs, or just of ordinary things, of meals and neighbors and schedules. It didn't matter what was discussed. Never did the Darbys speak to each other with raised voices or expressions of blame. No matter what the subject was, I loved to hear the things they said, the simple, everyday things that I always imagined a husband saying to his wife, a wife saying to her husband.

On those long-ago trips, I would take in a deep breath, close my eyes, and pretend I belonged to the Darbys, that Daisy and I were not a part of a family where a father never existed and a mother was almost always drunk or high, always talking a little too loud, laughing or screaming a little too harshly. I would pretend that my sister and I somehow belonged to this large and raucous family, somehow ordered in between Nancy, the teenager, and Louie, the littlest one, still resting in his mother's lap. I would close my eyes and pretend, and for however long it took us to reach our grandparents' place, where Mr. Darby stopped the car and carefully lifted Daisy and me from among the other children, opening the door and carrying us out, I belonged to something big and wonderful and safe.

I reach down now, feeling for Clementine's neck, and think about how the six of us crammed ourselves into the florist van today, how Lucy was convinced she had lost her glasses and how we returned to each department we'd visited, searching for them, until Carl finally discovered that they'd been hanging around her neck the whole time; how Jimmy pulled Will into the backseat, tugging so hard that he slid from one side of the van to the other, crashing into the door and then laughing so hard he got the hiccups; how we all groaned when Nora needed to make a stop before we even left town so that she could go to the bathroom again; and how we all decided together that everyone having an ice cream cone would help keep me awake on the drive home, stopping at the Dairy Queen, piling out and then piling back in, our fingers and lips still sticky.

The drive to and from Spokane with my friends was as loud and rowdy as any I took with the Darbys—and even though I know I spent way too much money, I also know that on that ride home I felt happy and safe. And as I glance over at my purchases, which I will likely still be paying off next year, I feel delighted and exhausted and I find myself grateful to Captain Miller for already giving me the best night I've had as a grown-up even if we haven't even gone out yet.

"Well," I say to Clementine, who barely lifts herself as I find the spot behind her ears and give her a good scratch. "I may have spent way too much for this outfit, but I have to say it was worth it."

She sighs in agreement and I lie back in the chair and close my eyes, imagining Mr. Darby reaching in and lifting me tenderly from the backseat. He smiles and I pretend I am asleep as he carries me all the way to my grandmother's door.

·Twenty-One·

"How do you know it wasn't for his mother?"

Nora started pestering me about the new veterinarian when I got back from making today's deliveries. She thinks I should go to his house or his office and take him a welcome gift. She suggested an amaryllis or one of the new primrose plants I just bought online. I reminded her that he already bought the bamboo and then I mentioned the bouquet he bought for Valentine's Day.

"That wasn't a son-to-mother flower arrangement," I tell her.

She makes that huffing noise she makes a lot when she's exasperated.

I keep leaving the design area and heading to the cooler or to the storage room in the back to select the flowers and the supplies for the missionary supper at the Baptist church this weekend. They want small floral displays for sixteen tables. I had Jimmy bring up a box of vases from the basement. She keeps following me.

"Ruby, not everyone sees what you see when you make the arrangements. Not everyone knows that marigolds increase positive energies or that the rose is the ultimate gentle healing herb of love. Not everyone knows what you do when you make a bouquet. They don't feel what you feel."

I go inside the cooler to check out my inventory once more. I'm thinking that creating something simple is best, Matsumoto asters and some hot pink miniature carnations, a few stems of alstroemeria and a little heather.

"He picked the biggest one in the refrigerator. That's all he did. He saw a bouquet he wanted and he bought it. That *does* sound like a son-to-mother gift. He didn't know the particular qualities of each stem or bloom. He just liked the colors."

I don't answer. I know that Nora wasn't in the shop when the order was placed on February 14. Jimmy was running the counter. She had stepped out to get them lunch when Dr. Cash arrived, wanting flowers. She doesn't really know what he liked or why he bought what he bought.

The truth is that it doesn't matter to me anyway; I actually feel a little relieved that Dr. Cash is involved with someone. I'm glad I don't have to think about the kinds of things new lovers have to think about, and I'm especially glad I don't have to think about that today. I'm trying to figure out what I can use on the tables in the fellowship hall at the Baptist church. I'll need to come up with arrangements that fit in their budget but are still beautiful and celebratory of the work of the visiting missionaries. I have work to do. I pull out a few stems of orange and yellow alstroemeria from the bucket by the door, and when I turn around to head back to the design table I run into Nora.

"Geez, you're going to make me fall!" I tell her. "Look, I don't want to talk about this right now."

She steps aside to let me pass, but she stays right on my heels. I feel her breath on my neck; she's that close.

"You need to talk about this. In fact, I think you need an intervention, Ruby Jewell."

I glance up and see Jimmy standing in the doorway. He's holding the box of vases. He hears the conversation and he turns around to leave. I guess he doesn't want to be a part of intervening with me.

"Jimmy," I say as he's walking out. "It's okay. I'm not listening to her anyway. Just bring me the box."

He turns around, comes back in the room, and places the box of vases on the design table. He turns to Nora, shakes his head, and makes another exit.

"Jimmy, come back here and tell Ruby what happened when the veterinarian came and bought the flowers."

He has a defeated look on his face. It's easy to see that he really doesn't want to be involved. He sighs in resignation, however, because we all three know that he does whatever Nora tells him to do.

"Nora had left to get us a bite of lunch," he reports. "Dr. Cash came in and asked if you were here. I told him you were out making deliveries. He wanted to know what bouquets I had left and I pointed to the refrigerator. He looked through the door and pointed to the big one on the top shelf and he asked me if anybody had bought that one. I said no, that it was for purchase, and he said he would take it. I got the arrangement out, wiped off the vase on the bottom where some water had spilled, asked him if he wanted a card and he said no, and then he paid with a credit card, a Visa. The receipt should have been in the day's stack." Jimmy takes a breath.

He's obviously already gone over this with Nora.

"Did he say who he was buying the flowers for?" Nora asks, and stares at me while Jimmy answers.

"No."

She nods.

"Did he say that the bouquet was romantic and filled with flowers that provoked feelings of passion within him?"

"Uh, no, I don't recall him saying anything like that either."

"And he asked if Ruby was here, yes?"

Jimmy nods.

I roll my eyes, place the flowers I had in my hands on the table, and start pulling out the vases that I want to use from the box.

"See, he came by, he was searching for you, but he picked out some flowers for his mother or his aunt or some woman he's related to and he bought them."

"Nora, he picked out the Graceful Heart Bouquet. It used all the roses I had left over. It had bear grass shaped like a heart. There was pittosporum in it; I even stuck in a little jasmine. Jasmine, Nora, jasmine."

"Jasmine is not just for increasing sexual desire. You told me yourself that it's used for PMS. Did you think of that?" she asks. "Maybe he wanted the arrangement to help a friend suffering from cramps." She seems satisfied with herself.

Jimmy shifts his weight from side to side. He is waiting to be excused.

"The vase was a ruby red cube. It was a romantic arrangement. Even someone clueless about flowers would know this is a gift of romance, a gift of passion." I snip off the ends of the blooms I've chosen and start placing them in the vases. "And I told you that I don't want to talk about this right now!" I say again, my voice raised and sharp.

Clementine slides under the table, out of my way. Jimmy walks out of the room without permission. Nora is studying me.

I feel her watching and watching. I blow out a long breath. "What?" I ask.

"When did you start getting so snippety?"

I put down the flowers and I wipe my hands on my apron. "I am not trying to be snippety," I say, lowering my voice. "I just have to finish these arrangements and take them over to the church," I add.

She's still watching me, waiting for something more.

I pinch off a few leaves so that the flowers arrange more easily.

She doesn't respond.

"He hasn't come by since then," I tell her, and when I look up, the silence not being quite what I expected, I can see she is surprised.

"I haven't seen him since before Valentine's Day," I add. I figure I might as well lay it all out there.

Now she looks like she feels sorry for me. I hate that.

"Then that is all the more reason for you to drop by with a primrose or a bromeliad." She cannot let this go.

"Nora, I'm not chasing John Cash. I haven't chased a boy since I was in sixth grade and Tommy Locklear stole my homework. I chased him from homeroom to the playground and then behind the cafeteria and I promised myself I would never do that again."

She turns away from me.

"Nora . . ."

She won't look at me.

"I'm happy," I tell her, taking her by the arms. "I don't need a boyfriend. I have you and Jimmy and Clementine and Will. I have this shop to think about, and all the people I try to help. I have a date with an astronaut in two weeks. John Cash is a nice man and I'm sure he is lovely to the animals he treats, and to their owners, and I hope he will be successful and happy in Creekside. I don't want a boyfriend," I say again. "I don't need an intervention or a special potion. I'm good, okay?"

She doesn't respond.

I tug on her arms a little. "Okay?"

She nods reluctantly.

"Okay," I say, dropping my grip on her and turning back to the table and my work.

"I just don't see why it is that you assist everyone else's love life but don't do a thing for your own."

"Nora . . ." I shake my head.

She makes a kind of humming noise and goes over to pick up the broom. She starts sweeping up.

"So I'm right," she says with a kind of smirk. "It is a date with Captain Miller."

I just have to laugh.

·Twenty-Two·

"I want to ask her to m-m-marry me." Henry Phillips has waited until everyone has left the shop before walking across the street to talk.

He finally told me last week who he was buying the yellow bouquets for, even though Will let me in on that secret the first time I met the boy. Henry has bought daffodils and freesia, daisies and blazing stars every Thursday for more than a month now. I'm not sure how long he's been checking out stacks of books in the process of falling for the librarian, but it seems a little early for a marriage proposal. Still, I am not one to squelch love.

"That's wonderful, Henry," I reply. "How do you plan to ask her?"

"Well . . . well, that's why I'm he-here."

"You want to give her flowers?" I ask, knowing that I have just the bouquet in mind. I used it with Dennis Duncan from Valley when he proposed to Clara, and I also sold it to James Harvey and

Bill Durham for their special occasions. "I have a beautiful one with white flowers."

I call it the You're the One Bouquet and it includes crème and white roses, white gladioli, white miniature carnations, white lisianthus, and delicate white waxflower with just a touch of variegated pittosporum. I am already running inventory in my mind before he answers. I have everything but the lisianthus. I'll need to tell Nora to add that to my order.

He turns away. I guess he has something else in mind.

"I-I think sh-she really likes the yel-yellow ones."

I nod. I guess You're the One won't work for Henry and Lou. Still, I can do a nice proposal bouquet with the blazing stars and snapdragons. I can make the same bouquet I've made every week for Henry to give to his beloved, only I'll add a few tulips and yellow roses to make it special.

"I-I don't know if sh-sh-she'll say yes."

I smile and reach under the counter and pull out my order forms. I figure he'll tell me what he wants and I'll just make the list.

"I guess no man asking the woman he loves to marry him knows her answer for sure," I respond. I take out my daisy pen and write his name at the top of the form. "I suppose a big proposal like that bears a certain amount of risk. Have you been out together a lot? Do you have a favorite place you'll go to pop the question?"

He doesn't answer and I glance up, waiting. He shifts his weight from side to side. He clears his throat.

"We have-haven't been ou-out at all."

I am surprised. I know I seem surprised. "But all the bouquets? Doesn't she know how you feel with all the bouquets you've given her?"

He shakes his head. His face is bright red.

"You didn't tell her that the flowers are from you?" I understand the blush now.

He shakes his head again.

"Well, Henry, who does she think they're from?"

"I-I don't know."

"And you want to ask her to marry you?" Oh my, this is not sounding good.

He nods.

Okay. I try to think of how to respond with delicacy, being truthful but gentle. I put down my pen and slide the order form back under the counter. I look him in the eye. "I don't know, Henry. I mean, I'm not a relationship expert, but I think you need to go out together a few times before you rush into marriage."

"I-I love her and I-I think sh-she loves me."

"But you've never been out."

He drops his head, nodding.

"Do you talk to her?"

He shrugs.

"Have you ever spoken to Lou?"

"Sh-she knows I like bi-biographies of pr-pr-presidents. She f-finds me ones I-I haven't read and h-h-holds them for me at the d-desk."

"And when you pick these up, do you talk?"

He nods. "I-I say thank you."

I am at a loss here. I don't want Henry to get his heart broken, and if in his first conversation with her, he asks Lou Ann Peterson to marry him, he's definitely on his way to heartbreak. I think of what flower or herb might help here, but I'm not sure exactly what I'm dealing with. Is it a need for confidence or a desire to express strong feelings positively? I could go with paperwhites or something from the passion variety, but I'm not really convinced flowers are the answer here.

"Okay, let's pause for just a second." I'm trying to organize my thoughts. "Why don't you start by giving her another bouquet and this time adding a card, letting her know it's you sending the flowers?"

He bites his bottom lip, thinking, thinking.

"Then, after a day or so, you could see her and ask her out for a date."

"C-c-could I write that o-on the c-c-card?"

"The request for a date?" I ask.

He nods.

"I guess." I think about it. "You could say something along the lines of, 'I hope you have liked the flowers I have sent and now I'm wondering if you'd like to have dinner with me?' And sign your name. Then you show up and ask her."

"What if I-I write s-something like, 'Few people dare now to say that two beings have fallen in love because they have looked at each other. Yet it is in this way that love begins and in this way only.'"

I am stunned. Henry didn't stutter at all saying those two sentences. "That's beautiful, Henry. Is that Shakespeare?"

"It . . . it's from the play *Les Misèrables*."

"I think that should definitely go on the card."

He smiles.

"So, you want me to make the arrangement now?"

He nods. "I-is it o-okay if I wait?"

"Sure," I answer. "Why don't you have a seat around here on the stool?" I motion him around the counter and he complies. Clementine stands up and goes over to welcome him into our private space. I watch him give her a pat on the head. She drops down at his side. She and Henry have been friends a long time.

"You want it all yellow, right?"

"Sh-she likes ye-yellow."

"Then yellow she shall have."

I go back to the cooler and take stems of all the yellow flowers I have. There are the usuals that I keep on hand: daisies, daffodils, alstroemeria, blazing stars. And I also take a couple of stems of yellow roses, two new tulips. I walk back into the main room of the shop and place them on the table. Henry watches.

"You know, yellow stimulates the nervous system. It helps balance emotions." I search on the shelves for the right vessel. "How about a nice clear vase?"

"I-I don't carry th-these in t-t-tissue paper?"

I shake my head. "No, not this time," I answer. "This time, with that quote and this revelation, you have to put these flowers in a vase. With all that sentiment and disclosure, they need to be contained."

He nods as if he understands.

I find a round glass vase, a tall one with a sculpted ring design wrapped around it. It's pretty but not too showy. I never want the vase to outdo the bouquet. I take it off the shelf, go over to the sink and pour just a little warm water in it, set it beside me, pick up my scissors and start clipping off leaves and cutting ends of stems. I place the flowers in the vase, one by one.

"How d-did you l-learn about flowers?" he asks.

I continue my work. "I took some classes," I answer.

"E-every . . . body th-thinks y-you make m-magic. Th-that you a-ar-range more than just flowers here."

I turn to Henry. "Do they?" I ask. I hadn't really heard this before.

"Th-they th-think you a-range h-hearts."

"You mean like heal broken hearts?"

I can see out of the corner of my eye that he is shaking his head. "L-like m-make h-hearts f -f-feel a cer-cer-certain way. F-f-fix them."

"Fix, like fixing a bet or a race to make it go the way I want it to?" I had never thought about my arrangements being used in that way.

He nods.

"Do you think I can do that with Lou Ann?" I ask. I stop my work and turn to Henry. I don't want to be a part of something false, something unattainable for him.

He waits and then he shakes his head again. "I-I th-think you bl-bl-blossom what is al-already there. I-I d-don't th-think you ca-can make s-somebody feel s-something th-they d-d-don't."

I go back to the arrangement. "Well, that's the truth."

"S-so, h-how d-do you do it?"

"I believe in the power of love, Henry. And I believe it's always present," I say, tucking in the snapdragons and the stems of greenery. I snip the ends of the tulips and place them in the center of the arrangement and then I spin the vase around, checking it from every angle. "But I do believe that beauty somehow opens us to it," I add. Suddenly I am remembering the brilliant blue of the hydrangea bush outside my window the day I finally left my bed weeks after Daisy died, the tiniest pink crocus, brazen, rising from the frozen earth, the narrow escape I found.

I add the last of the daffodils to the vase, the yellow rosebud, and a narrow stem of statice, and then I go to my shelf of herbs and take down a jar of Job's tears. When I get back to the design table, I add three seeds to the bouquet for luck. I figure Henry can use all that he can get. I find the yellow chiffon ribbon, wrap it around the glass vase, loop and tie a broad bow. I give it a good final examination, approve, and then walk the arrangement over to Henry. He holds out his hands and I give it to him. I then go over to my box of cards near the cash register and pick out a yellow one, plain except for a tiny hand-painted daisy centered at the bottom. I bought these from Molly Lipton, a high school student who happens to be a very talented artist.

"Do you want me to write it or you?" I ask, thinking he will need to repeat the quote, because I don't remember the exact wording.

"I-I will d-do it," he replies.

I smile, put the card in its matching envelope, find a small plastic bag to place it in, and then hang the bag on his finger, which he sticks out beside the vase.

"I will add this arrangement to your bill," I explain. "You can pay me at the end of the month."

Henry stands up from the stool and Clementine joins him.

"I-I th-think this is just right," he says. "I-I will w-wait to pr-propose until after we g-g-go out."

I place my hand on his as he cradles the vase of flowers. "Come back and tell me how it went," I say with a squeeze.

He nods, turns, then walks around the counter and out the door.

Clementine sits and then lifts a paw to brush against my leg.

"I know," I tell her, watching Henry cross the street. "It's not up to us now; we can only hope for the best."

·TWENTY-THREE·

I AM to meet Captain Miller at the small airport that is located just behind the sixteenth green at the public golf course. Both of these facilities were built at the top of the hill, straight up Sand Crane Drive. It's a beautiful part of town up there, mostly homes of retired people, mostly golfers and pilots. I guess Captain Miller is all three.

Nora helped me dress. She arrived just before noon even though I wasn't leaving the house until three. She claimed there was much more to the ritual of preparation than just yanking the dress off the rack and throwing it on. And she spent two hours proving she was right.

She brought rose petals and lavender for a tepid bath since a hot one would make me sweaty; a special moisturizer for my legs, which she said would render them silky smooth; and she had arranged for Cora Salisbury, the local hair salon owner, to drop by before two o'clock to wash and style my hair. She even brought sparkling water for herself and a small bottle of champagne for me.

She waited with Clementine in the living room while I soaked, giving me two slices of cucumber, which I thought was an odd snack but was just about to eat them anyway when she snatched them from me, explaining that they were to place on my eyes. She lit a vanilla candle before she left the room, turned on my radio, the jazz station already programmed, and then reappeared after about twenty minutes with a small plate of cheese and grapes. When she knocked on the door and told me why she was there, I worried that she might want to feed them to me, which I must admit made me a tad uncomfortable, but then she entered, carefully placed the saucer by the tub, and quietly backed out.

"You don't have to walk on your tiptoes," I said, "I'm not asleep." But she didn't respond and simply closed the door behind her.

After the bath and my home hair appointment, Carl arrived and did my makeup. He worked for a cosmetics company when he was in college. He came in carrying two suitcases, and I thought he was spending the night, but it turned out he still has a cosmetologist's discount and enjoys purchasing cosmetics and supplies from the headquarters of Estée Lauder.

He started me in corals: lipstick, eye shadow, blush, all of them from the same color format, but then once he got a good look at me he shook his head and made me wash it all off, starting over with what he called his "rosy palette." It was rooted in pink, and after he finished I felt like I had been sprayed down in Pepto-Bismol, but both he and Nora seemed pleased. After all the color, Carl applied mascara. At first there was so much I was afraid my top and bottom lashes were going to stick together and I wouldn't be able to open my eyes. I told him that I didn't really want to miss having a good look at the president because of an overabundance of eye makeup, and he stormed out of the room and then stormed back in, handing me a tissue and telling me to blot it gently against my lashes. He must have said "gently" ten times. So I was careful and it seemed to help.

Jimmy came over to the house as well and took pictures. Now I know how a girl must feel getting ready for the prom. Since I never attended the high school socials, I don't have anything to compare this experience to, but I do know that I feel polished and shined. And now I think I know what Daisy meant when she used to say she was "done up and going out."

Nora has even made me a pearl wristlet. I had shown her the boutonniere I had arranged for Captain Miller, and somehow she found a way to sneak behind my back and make a corsage that matched it. I had used a purple dendrobium with three small white roses, and a sprig of ivy, tying them all together with a silver-gray grosgrain ribbon. She found a matching orchid and added white spray roses with tiny rhinestones strategically placed so they accented the blooms. She must have worked all morning on it, because Nora doesn't do corsages or nosegays. She claims her fingers can't handle the small bouquets, so I don't know how she managed it, but she did. It's beautiful and when she hands me one of the narrow white boxes that I have given out more than a hundred times to other girls, I am completely surprised. I feel special.

Finally, after all this time, they tell me I am finished and can see for myself their magic-making. Carl makes me close my eyes, and he and Nora guide me to the living room, where Carl has brought and set up a full-size mirror from home. Somehow, he knew I wouldn't have one. And then I feel them both jump behind me.

"Okay, open your eyes!" Carl instructs me, and just for fun, I act like I can't pull them apart.

I am laughing when I catch the first glimpse of myself. Jimmy snaps a picture and I swear I almost cry. I look like no one I have ever seen in a mirror before.

Nora, of course, does cry. She can't stop blubbering about how beautiful I am, and she and Carl embrace. Then Jimmy and Nora embrace. And then it's Carl and Jimmy. And then Clementine wants a hug. And I'm just standing here, thinking maybe I need to start paying more attention to my appearance day to day, because obviously this is a very big deal.

"Okay, okay," I say, waving away their emotional outbursts.

Jimmy takes a few more photos. I tell them all good-bye, give Clem a snack, grab the silver and black purse I borrowed from Kathy Shepherd, and head out the door, leaving my friends to clean up the mess.

"Text us to let us know what he's wearing," Carl says as I get in the van. "I'm thinking it's a classic tuxedo but Nora thinks he's bought something contemporary."

I roll my eyes. *Like I will know the difference*, I think.

"Don't make a face," Nora yells. "You have on too much makeup for that."

I turn on the engine and back out of the driveway, having no idea what that sentence means.

When I get to the airport, I see a plane pulled out on the runway, and a man dressed in coveralls directs me to an opening in the hangar, where I see another vehicle, which I recognize as Captain Miller's. I park beside it, turn off the engine, pull out the keys, and drop them in my purse, and when I reach for the handle to open the door, the Captain is standing beside me, holding out his hand.

I don't know if he's wearing a classic or a contemporary suit, but he looks very snazzy. I'm sliding out, trying to be as ladylike as possible, when I remember the boutonniere and then quickly duck back in the driver's seat. When I emerge the second time, Captain Miller looks confused.

"I thought you had changed your mind," he says, reaching out once more.

I'm stumped. "Oh, because I sat back down," I say, nodding and taking his hand. I grasp a little too tightly when I suddenly remember Carl showing me over and over again how to shake the president's hand.

"Delicate, Ruby," he told me when I demonstrated what I would offer. "You aren't arm wrestling."

I loosen my grip on his hand. When I stand up, he is smiling.

"As if you were on fire from within. The moon lives in the lining of your skin."

I assume that's some famous quote, but I know nobody has ever said it to me.

"It's Neruda," he explains. "Pablo Neruda."

"I like him," I say, and I hand Captain Miller the boutonniere.

He takes it from the box, notices the corsage on my wrist, and smiles. "You have brought me flowers," he says. "I am indeed a lucky man," and then asks, "You'll assist me?"

I glance around for a place to put my purse and he politely offers a hand.

I pin the orchid on his lapel and then stand back to admire my work. It's lovely, and while studying it I notice a tiny sprig of jasmine that's just behind one of the roses. Nora had sneaked into the box and added a little extra touch. It is, of course, our own private florist joke, so I do not mention it to the Captain.

"Shall we?" he asks, holding out his arm, which I take as delicately as I can.

·TWENTY-FOUR·

"WHAT was the main course?"

"What was the First Lady wearing?"

"How was the flight over to Seattle?"

There are way too many questions thrown at me at once. They are standing at my door like Jehovah's Witnesses or trick-or-treaters, waiting to be invited in. I wonder if they'd settle for a piece of candy.

Clem and I move aside, making room for all three.

"I brought a cheesecake," Carl reports. "It was left over from an event at the club last night." He shakes his head as he places the dessert on my kitchen counter. "It was the Spring Ladies' Golf Social. They brought silk flowers, Ruby," he says to me, shaking his head. "Hideous."

Carl hates artificial arrangements almost as much as I do.

"But they did select the best dessert choices and since most of the women at the club are anorexic, we have leftovers! The cheesecake has a fresh cherry topping so it's perfect for breakfast. Where are your dishes?"

"The plates are right above the stove. Should I make coffee?" Nora has made her way to the kitchen.

"Hey, Ruby."

"Hey, Jimmy. You can sit if you want." I motion to the sofa and he takes a seat.

We both listen as Nora and Carl go through all my cabinets, taking things out, putting things back, discussing my brand of coffee. Apparently I buy the cheap kind.

"You have a good time?" he asks.

"I did," I answer, and yawn, wondering what time it is and how somebody like me got to do what I did last night. I feel like Cinderella after the ball, only I don't have to clean up after a mean stepmother and I came home with both shoes.

"Is Captain Miller a good pilot?"

I think of the long, slow way we took off, the strength of his hands, the calm manner in which he spoke into the radio microphone spouting off speeds and latitudes, the polite means by which he transported me.

"Very good," I answer. And I sit down in the chair across from Jimmy, lean back, and close my eyes, recalling how our conversation in the cockpit began. "Do you like to fly?" he had asked.

I had my arms wrapped around my knees and I was leaning against the door, staring out the window. It was spectacular, the narrow tops of trees, the winding rivers and creeks, our movement in and out of clouds. The late-afternoon sun. I was transfixed. It was actually my first airplane flight, so how could I answer? I simply nodded, and as if he understood my enthrallment completely, he didn't ask another question. He did not try to take me from where I had ascended.

"It is beautiful," I finally said, sitting back, breathing deeply, and he nodded knowingly.

"Wake up there, missy." It's Carl standing over me with a piece of cake. "It was a classic tux, right?"

"Does classic have a narrow satin ribbon along the side of the pants?"

"Was there one on the lapel of the jacket?"

I think for a second and then get up from the chair, walk over to the kitchen counter, and get the purse I used last night. I open it and take out a piece of paper, which I hand to Carl.

He unfolds it and reads, "Two-button black satin with an edge notch lapel, pleated pants with a Venice champagne cummerbund, vest, and tie. An ivory microfiber point collar shirt and black patent leather round-toe shoes. Versace." And he clasps the paper against his chest like it is a love letter. "Perfect," is what he says in response, "Absolutely perfect."

"What is he reading?" Nora wants to know as she makes her way out of the kitchen and onto the sofa next to Jimmy.

"Dan wrote down what he wore because he knew Carl would want details." I walk back, take the piece of cake Carl is holding, and plop down cross-legged on the chair. I smell the coffee brewing.

"Dan?" Nora asks, lifting her eyebrows in a huge question mark.

"Yes, Dan," I answer, feeling my cheeks start to burn.

"Okay, give it to us all, and don't leave out a thing," Carl says, going back for his slice of breakfast cheesecake.

I chew and swallow. "It was like a fairy tale," I reply. "In all my life I have never felt so pretty, so elite, and such a part of something so glamorous." I put the fork on the plate and put the plate down so I can better explain.

"On every table there was an arrangement that I can only call a masterpiece. I only wish I could afford to make such exquisite art. There were pink orchids, pink tulips, the blooms just dusted in a hint of blush, pink hydrangea, white roses, lavender roses, pink and white spray roses, pink alstroemeria and lavender button spray chrysanthemums with just a few stems of viburnum. There were so many flowers I couldn't even count them and they were perfectly arranged, at just the right height for table conversation, overflowing these thick mercury glass bowls. It was . . ." I stop and close my eyes, recalling these floral works of art. "It was like little gardens of rhapsody on every table. They were divine." I shake my head with the memory of such beauty.

When I open my eyes, all three of my friends are staring at me as if I just grew another head.

"What?"

"That's what you got?" Nora asks. "You go out with an astronaut, you meet the president, you're having dinner at an event where people paid thousands of dollars to attend, and you tell us about the flowers?"

"Well, the mercury bowls sound pretty special," Carl says, and I don't know if he's being snarky or if he really means it.

He rolls his eyes at Nora and I know he's being snarky.

"We had salmon, wild king salmon, grilled with a kind of tangy sauce that made the fish melt in your mouth. There was champagne and these perfect little desserts. It was the best meal I've ever eaten. The president was charming and smart and seemed to like a good grip with his handshakes." I smile at Carl.

"The first lady wore a pink dressy dress. She matched the flowers on the tables; I guess her people called the governor's people and made sure she would shine. She is tall and beautiful and kind and she said she loved my wristlet."

I wink at Nora.

"We sat with three other couples; the men were all astronauts. Dan was the only one of the four who walked on the moon. The women were sweet to me but I wasn't so comfortable with the small talk. Dan is an excellent pilot, very knowledgeable, and prefers flying piston twin engines, and he is partial to the Cessna 337. He was married once but she was a behaviorist and could not understand how an astronaut could give up being in the space program to delve into the world of noetic sciences. They didn't have children and he sometimes regrets not having a family with him in his retirement years. He was the perfect date, attentive but not clingy, formal but not stiff, a true gentleman in every detail."

I pick up my cheesecake. "We left at three o'clock, arrived at the Seattle airport at five thirty, and had a car pick us up and take us to the dinner. We were back in Creekside by midnight and I hurried home before my perfect Nordstrom's dress turned into an apron and rags and my truck turned into a pumpkin." I take a bite and await the questions even as I know what I will and will not tell.

·TWENTY-FIVE·

THERE are things that happen between two people that, no matter how you try to duplicate the conversation or replay every detail, will always be something that only those two people understand.

That's the way it was with my date with the astronaut. I can tell my friends all the facts and even share all the pleasures. I can paint the picture of the room where we ate, the sky at sunset, the flowers on the tables—but I will never be able to explain what it was to feel so special, to dine and dance in such opulence, to have someone hold out his hand for me. The sheer delight of flying above clouds, the intimate way our conversation shifted. . . . The entire night was magical and perfect and I cannot explain it to anyone who wasn't right there with me; even to try and relive the event with Dan or even myself, I'm not sure I can tell it exactly like it was.

Nora, Jimmy, and Carl left when they had exhausted their questions, when they had gotten as much as I could give. Now it is just me and Clem sorting through what happened. I have coffee and I am still wearing my pajamas. There is sunshine pouring through the window and jazz on the radio.

"Dan has cancer," I tell my dog. "He's healed himself twice already but he's not going to do it again."

Clementine stares up at me.

"He thinks it is his time."

There is a nod from my dog, and then she decides to take a nap. She jumps up on the sofa to join me, settling at the other end.

"I didn't try to change his mind," I continue, even though it's clear my companion has heard all she wants to hear. "With him, I didn't feel like I needed to. As odd as it sounds, I think he's right."

I lean back and put my feet on the coffee table, close my eyes, and remember the night.

"Tell me about the moon," I said after we were back in the plane, after Dan had taken off from Seattle, the lights of the city dancing below us.

He engaged the autopilot and I watched as we climbed in the sky.

"It is full and silent," he replied. "It is like a woman with a secret." He looked at me and winked.

"Was it dark?"

"Yes," he answered. "Very dark."

"And how did it make you feel to step out on it? Were you afraid? Did it change you?"

He shook his head. "No, not afraid," he replied. "I was mentally and emotionally ready for the exit from the shuttle and how I needed to ambulate once I got outside. We had spent a lot of time preparing for that door to open, for that jump out; and no, the moon itself didn't change me, but I was different after the landings."

I waited.

"I had an epiphany on my second mission."

I turned in my seat to be able to listen more intently. I was still a little tipsy from the champagne, but I was alert enough to know this was important, this was something I didn't want to miss.

"What kind of epiphany?" I asked, remembering what I had read in his book and wanting to hear it all in person.

"My work on the missions included getting us to the moon, and then I had tasks once we landed. On the way home I had very few responsibilities, so I just sat and watched the sky out of the big window in front of us. And every few hours I would have the same view. I would see the sun and the moon and the Earth all lined up, like three balls in a row." He rested his hands on his knees and stared out the windshield. "There was a perfect order to them."

I know so little of planets and suns and moons, I cannot even imagine how such a thing must appear. I made no comment.

"And the stars . . ." He shook his head, recalling the sight, I suppose. "They were so bright, so big and bright."

I stared straight ahead as well, trying to get an idea of what he must have seen flying in space, returning home after walking on the moon.

There was a pause.

"Have you ever felt connected to something or someone, had a sense that you had always been together and that no matter how much distance there is between you, you are always and forever linked?"

I immediately thought of Daisy, how deeply attached I was to her when we were together and how it is that even after her death I feel her with me, around me, inside me. I know she is still here.

I nodded.

"When I was in space and saw the stars," he continued, "I felt as if I were seeing something of myself, something that belonged to me but that I hadn't seen before. I didn't feel it was something I had conquered or mastered. I felt as if I were somehow connected to these great beings, these masses of light and gas, as if everything I was made of could be found in them as well, that everything lines up, like the sun and the moon and the Earth, that everything is ordered and intersects."

It was quiet in the cockpit as I considered such a thing.

"Is it strange, what I am saying?" he asked.

And when I turned to him I simply shook my head.

"For the longest time," he said, "I couldn't find anyone to understand. My family thought I was a little off, that I had been in space too long. My colleagues, even though a couple of them had experienced a similar kind of thing when they were up there, didn't want to discuss what happened. I know it sounds odd and perhaps I shouldn't have told you about this, but somehow I thought you might understand."

I smiled.

I turned to watch the sky again. I could see blinking lights below, the moon ahead of us. I could see how he would discover such a thing.

"When I arrange flowers," I said, thinking about my craft, "I know which stems belong together. I feel a certain energy that guides me. I think of the person who placed the order, their emotion when they call or stop by. I think of what they want to tell someone, what they need to say, and somehow, when I go into the cooler, the refrigerated storage room where we keep the inventory, the flowers have this kind of energy to them and it's as if I know which ones need to be taken and exactly how they should be arranged." I turn to Dan again. "I've never told anyone that before."

He nodded.

And that was when he told me about the cancer, how he had been healed twice before but that this time there was a kind of weight to the doctor's pronouncement, a different view on the x-rays. This time, he told me, was a final time, and he found this information not unsettling at all. He felt almost comforted by the news, he said.

"There used to be this janitor at the NASA headquarters," he told me. "His name was Josiah but everybody just called him Jo. Jo must have been a hundred when I met him, but he worked another twenty years after that and he never missed a day."

"I'd see him every morning. He'd stand and salute all the astronauts when we came in the building and he'd always say the same thing when we asked him how he was doing. 'Everything's good with my heart,' he'd tell us, and being young and brash we'd just hurry past him, slap the old man on the back without too much thought; but you know, I always knew that what he said was important and I always thought that was the thing I wanted to be able to say, too."

I sat, listening.

"And it took a while, but you know, I can finally say the same thing as Jo. Everything is good with my heart." And he tapped his chest and nodded. "I have a few more things I need to do but mostly I am finished with my time on Earth. I feel ready to return to stardust. Everything is good with my heart."

And I reached over and took his hand and we stayed that way, in darkness and silence, touching and linked until we began our descent. Except for my brief thank-you and a moment when we stood at my truck, the breeze stirring all around us, a polite and tender kiss good-bye, we said nothing else.

What we had shared was more than enough.

·TWENTY-SIX·

I AM counting the Easter lilies, making sure I ordered enough, when I see the old Jeep pull across the street and park. It's John Cash and he's going to get his hair cut. He glances in my direction but he can't see me through the tinted window. He goes inside Henry's shop. I realize I haven't seen him since before Valentine's Day, when he stopped by the shop to tell me about the house he bought, and I wonder how it is that we can live in such a small town and not run into each other. I have not heard whether he's moved into the Chatham house, if he's settled into his practice. I haven't heard much talk at all about the handsome veterinarian, which is certainly peculiar in Creekside since we have a fair number of both gossips and pet owners.

It's a busy week but not overwhelming. Once I get the lilies delivered to the three churches, I have only a couple of birthday bouquets to make. Stan's mother turns ninety and I have ordered her a china doll plant, a healthy one in a ten-inch pot, and Jessica turns eighteen and Steven asked for that many tulips, all different colors, and that they be tied together in tissue; a spring wreath of ivy and yellow bells for the nursing home; and a few arrangements for a banquet at the country club, orange Asiatic lilies, hot pink roses, miniature red carnations, with a few stems of myrtle, nothing too difficult.

Lucky for me, there have been no deaths and no births this week and the school dances don't start for another month or so. On Saturday, I may close early and go exploring at the lake or take a drive to the Cascades. I don't usually pick the wildflowers since the blooms are fragile and because it's not healthy for the landscape, but I do enjoy seeing how Mother Nature arranges her meadows and hillsides. Her color palette and her choices of combinations are always inspiring. I am writing down the numbers when the front door opens, the tiny bell sounding.

"You're early," I say to Will, who has come to walk Clementine. He usually doesn't arrive until later in the afternoon.

Already, my dog is up and coming around the counter. She recognizes the boy's name or his smell, I don't know which, but somehow she is ready for the outing even if it is a couple of hours ahead of schedule.

"We don't have school this week," he reports as he greets Clementine and then comes around to get the leash. He stands behind me.

"I made a B plus on my math test."

"That's a fine grade," I respond.

"I've never made a plus before. I think that's good, right?"

"Very good, yes," I say with enthusiasm. "It's like a super B."

I turn around and he's grinning at me. "Super B, you're funny, Miss Ruby."

"Am I now?" I have never thought of myself as funny. Daisy always had the gift of humor; I was better with money than jokes.

"Yeah." He walks back around to the front and attaches the leash to Clem's collar. "Why do you have all those plants?"

The counter is full; the design table is full. There are lilies everywhere.

"It's Easter," I reply. "Everyone buys a lily at Easter in memory of someone who died. And they put them in the church for the Sunday service."

"Why?"

"It's just a custom, I guess, a way to remember loved ones, a way to celebrate life."

"Why those flowers? Why not daisies or roses? Why not those snapdragons? I like those."

He's been hanging around the shop too long, I think, and I hope he doesn't go around talking about flowers at school. That's grounds for getting beat up, for sure.

"Well, the white Easter lily symbolizes purity, hope, and life; I guess it's like the meaning of Easter, Jesus rising from the dead, life coming from death, spring coming after winter. It's a flower that everyone thinks of when they think of resurrection. But I have to say, I'm like you when it comes to this ritual. I'm sort of partial to the snapdragon as well."

He smiles, keeps glancing around. I think he's counting the plants too. That B plus must have sparked a new interest in numbers.

He stops counting, looks me in the eye. "Do you think Jesus really rose from the dead like they say?"

It's been a very long time since I was asked that question. The last time I got that one was in front of a congregation when Daisy and I joined the Baptist church. I was about Will's age. Daisy was a couple of years younger. She shrugged when they asked her and I'm pretty sure I jumped in and recited a Bible verse that my Sunday school teacher had taught me. I was quite proficient at memorizing scripture. Anyway, it got us both on the membership roll so we could go to summer camp, which was, of course, our real reason for joining.

"I don't know, Will."

He ponders his own question.

"I think it was easier back then to rise from the dead. All Jesus had to do was move a big stone since they put the dead bodies in a cave. Now he'd have to dig out of all that dirt and grass. I think it'd be harder to come back now."

I consider his logic. I hadn't really thought through the ease of resurrection in the first century.

"Do you think anybody can do that?"

It's clear that Will isn't all that interested in Jesus and the Great Christian Doctrine of the Resurrection of the Body. Will wants to know about his mom.

"You mean come back from the dead?"

He nods.

"Not like they say Jesus did; not like they can come back and be the same way we are, the same way they were before they died, but I think they're still with us."

"Just in our hearts, right?"

It's easy to see the lesson of some well-meaning grown-up.

"No, not just in our hearts."

He's watching me very closely now; I better have something. I think for a second but I'm afraid I don't really have what he needs.

"Are you missing your mom?"

He turns away, but I can still make out the slightest nod.

"She liked Easter," he answers.

"Yeah, what did she like about Easter?"

"The baskets, the chocolate bunnies, the ones with marshmallow. And she always made me go on an Easter egg hunt. It was pretty lame since I watched her hide the eggs and I always knew where they were, but she'd make me go outside and find them anyway."

He stops, looks up at me. "She'd make these teeny holes at the ends of the eggs with a straight pin. And then I blew out the yolks into a bowl because I was really good at that. And then we colored them with dye and watercolor paint, and when they were finally dry, she'd go in the front yard and hide them. After I found them all, we got to eat scrambled eggs with ham mixed in. It was good."

"Sounds good," I reply.

"Is your mama dead too?"

It's a fair question.

"Yes," I answer.

"Is that who you visit at the cemetery? Is that where your mom's body is?"

I shake my head and then I wonder when he's seen me there, since I usually only go at night.

"My sister died too," I say.

"Daisy," he responds. "I read her name on the stone."

I nod.

"Do you ever wish she'd come back from the dead? Do you ever wish for her to resurrect?" He stumbles over the word, and it makes me smile.

"I used to."

He's watching me very closely.

"I used to beg and cry and tell God that I would do anything if he'd just let her not be dead. I even used to pretend she didn't really die."

He nods. I can see that he knows exactly what I mean.

"But now, I think she's happy and I try just to let her be with me in a new way."

"Like an angel?"

I shrug. "More like a very smart person."

"Like thinking of an answer on a test that you didn't know before?"

"Yeah, something like that. Although I did still have to study in school." I didn't want him to try that kind of magical thinking, just getting his first B plus and all. "If I get very quiet and close my eyes and try to empty my mind of all the worries or the sadness and all the words I hear all day and just listen to the wind, I think I hear her talk to me."

"Yeah," he says, and then waits a second.

I listen. I can see he has something else to say.

"I dream about my mom sometimes. Do you think they tell us stuff in dreams?"

"I do think that," I answer, and resist the urge to ask him what his mother has told him. I think some things need to stay private.

"Well, whether Jesus got through that stone or not, it's a good story, isn't it?"

I nod.

"We all really want to think people who die will come back, don't we?"

"Yes, I think we do."

He studies all the plants again. "Do you think I should buy one of those so my mom knows I'm remembering her?"

"Nah," I answer. "When you come back I'll give you a few snapdragons and we can go give them to Daisy and your mom. And we can make colored eggs later if you want."

He grins and nods and walks out the door. Clementine is close behind.

TWENTY-SEVEN

H E was over here looking for you."

Nora is back from the shopping trip. I had run out of white satin ribbon that I tie around the baskets of lilies. She went to Colville to buy a few rolls, and then when she returned I left and made the deliveries.

"Well now, who is he?" It's closing time and Cooper has stopped by on his way back to Spokane. He brought me three more buckets of tulips. It seems the company ordered too many, so he's giving them to me at a steep discount.

Nora is helping us unload the flowers. She waited around because she wanted to tell me about the veterinarian. Apparently, he dropped by after his haircut.

"Did he ask for me?" I am ignoring Cooper.

"He asked how to take care of the bamboo, but he kept trying to see around me to the back of the store. I finally told him you were out."

"Even though he didn't ask?"

"He didn't have to."

"Who is he?" Cooper asks again. He shuts the rear doors of his truck and follows us into the shop.

I roll my eyes. "What did you tell him about the bamboo?"

"I told him to use distilled water to prevent algae from growing in the vase."

"Does he have algae growing in the vase?"

She thinks for a second, shakes her head, puts her bucket of tulips on the design table. "He said that he uses tap water."

"Are the leaves turning yellow?" I place mine beside hers.

She nods. "I told him about the bottled water, how the spring variety is best."

"That's good," I respond, and start examining my discount flowers. They're perfect and I decide I'll give a few to Will for his mom's Easter bouquet.

"He wasn't here about the bamboo," she adds.

"Who is *he*?" Cooper is not letting this go. He walks in behind me, jumps up on the counter, and sits.

"And you know this because of your secret psychic powers?" I ask, still refusing to answer Cooper's question; he knows I hate it when he sits on my counter. I throw him a look and he jumps down.

"I know this because I understand a man's hunger."

"He was hungry?" I walk over to get a pitcher to add some water to the buckets.

Clementine moves away from her spot under the table. She knows that sometimes the water spills, and she's not particularly keen on water spills. Nora waves away the comment. "You know what I mean."

"Will you please tell me the hungry man's name?"

We both turn to Cooper. "JOHN CASH!" we say together, and I pour the water, sloshing it over the sides. I glance at Clementine, who just shakes her head and settles down against the wall.

Cooper looks confused.

"I told him you'd call him this evening."

"What? Why?" I put down the pitcher and stare at her.

"To help him with his bamboo." She grins. "Here's his cell number." And she hands me a piece of paper.

"Johnny Cash is in Creekside? I thought he was dead or in Tennessee. What's he doing here and why was he looking for Ruby?" I shake my head at Cooper.

"Nora, I am not calling him."

She blows out a long breath. "Well, why not?"

"Because he's dead," Cooper answers. "How is she supposed to call a dead man?"

"Not Johnny Cash," Nora says to Cooper. "John Cash, the new recently divorced veterinarian."

"Oh." Cooper seems disappointed.

"I am not calling him because . . ." I pause. "Well, because I'm not calling him." I grab both buckets, put them under my arms, and take them to the cooler. I hear Cooper behind me.

"What kind of mother names her son John Cash?"

I let the door close and I put down the buckets. I can't believe Nora has told him I would call him. Who does she think she is? And why can't she just let me be?

I glance around at my inventory and take out the stems I want to use for Will and me. I try to forget the conversation I just had, and I decide to go with the main colors of purple and yellow. Purple banishes what lies in the past, and yellow balances the emotions.

I doubt the dead have any real need for the healing properties of flowers, but Will and I could certainly still use some help. When I've taken what I want, I head back into the main part of the shop. I stayed gone long enough that I am hopeful Nora and Cooper are getting ready to leave, but they haven't moved from where they were a few minutes ago.

"Cooper says you're a bullet," Nora announces.

I place the flowers on the table. Cooper is leaning against the counter and Nora is standing in the doorway. Her arms are wrapped around her chest.

I shrug. Calling me a rose that doesn't open stings, but only a little.

"He says bullets have turned in on themselves so tightly they can never release their fragrance."

"I know what a bullet is," I answer. I have thrown away my share of the unopened buds.

"Are you a bullet?" Nora is asking.

"Am I a flower?" I turn to her. "No, I am not a flower. I am a human being."

"You know what I mean."

"Nora, we have had this conversation before. I do not wish to start a relationship with John Cash. Please, let it go."

"I told you," Cooper weighs in.

And just like that I snap.

"You have no right to judge me, Cooper Easterling. Just because I haven't slept with you or succumbed to your lame one-liners like every other florist in Washington State does not make me rigid or closed. It makes me smart. And just because I don't want to fling myself at the first single man in this town doesn't make me a flower that doesn't bloom. I choose not to be in a relationship and I am tired of having to defend what I choose. Nora, why don't you worry about your own love life? Are you screwing Jimmy because you love him or are you just *releasing your fragrance* to keep him from getting drunk?"

And as soon as the words leave my mouth I see that someone else has come into the shop while I was in the other room. I look behind Nora and I am suddenly and completely appalled at myself for saying what I have just said.

"Jimmy . . ."

And he turns and walks out the back door. Nora quickly follows him.

·TWENTY-EIGHT·

WELL, can't you just apologize?"

Will, Clementine, and I are sitting at his mother's grave. We have already put some flowers at Daisy's plot and after cleaning up Diane's, we have put her arrangement in the vase by the headstone and now we're just resting.

Will asked me what was wrong with Jimmy and Nora because he walked in right as they drove away. He told me that he had waved at them but that Nora was crying and Jimmy wouldn't even look at him when they passed. When he asked me at the shop what had happened, I explained that I had said a horrible thing and I had hurt their feelings.

"I will apologize," I answer him. "Just as soon as I talk to them again." They weren't answering their phones. I figure they either went to a meeting or were just refusing to take my calls.

"What was it that you said?"

I look at the boy and try to think of what to tell him, how to edit the grown-up version. "I told Nora to mind her own business and

I said something bad about her and Jimmy. I didn't think Jimmy was there, but he was, and he heard me."

Will is sitting cross-legged facing his mother's headstone. He has a stick and he's drawing lines in the dirt. I am sitting beside him. Clementine leaves us and starts sniffing along the line of the trees that borders the cemetery.

"I said something about Mama's boyfriend once. I thought he was gone and I yelled at her for dating such a loser. He was in the bathroom and when he came out, he hit me with his fist."

"Yeah, well, I wish Jimmy had hit me," I say, recalling the long, silent way he had looked at me, the hurt in his eyes as he turned and walked away.

"Not like this guy hit. He almost knocked my tooth out."

"Ouch!" I reply, and rub the top of his head. "You're right, I wouldn't want to get hit."

"Why did Nora make you mad?"

I didn't really expect to be analyzing my recent argument with a ten-year-old.

"She thinks I need a boyfriend," I answer.

"Do you?"

I smile. "I don't think so," I say.

"Mama always had a boyfriend," Will tells me. "Some of them were okay, but some of them were not very nice."

"Like the one who hit you in the mouth."

"Yeah, he was the worst."

Clementine makes a dash into the woods. She's chasing something, but I know she'll be back soon. She never strays too far away.

"I asked her once why she needed a boyfriend all the time," Will says. "Especially because she would always tell me that we were a good team together, that we didn't need anyone else."

"What did she say?" I lean back on my elbows and watch the stars begin to appear.

"She said she gets lonely sometimes when I'm at school and that she thought I needed a man around."

"Did you think you needed a man around?"

He shakes his head.

"Did your mom ever marry any of the boyfriends?" I realize that I don't know much about Will's family, about his mother, his father.

"She wanted to marry them all," he says. "But I guess they didn't want that."

I glance up to see if Clem is heading back in our direction. I don't see her.

"I think it was because of me," he adds softly.

"Why would you think that?" I ask.

He shrugs. "I heard somebody say one time that a child changes the situation."

I look at Will and it's easy to tell that he too had been privy to a conversation not meant for his ears. "Did you hear your mom say that?"

He turns away so that I can't see his eyes. He doesn't answer.

"Will, I didn't know your mom so I can't speak for her." He's still facing another direction. "But what I know is that she came back for you when she could. She came back and got you from your grandparents, and she didn't have to do that."

I hear a sniffle.

"Right?" I ask.

He doesn't respond.

"If she had wanted to get married, and if having you kept her from that, she wouldn't have come for you. She wouldn't have fought for you in court. Maybe some of those guys didn't want a child, but your mom did. She wanted you. She came back for you."

I wait to see if he's going to say anything.

"Right?" I ask.

He nods slightly.

"That's right," I answer myself. "She may have wanted a boyfriend or a husband, but she wanted you more. And that's something," I say, thinking about my mother's choices, remembering how she left and never came back, how she walked away from Daisy and me and never came back.

"The doctor said she took too many pills," he tells me. "He said she died because she took a lot of pills."

"Yeah, that's what I heard, too."

"How did your sister die?"

And I breathe out a long, slow, deep breath. I haven't told this story in a long time. But I suppose if anyone deserves to hear it, it's Will. Still, I would rather tell the short version instead of the one I remember, the one reliving every single detail. I don't think anyone wants to hear that one anyway.

"Even when she was a little girl, Daisy would sometimes get very, very sad. And when she got that way, she would go to the hospital and they would give her some medicine that would help her not feel so sad. And then she'd come home and she'd feel better for a while. One time—the last time," I say, remembering that terrible day, "she went to the same hospital but it was a different doctor and he gave her the wrong medicine and it made her really, really sick. And by the time they knew what had happened, by the time they figured out she wasn't just pretending to be sick, she died."

I feel my voice catch in my throat, the tears gather in my eyes.

"Did the doctor say he was sorry for giving her the wrong medicine?"

"No, he never did."

"Are you still mad at him?"

I look at the little boy and I think about the question I have never thought to ask myself, and in the same way he had answered my last question to him, I nod, ever so slightly.

And for the longest time we don't speak. Will makes lines in the dirt with his stick and I just sit and watch the sky. It isn't for almost half an hour before I realize Clementine hasn't returned.

·TWENTY-NINE·

I T is exactly how it was when Daisy died. I feel completely pulled out of my body and it is as if I am watching everything from some other angle, from some other person's viewpoint. I can see everything that is happening but I am not within myself. I am not who I think I am.

I don't know how I got from the cemetery to John Cash's house. I don't remember picking up my dog and carrying her for more than half a mile to the truck, Will running ahead of me, yelling and screaming to hurry up. I don't know how I knew where to go, how I didn't crash driving up the mountain, then back down to his office, and I still don't know how Nora and Jimmy found out and met us there and I don't even know if they have forgiven me. I don't feel the porcupine quills in my hands and chest that dug into my skin when I pulled the spiny rodent away and gathered up my dog. I don't feel my ankle swelling from the second fall I took when I put Clem in the truck and tried to run around to the driver's side, slipping and falling and trying and trying to get up.

I am in a fog, some unbelievable, indescribable, terrible, terrible fog.

I hear the vet telling Nora to take me to the hospital, to get me to a doctor to check my foot and to pull out the quills, but there is no way I'm leaving Clem.

Will is crying and Jimmy is talking to his grandmother on the phone, holding him, and I cannot even speak to tell him it's going to be okay. I cannot even console this little boy who saw what I saw when we rounded the corner at the end of the line of trees after we walked away from his mother's grave, trying to find my dog.

I knew porcupines lived around Creekside. I knew they foraged for food in forests, that the drought had forced them closer to human habitations. I knew they were dangerous to dogs, their quills sharp as needles, and that they would attack if provoked. I know I heard a story once about a family pet being killed by a porcupine, an infection taking over and causing death, pictures on the Internet of the quills covering the face of an unsuspecting bulldog; but I had never known to be afraid. I had never worried that Clementine would be in danger from a porcupine. I had thought of cars and cancer and poisonous food; I knew of dysplasia, bad joints, decaying teeth; but I had never worried about a rodent at dusk. I have never known to be afraid of that.

What else? I think. What else have I overlooked? What other calamity can strike and put an end to this life I have made for myself? What else have I missed?

"Drink this." And Nora puts a cup of something warm to my lips. It is tea or coffee, I don't know which, but it is bitter and I obey. I swallow.

I cannot see what the vet is doing. I am sitting in a room outside but sometimes I hear a movement from the other side of the door. Sometimes I hear him speaking softly and I want to go in, but Nora holds me back.

"Drink some more." And I do as I am told.

"Now, take this." And she hands me a pill and without asking what it is or what it will do, I swallow that, too.

There is an ice pack on my ankle. I do not remember who put it there, how long it has been resting on my foot. I think it should be cold but I don't feel it.

"I'm going to pull out some of these quills," Nora says, and I lean back against the chair.

"I don't understand how you got these stuck in you." She takes in a breath. I see her turn to Jimmy, who just shakes his head.

"Did the animal attack you, too?" And she pulls at one and I watch it come out of my hand. There is a little blood.

"Maybe you got them when you picked Clem up." And she yanks out another. "Do these stick on both ends?" She is placing them on the floor beside her and I see them, these tiny narrow spines that had covered my dog and then covered me. I see them and I want to pick one up, hold it close to my eyes, study it, try to understand how it could render my dog motionless, how it made her so quiet, so still. But I only look at them from where I am sitting. I do not try to reach down.

I see Juanita when she pulls up and I watch as she walks into the office. I see her go over to Will and I hear him cry and scream that he doesn't want to leave, but I watch as Jimmy picks him up and carries him out, places him in the backseat of her car. I watch as she drives away.

I wouldn't let him touch Clementine. He tried to help me get her in the truck, but I told him to get away until I could cover her with a blanket and then I let him get in, kneel in front of her, out of a seat belt, out of a seat, to keep her from rolling onto the floor. Clem was in shock or already dead, I don't know. She didn't cry or try to move. She didn't flail around or yelp in pain; she just lay there, so very, very still. And I kept touching her where I could, where there were no quills—her back, a tiny place on her neck—telling her it would be okay, telling her I wouldn't let anything bad happen, telling her the very same thing I said to my sister when she took her final breath and I knew I had failed.

"Just a few more," I hear Nora say, and I look down at the bloody mess on the inside of my hands and I keep thinking I should be feeling something, I should hurt or wince or somehow know physically what she is doing, but there is this absolute and complete absence of pain or ache. I am still somewhere beyond myself.

"He's a good doctor," she adds. "Clem will be fine." And she pulls another quill and I think that perhaps I shall be full of holes when she is done. I think I shall look like a cartoon character shot in a hundred places. I imagine drinking some juice and watching it squirt out of all the holes. I think of a garden hose punched with tiny openings, made to irrigate a flower bed.

Jimmy returns to the room where we sit and takes a chair across from me.

"Get me a wet towel," Nora instructs him, and he leaves and returns with a small towel, dripping with water. She holds it against the palms of my hands.

"I need another one."

He leaves and comes back with another.

She places it on top of the first one.

"Get me the peroxide," and he goes out again and then reappears at my side. And then she nods at him, and I think I see him leave.

"Lift up your shirt."

And I think I must be wrong and that Jimmy is still there, just out of my view, and maybe she needs his clothes for something, but then I realize she is talking to me and I watch her pull at the bottom of my shirt and feel it lift off my head.

I look down and see the quills stuck all across my chest and I wonder if one has pierced my heart and if that is the reason I cannot feel anything, if my heart has been punctured and everything has drained away. I wonder if I am already dead, watching things just before I'm sucked like a vapor into heaven. I wonder if this is what all those books are written about, if this is one of those near-death experiences I have heard about.

"Jesus," Nora says, and I close my eyes and feel her lay me down on the row of chairs as she begins to pull the needles from my skin.

I must stay there for a long time. I feel her near me, yanking and pulling, blotting a towel or gauze pad on my chest. I hear Jimmy coming and going. I hear voices. I sense people floating around me, talking about me, saying how awful such a thing can be. But I do not see Clementine. I keep searching and searching but I cannot find my dog.

I start to feel a kind of throbbing in my ankle and I wonder whether I have come back. I think about all those people who write those books, about Jesus and the stone, and I wonder if I have died and come back.

"Ruby," I hear, and I open my eyes and Dr. Cash is standing over me.

·THIRTY·

"Sᴏᴏᴏ's stable," he says, and I begin to weep. "She was in shock after the attack; one of the quills was lodged in her throat but she's okay now."

I am a river of relief. I cannot even say thank you or ask when I can see her. I can only let the tears fall, the air fill and leave my lungs.

"But you're not okay," he adds. "Your ankle is fractured and I'm worried you've gone into shock. You've been here too long already. You need medical attention and you need it now. So Jimmy is taking you to the emergency room at the hospital."

I shake my head. I'm fine. I know I'm fine.

"Ruby, you need to go. I will not leave Clementine until you are back. She's sedated and she doesn't need you to be near her because she needs to focus on herself, not on you. She knows you are hurt and the reminder of that, you here and hurt, will keep her from healing. You don't want that, do you?"

I see that he is waiting for an answer, so I shake my head.

His face is close to mine, to make sure I've heard him, to make sure I'm listening, or maybe to make himself sound big and authoritative so I will obey. I don't know why he leans in so near, but he smells of castile soap and fatigue and what he says sounds like the truth, so I nod in agreement.

He stands and Jimmy moves over to where I am sitting and the two of them kneel over me, lift up my arms, and pick me up. One of them is on each side and I feel like a football player being carried off the field. I am carefully walked through the office door, placed in the car, the passenger side, the seat belt wrapped around my chest, the tiny punctures stinging, and Jimmy gets in on the driver's side. Nora takes the backseat and I think I should mention that Jimmy should not drive, that his license is still suspended, but frankly, I do not care. Frankly, I am a thousand miles away already.

The hospital is bright lights, questions and introductions, quick movements, first a nurse, then a doctor, then another nurse, first one room, a curtain yanked around me, my clothes peeled off, needles inserted, fingers probing my arms and legs, my chest, my foot, then another room, x-rays, then back to where I started. I am dizzy and confused and I hear the voices all around me, talking to me, talking about me, but I feel so far away. I answer what I can with nods and shakes of my head, but I try not to talk because I don't really know how to say the words that will satisfy their questions. I cannot give them what they seem to need to know. Finally, I am shown pictures of my ankle, thin white bones on black film, a long nimble finger pointed to show me what has cracked, what must be pulled back and wired together. I am given a form to sign and next I am soundly and deeply asleep. For all I know, I may be dead again.

I dream of flowers and soft light, of leaves unfurling, and bright bursts of color. There is the deepest, clearest blue and I fall into it, caught and held like I am in the narrow cup of a mountain gentian, the stem, long and sturdy, leaves like tiny green steps leading me to a meadow floor. Everywhere I look there is color and there is fragrance and I am as light as a feather, every burden, every weight that I have carried for so long, removed from me, gone.

In this garden, this dream of paradise, there are no greenhouse tricks, no irrigation hoses, no fertilizers, no fields plowed and seeded. There are only wild blooms, flowers found in rich woods and sagebrush plains, alpine ridges, and thick swampy bogs. Monkshood and larkspur, sky pilots and shootingstars, fireweed and globemallow, plumed avens and parrot's beaks, harebells and chickweed. These flowers are not the ones I get from the back of a truck, not the ones I keep in buckets, in refrigerated air, not the ones I snip and trim and domesticate.

These are divine flowers, tiny pieces of indescribable beauty like patches of some heavenly quilt, and all I want to do, all I have to do, is breathe, open my eyes, open my heart, and see. It is the easiest thing I have ever done and I let myself go, let myself come undone in this brilliance. And even as I am immersed in this otherworldly revelation I hear myself say, "This is what he meant. This is the epiphany. This is the thing that changes you forever." I kneel and then fall back and I stay in this wonder for what seems like a very long time.

When I finally begin my return, finally start to come back to myself, to my world, to my body and hospital bed, the first person I think I see is Captain Dan Miller smiling at me from across the room. He knows. I can tell he smiles at me because he knows and I need not tell him a thing about where I have been and what I have seen. He has walked this splendid field.

"Ms. Jewell . . . Ms. Jewell . . ." I feel someone tugging at my arm, shaking me, pulling me back, yanking me away from the meadow, away from the dream, the astronaut.

"Ruby . . ." The voice is sharp, demanding, and I open my eyes as I know I am being told to do. "You need to wake up. You've been under anesthesia too long now. Wake up!"

And I do. And as I look around, a heavyset woman dressed in white is standing right beside me, the one who calls, the one who will not be denied. And sitting in the two chairs situated around my bed are Nora and Jimmy. I guess they have been here all night. Captain Miller is nowhere in the room.

"Hey." It's Nora. She gets up and stands at the other side of the bed while the nurse shines a light in my eyes, raises my arm, slips a cuff around it, and begins to pump a small black bulb. She is checking my blood pressure. She places the tiny cup of the stethoscope on the inside of my arm, which I can see is just like the palm of my hand, welted and red.

"Are you in any pain?" the nurse asks.

I shake my head.

"Right here is the pain medication."

I follow her eyes to an IV stand, a small box, a bulging bag hanging at the top.

"You see this little lever?"

I nod.

"You just squeeze it when you start to hurt, okay? You're in charge of your medication."

Again, I nod.

She checks the numbers on the cuff, releases the air, pulls it off my arm. She moves the stethoscope to my chest, delicately, and listens to my heart.

"The surgery went well. And we've got you pretty numbed up so you shouldn't be in too much pain tonight. But you've got a lot of wounds." She studies the tiny holes, makes a kind of clucking noise as if she disapproves, checks the IVs and lines coming from my arm, and then finally raises the sheet and checks my feet. I feel her cold fingers on my legs.

"Do you need anything?"

I shake my head.

"Ice chips, water?"

"No," I whisper.

"Okay, you can talk to your friends a little bit, but then they need to go so you can rest. It's very late," she says, and gives them a look like a third-grade teacher.

They nod, dutiful students.

I smile and she is gone.

"Clem?"

I see the tears gather in Nora's eyes. "She's fine. Dr. Cash just texted that he removed all the quills. Not a one got in her eyes and he removed the one from her throat. He's pleased with how she is doing."

I glance over at Jimmy and suddenly I remember what happened between us. "I'm sorry I said what I said," I tell him.

He looks at me carefully. "I don't know what you're talking about," he replies.

I feel the sweet relief of forgiveness and even though I want to say more, I don't.

I close my eyes and drift off to sleep. I doubt I will return to the meadow of my dreams, but I am hopeful there might be more color.

·THIRTY-ONE·

I MISSED Easter and the high school spring dance, the social at the club, and at least three birthdays, what else?" I have been out for only two weeks, but for a florist used to a tight community schedule, that can feel like an eternity.

We closed the shop for one week and Nora has been filling the orders for the last several days. She had some help from the florist in Deer Park, Edna Lane, a woman who helped me start my business and has always assisted me when needed, and from what I hear, Cooper arranged the bouquets for the two church services and the one funeral for Miss Lucy Waller, who has lived twenty years over at the nursing home.

Cooper stayed with Jimmy a couple of days in Creekside, even stopped by the hospital to check on me, brought me a thick bunch of fresh daffodils and a few stems of fancy leucadendrons that he found at the market in Seattle. And he was quite the gentleman, didn't try to get in bed with me but once. Still, even with all the help, it's time I get back to business. It's time I get back to what it is I do.

"Henry's come by a couple of times, but he won't tell me what he wants or who he's buying for, just keeps saying he'll come over when you're better."

She glances across the street in the direction of the barbershop and then she glances back at me. I wait for the questions, but she seems to think better of it and doesn't ask what I know about Henry's love life.

Without saying anything to Nora, I do wonder how things are progressing between Henry and Lou Ann. I wonder if he's found the courage finally to speak to her, tell her that he's the secret admirer who has been sending her flowers. I wonder if they went out on a date.

"Conrad proposed to Vivian. He came by and wanted the same arrangement you made when he took her out for Mexican food in February." She has picked up the stack and is going through the receipts of the past week. "He said it gave him good luck."

"Dendrobiums," I respond, reminded of the other couple I have been trying to help along. I think of Vivian and Conrad and remember the purple orchids and the date to Rancho Chico in Colville, the risk I took in giving him those blooms.

She nods. "Cooper was here when he stopped in. He seemed to know exactly what you had put in the arrangement, made it up in a few minutes. He said that he was here when you put it together and that the floral choices were actually his idea."

I smile, recalling the conversation from months ago that Cooper and I had about the couple, the way he persuaded me to do what I did. "I guess he's right. He was pretty pushy about the Thai blooms." I think about Conrad and Vivian, how long they've been dating, the heat that finally rose between them this winter. "Did you hear her answer?"

"They already set a date for July."

I count the months on my fingers. "Wow, that's not very far off," I say.

"She's going to call about the arrangements," Nora tells me. "She's thinking sunflowers and blue irises. Who knows where she got that combination."

I consider the two plants and sort of like the idea, tall slender stems of long azure blooms mixed in with the round full faces of sunflowers. I hadn't expected that Vivian had such a creative mind or that she was so confident in her choices of wedding flowers, and I wonder if it was the orchids that sealed the deal for the couple or if Vivian had been ready and waiting all along and it was Conrad who had actually needed the extra push.

Clementine gets up from her spot near my wheelchair and moves under the design table. I watch her carefully even though she no longer seems to be in pain or have trouble walking. She has recovered much faster than I have and except for a few welts along her snout, some loss of appetite, she is fine. A little more to herself, reserved, less social, as if she's still trying to process a fight with a porcupine, but fine.

The vet has her on antibiotics for another few days and wants to see her in a few weeks for a follow-up, but beyond that she is released from her doctor's care. I suddenly think about John Cash, his kindness, his gentle way with Clem and with me, and I feel a slight fluttering inside. I shake my head when I remember the phone call he took during one of Clem's appointments, the way he left the room and returned, the flustered way he finished telling me about the medications, the way he kept rubbing his left ring finger.

"I still don't see how you can make arrangements sitting down." Nora is looking first at me, then at the table, then back at me. She is shaking her head. "Even with that contraption that Jimmy made you, I don't know how you can balance a vase with all the flowers you put in. Why don't you just limit your orders to what I can do until you're back on your feet? People will understand."

I continue trimming the ends of the stems of freesia on the narrow board that stretches across the arms of my wheelchair. Jimmy measured and cut a piece of wood, sanded it down, and sealed it, and I think it works perfectly. As long as Nora will bring me the flowers from the storage room, I can do my work from the chair.

"It's just for a couple more weeks," I reply. "Then I get a soft cast and a boot and I'll be able to stand and hold on to the table," I add, thinking this will be a long spring season trying to do my work on one leg. I hold up another stem and cut away the thin narrow leaves at the bottom.

I am making a bouquet for Evelyn Barr, the nurse who took care of me after the surgery. She said she loved freesia, that the smell always made her think of goodness and that the funnel-shaped blooms were to her a symbol of grace. She told me the story of her favorite flower when she helped me get out of bed for the first time and when she learned I was the town florist. She isn't from around here, so we had never met.

"There was a teacher at nursing school who used to wear a perfume with that scent. She was old, had been teaching for thirty years when I took her class in pharmaceuticals. One day I was sure I had failed a test and wouldn't graduate and she found me sitting outside on the back steps crying. She made me get up and she gave me a big hug and told me she was certain that I had not failed the test and that even if I had it wouldn't keep me from graduating. She told me that I would make a fine nurse and I remember that she smelled like a garden of freesias. Since then I have always loved those flowers." She let me lean against her while I hopped on one foot. "That fragrance takes me back to one of the most important moments of my life and reminds me of someone who made me feel good about myself."

I ordered ten bunches of them as soon as I was discharged. Evelyn is a very good nurse and she deserves to feel special.

"Jenny's back in the hospital," Nora mentions, changing the subject. "Justin's mother stopped by a couple of days ago to buy a plant for her sister-in-law in Idaho Falls. She said the treatments have caused an infection and she has to stay on IV drugs for a few days. And she's having some heart problems now." She puts the receipts back by the cash register. "Poor girl, she has certainly been through it." She pauses for a second. "At least she's here at St. Joseph's and not on the cancer ward in Spokane. Makes it easier on Justin."

"Call Cooper and see if he's left the warehouse yet. If he hasn't, tell him to bring me a few dozen stems of lily of the valley when he comes in the morning." I know they help with cardiac issues. "I'll add them to the pink and yellow peonies I ordered. That'll lift her spirits."

Nora gets a pen and writes down the instruction.

"When I go to take these to Evelyn tomorrow, I'll stop by and drop them off."

"Are you supposed to be driving?" she asks.

"I can get around town okay," I answer, remembering the doctor's order. I'm not officially released to be behind the wheel until the cast comes off, but it's Creekside. You could drive in reverse around here and still be safe. I'll be fine for a couple more weeks.

"You want to have dinner with me and Jimmy tonight? We're going to the Chinese place. They have a new fish platter that Carl has been raving about."

I just shake my head.

"I thought you liked Chinese food," she says, and she studies me. "Wait a minute. Do you have something else to do?"

I smile, thinking about the visit a few days ago, glad for the chance to spend time with Dan and tell him about my dream, compare notes of epiphanies.

"John?" she asks, the hopefulness ringing in her voice. I have not told her about my suspicions. I have not mentioned the phone call that was such a distraction or the way he seems to long for his wedding ring.

"Captain Miller," I reply.

She raises her eyebrows. "Another date with the astronaut?"

And I want to tell her the truth. I want to tell her that Dan and I are friends, that I have felt a deep connection to him since we flew to Seattle, since I walked out of the meadow and saw him waiting for me. That he is sick. But like so many things that I think and even know, I keep it to myself. After all, these last couple of weeks Nora has seen me wounded and broken and bloody and naked. As far as I'm concerned, for at least a while in this relationship, I have shared enough.

·THIRTY-TWO·

It's called spontaneous remission." Dan is at the stove. He is making spaghetti, his favorite, he told me, angel hair pasta in a red clam sauce. He stopped at a fish market on his way out of Spokane this morning. The clams are fresh.

"But *spontaneous* isn't really the right word. It's more like *unexpected* or *unanticipated* because most things in life are not really spontaneous. I don't believe that things occur purely by accident. It is more likely that these remissions have a cause that just hasn't been identified yet."

I asked Dan about the healing he said he experienced two other times when he was diagnosed with cancer. He's telling me what he knows about the science of what happened to him.

He stirs the sauce.

"Based on what is published in medical journals, unexpected remissions occur in one out of every sixty thousand to one hundred thousand cancer survivors, but the number is probably higher than that because not all of these cases get reported."

He turns around to face me. I am sitting at the bar in front of him. He's wearing a red apron and has a dish towel thrown over his shoulder. He looks like a man comfortable in the kitchen. He reaches for his glass of wine and takes a swallow. "It's breast cancer, right?"

I told Dan about Jenny and asked about his remissions and whether he knew someone who might help her.

"I think it's spread."

He nods.

"I can call someone. The man I worked with is still in the States. He's actually from India but he's lived here for the last twenty years. He's in New Mexico. Do you think Jenny will be open to nonallopathic procedures?"

"What?" I ask.

"Nonallopathic; it refers to treatment that doesn't follow the principles of mainstream medical practice. Allopathy is the treatment of a disease using remedies whose effects are different than those produced by the disease. Nonallopathic would be the opposite of that. It is primarily focused on dietary changes as well as cognitive therapy."

I shake my head. Talking to Dan is like talking to a rocket scientist, which, now that I think about it, is sort of what he is.

He smiles, turns back to the stove and his clam sauce.

I take a drink from my glass. The wine is from California. Dan told me the exact location where the grapes are grown, somewhere in the southern region of Napa Valley, and how the grapes are picked at night and brought to the winery in darkness and that they are pressed in whole clusters and stored in oak barrels. I have no idea about the reasoning for any of these things, but he seems to believe they make all the difference in the world and I must agree it is a very good wine.

"Tell me about the stars," I say. I try to arrange myself so that I am sitting more comfortably, but it's hard since I need to prop up my foot. It hurts if it starts to swell, and letting it dangle makes it swell.

"Here." He has turned around and is watching me fidget in my seat on the stool. He walks over to the table, brings back a chair, sets it near the stove. Then he goes somewhere in the other part of the house and brings a small footstool. "Try this."

And I hobble over to the place he has made. He returns to his spot at the stove and puts a loaf of bread in the oven, checks the pot of water to see if it is boiling. He turns up the temperature.

"A star is a massive, luminous sphere of plasma held together by gravity. It begins as a collapsing cloud of material mostly composed of hydrogen, along with helium and trace amounts of other, heavier elements. When the central core is sufficiently dense, some of the hydrogen is converted into helium through the process we know to be nuclear fusion." He stops and glances over at me. I guess he can see the glaze across my eyes. "You're not really interested in what they're made of, are you? You want to know about the stars that changed me, the ones that altered my consciousness."

"I think I'll have a better shot of understanding that," I answer.

He takes another swallow of wine. "Your flowers," he says. "In your dream, can you adequately describe what they were like?"

I see what he's trying to tell me. I had told him about the meadow and how he appeared as I was leaving and he is explaining to me that his stars are like my flowers; to describe either of them is to undo the hold they have on us. I nod.

"Were you ever in love?" I ask, feeling a sort of boldness I don't ordinarily have.

"What is it with you and all these questions? Is this the wine talking or did that porcupine and that epiphany suddenly make you extraordinarily inquisitive?"

I shrug because I have no idea why I'm asking him these things.

He smiles. "This morning as I walked along the lakeshore, I fell in love with a wren and later in the day with a mouse the cat had dropped under the dining room table."

I know I appear confused. I never knew Dan had a cat.

"It's from Billy Collins, the poet."

"Oh," I respond, still unsure of what he's trying to say to me.

"Yes." He gives me a real answer. "Yes, I have been in love: aimless love, familial love, platonic love, and the best one of all— once I knew what it was to experience romantic love. I have known them all."

I nod.

"And you?" he asks, and I know it's only fair to have the question tossed back in my direction.

I think about Stephen Bartlett in tenth grade, his curly blond hair, his lanky stance and perfect chin, the shy way he'd smile. I think about Anthony Jaramillo in college, the lilt in his Shakespeare recitations, the Latin bravado, the dark brooding eyes; Casey Merlin from the library at law school, so quiet and studious, so knowledgeable about constitutional amendments and contractual agreements, his small delicate hands. At one time I thought I loved them all, thought they had something that might fill the emptiness, open wide my heart; but now I don't know. I'm not really sure I have ever let myself know what it is to feel such a thing.

He seems to recognize the hesitation and doesn't press. "There's still time," he says, turning again to the stove and the task of fixing dinner, his response jolting me back to the conversation.

"Is it worth it?" I ask, not sure why I want an answer, what I would even do with what he might tell me. "All the anguish and struggles, the knowing and not knowing, the loss and the turmoil, is it worth all that?"

I think about my customers. Henry risking everything on the librarian, who only knows the books he reads, the facts and stories that fill his head. Justin, sitting in hospital waiting rooms for weeks at a time, watching daytime television and hoping for a miracle. Stan and his yellow roses for his high school sweetheart, Viola, who left once and came back. The fights and then the making up, the highs and lows, the proposals and weddings, the hospital stays and funerals, all the flowers arranged to say what is either breaking or filling their hearts.

Dan turns down the heat on his sauce, puts a lid on the skillet, takes the pasta from the plastic bag on the counter and breaks a handful in half, drops it in the boiling water, wipes his hands on the towel that is flung across his shoulder, turns to me, and is suddenly very serious.

"Loving only once—giving myself utterly and fully without ever really knowing it might actually be reciprocated, losing myself so completely to an emotion, to another person, only having the chance, only taking the chance just once—is my only true regret of this life-time." He reaches for his glass of wine. "I should have tried again."

He takes the last sip, puts the glass on the counter, and turns back to the stove. "Dinner is ready," he announces, and I say nothing more about love.

·THIRTY-THREE·

"HE made me drink grape juice for two days." Jenny is home from the hospital and has had two sessions with the healer from New Mexico. Dan brought Dr. Singh to Creekside after he talked to both Jenny and Justin and decided she was a perfect candidate for the man who put his cancer in remission.

"That's not so bad," I say. I am able to stand now for extended periods of time. The cast is off and I rest my foot and leg on the seat of a walker while I make my arrangements. Today I'm working on prom corsages. I have orders for forty. Roses mostly, wristlets, tiny buds, pink and red and white, clipped and pressed together along with slender leaves of ivy and pitta negra. There are a few orchids, one or two carnations, and spread all across the table are tiny satin bows.

Jenny is sitting in a chair across from me. She's giving Clementine a good rub.

"It's better than prune juice," I add. I know this because I was terribly constipated following the surgery and it was a suggested remedy. I gave it a try but decided I'd just as soon never go to the bathroom again as to have to drink any more of that stuff.

"Ick," she responds.

It appears Jenny has been given the same remedy.

"What does he tell you to eat?"

"Nothing yet. Dr. Singh told me that I needed to clean out my system before taking any more food."

I look over at Jenny. She's so frail, so skinny. She can't weigh ninety pounds. I don't want to say anything, but it worries me that she's only drinking grape juice.

"I actually feel better, though," she reports. "I don't have that metal taste in my mouth anymore and I don't feel nauseated like I was feeling when I was in the hospital." She shrugs and wipes her hands on her legs. "Maybe this guy is for real."

Clementine lies at her side.

I think about the healer, this Indian man from New Mexico that Dan introduced me to a few days ago. Dan brought him by the shop and at first it seemed he mistook me for Jenny, the one in need of his services. As soon as he met me, he knelt down and touched my leg. I immediately felt a kind of warmth in my calf and down into my foot, but I also felt embarrassed because I was standing and still had my hand out to shake while he was kneeling in front of me. When Clem walked over and gave him a big lick on the cheek, he finally stood up, met my eyes, and took my hand. I have to say, though, my ankle has felt a lot better since then.

"Well, it can't hurt to let him try, right?" I ask.

"Do you really think he healed the astronaut of cancer?"

I nod. "He says so. I don't think he has any reason to lie about it."

"I feel different when I'm with him," she says.

And that piques my interest. "What do you mean?" I combine the two pink spray roses with four blooms of alstroemeria. I hold the corsage up and Jenny nods her approval. I reach over and take the roll of pink ribbon and start to cut.

She ponders the question for a bit. "There's just something about him. It's like the way I feel after I've just woken up from a good nap, like I'm rested or something."

I consider again how it was when I met Dr. Singh. He is a very centered man, I can say that. "What does he do in his sessions?" I ask.

"Well, the first time he reached out his hands and held mine for almost an hour. I waited for him to say something but he was just real quiet like he was listening to something inside himself, so I just sat and closed my eyes. He didn't really say anything then, just told me to drink the grape juice and not to eat anything."

"And the second time?" I ask, hoping there's something more to what this man has to offer than just holding hands.

"The second time he did the same thing but only for maybe half an hour and then he asked me to think of a time when I felt really strong and he wanted me to tell him everything I remembered about it."

I stop making the corsage and listen.

"At first, it took me a while to think of a time and we sat there for what felt like an eternity, but then, I finally remembered something from when I was ten years old."

I wait for more.

"And then for about twenty minutes he asked me questions. Who was with me? What did I do? What did it feel like? So I told him the story."

She pauses, so I have to ask the question.

"What story?"

"Okay, it was my birthday and I got a new bike. That afternoon my cousin came over and we rode our bikes down to the elementary school. We were just riding and hanging out and when we rode around to the back of the school, there were these boys playing basketball. They looked like they were about thirteen or fourteen. I didn't know them. I was ahead of my cousin, and all of a sudden I hear a crash and her start to cry. When I stopped and turned around, I could see that she had fallen and that there was a basketball right beside her. That's when I noticed that the boys were laughing, and I figured out that one of them had thrown the ball and knocked my cousin off her bike. When I got to where she was, it was like something just came over me." She stopped and turned to me. "Do you know what I mean?" she asks.

I nod because I kind of do.

She continues. "After I made sure that she was okay, I stomped over to that basketball court and stood right in front of those boys. I told them they were jerks and bullies and that if they ever did anything like that again I would kick their butts." She shakes her head, remembering.

"And I think they were so shocked that this little girl had threatened them, they didn't say anything. So I stomped back, picked my cousin up and got her on her bike, and then I got on mine and I stole their basketball. As soon as they realized what I had done, they started chasing us, but we had a good head start and we flew home, both of us scared to death, and we hid in my garage until after dark." She laughs.

"It was the weirdest thing but when I realized that they had knocked my cousin down, it was like I became somebody else, somebody stronger and tougher. I wasn't afraid of any of those boys and they were at least twice my size." She slides her hands down her legs, smiling. "I kept that ball for the longest time, like it was some kind of trophy or something. Crazy, right?" And she shakes her head.

I don't answer. I am thinking about her story, the courage of a ten-year-old girl, the way she stood up to teenage boys, the care she took for her cousin. I think about Daisy and me when we were kids and all the scraps we found ourselves in, all the bullying, name-calling, the way we were always there for each other, the way she made me brave. I feel the sting of grief. "Why does he want you to think about that?"

Jenny shrugs, bites her bottom lip. "He told me I need to find that strength again. I need to be confident and unafraid of the disease that has entered my body, to be just as tough and just as angry as I was at those boys, to tell the tumors they cannot live in my body, to confront them and take their power away from them. He says I somehow lost that little ten-year-old girl and I need for her to come back, that only she can help me get rid of the cancer."

I finish the corsage and start another. I decide to use hot pink spray roses for this one. This one is for Madeline Marks's granddaughter, Katie Phelps, a young girl who graduates this year and didn't think she'd go to the prom because she didn't have a date. At the last minute she's decided to go with a friend. She called and ordered herself a corsage, so because I like her grandmother and because I know what it is like not to be asked to the prom, I want her flowers to be extra-special.

"I haven't told anybody about that," Jenny says softly.

"Why?" I ask, adding two green dendrobium orchids to the tiny bouquet.

"I guess I'm afraid people will think it's silly."

I twirl the finished corsage around in my hands. "Well, it's not really anybody else's business," I say. I wrap the flowers tightly in white tape and squeeze the ends together, adding three pearl pins. "This is about you and your body. You don't need to worry about what anybody thinks about what you're doing to try to get better."

She pauses and I see her watching the traffic out the front window. She's wearing a bright yellow, pink, and orange scarf to cover up her bald head. She looks like a bouquet of gerberas, the kind of flower she likes the best. She turns to me.

"I think he's right," she says, and I stop what I am doing to pay closer attention. "I mean, look at me. I'm not even able to think about the things he tells me because I'm worried about what somebody might say about me for listening to a healer." She shakes her head. "I can't believe I'm so stupid."

"Well, thinking that is probably not very helpful," I say, but it doesn't appear she's listening.

"I was so different when I was little. Nothing frightened me then. When I think about those boys, I see now they could have beat the crap out of me, but back then I didn't care."

She leans against the wall, stretches out her legs in front of her, clasps her hands, and drops them on the top of her head. She closes her eyes, thinking about everything, I guess.

And then she sits up and turns to me as if she's come to some realization.

"It's weird, isn't it, how we grow up and lose parts of ourselves that were so important to us when we were kids? I never used to back down when I was a little girl. I would fuss and argue about anything I thought deserved a fight; I was always asking questions and wanting explanations. I used to drive my parents crazy and my teachers crazy because I wanted them to tell me why things were the way they were. I never accepted anything I was told unless I believed it." She slumps back in her chair.

"And then, I don't know, it's like I just lost my voice, got afraid of what everybody would think of me and just started accepting everything I was told. It's like one day I just grew up and turned into somebody else." She takes in a breath and lets it out.

"You know, Dr. Singh is right. It's no wonder the cancer keeps coming back; it's like I open the front door to it and give it a place to live."

I watch her as she contemplates what the healer has told her, the story from her tenth year, the ways in which she lost herself. She sits forward, her elbows on her knees, thinking about all of this.

"Well, you know what? I'm not going to do that anymore," she says. "It's time I make a change."

I think about Katie Phelps, her resolve to go to the prom unaccompanied. I hold her flowers close to my face and take in a deep breath, the fragrance of the roses and the resolution of a young woman filling me. I glance back to Jenny, her chin somehow held a little higher. She watches me as I place the corsage in the narrow cardboard box.

"I guess you're going to have to steal some more balls," I say, folding over the top and setting the box aside.

And she smiles. "I think I'll just grow my own." And when she stands to leave, I swear she's gained a couple of inches and at least twenty pounds.

·THIRTY-FOUR·

Two weddings, homecoming at the Baptist church, a graduation party, and now, Bernie Wilson just called and asked for
a large arrangement to take to Cheney for his mother's birthday on
Friday. It is a busy week.

Nora is billing the accounts, organizing the vases, cutting the
ribbon, and trimming the foam. Jimmy got his license back earlier
than expected, provisional only for daytime hours, but he is now
available to pick up a few necessary supplies as well as make a few
runs, and Cooper, who has already made one extra delivery for me,
is planning to stop back by on his way from Metaline Falls and let
me have any flowers he has left over. Even Will is sweeping the
shop and changing the water in the buckets, bringing up boxes of
vases from the basement. Everybody is pitching in.

My ankle is much better, although it swells after a day of standing and it still aches a little at night. It's been more than two months
since the fall, but the doctor tells me it might be four to six months
before I'm able to run on it. I'm not sure which patient he has me

mixed up with, but I never asked about running; I only need to be able to lean against a table and arrange flowers. Walking is good; Clementine is glad to have me back in shape for that, but I don't even think she would be interested in taking up jogging at our ages.

"What are these for?" Will asks as he reaches up and puts the small cardboard box on the counter. There isn't any room on the design table. He takes out a bag of satin rose petals.

"The flower girl," Nora answers. "We just need one of those; you didn't have to bring the whole box."

"Oh." He stares at it. "I'll take it back." He glances down at the plastic bag in his hand. "What's a flower girl do?"

"She sprinkles rose petals on the floor before the bride comes out." Nora takes the bag from the boy.

He nods like he understands and then turns to me. "Why?"

I am working on the Saturday wedding. It's a small affair: daffodils, freesia, and golden alstroemeria. It turns out that Lou Ann Peterson was as eager to marry Henry as he was eager to marry her. It seems she was carrying her own torch for her most loyal library client, the one who read every book she gave him, thanking her every time. She knew the flowers were from him as soon as she got the first bunch. She had been waiting for him to get the nerve to speak to her, and when he finally asked her out, finally admitted that he had been her secret admirer, she confessed her love for him and they were engaged by the end of the date.

They're getting married behind his barbershop, a spot of yard hidden behind a tall wooden fence that I've never seen until he took me there last week. I had always wondered what Henry was doing back there, but now I know. He's been landscaping the little piece of property as if he has been planning his wedding venue for years. He has created a beautiful greensward with highbush cranberry, swamp rose, and red-osier dogwoods. There are tall, brightly colored hollyhocks all along the fence, goat's beard, lady fern, and small fruited bulrush in small clumps all throughout the garden. And in the northwest corner of the yard, along the rear fence, is his prize.

Henry has created a lovely pond filled with brightly colored koi. A waterfall, large slate rocks, elephant's ear, and lotus plants surround it. I was as surprised by his backyard as I was by the announcement of the marriage. It will be a beautiful place for the wedding. And with the reception planned to be held at the library, it is a perfect combination for the bride and groom, and I am making baskets and bouquets of yellow flowers for both events. "Just like sunshine," Henry had remarked when he saw my first arrangement and what he said he wanted when we discussed the floral arrangements for the backyard and the reception. "I-I want y-y-yellow f-flowers everywhere!"

"The flower girl is supposed to mark the path for the bride to find the groom," I tell Will, answering his question. "She sprinkles flower petals from where the bride stands all the way to where her beloved is waiting. It's a very important responsibility." I smile at Will, who rolls his eyes. Already at ten, he's convinced romance is gross.

"I never heard that," Nora responds. She takes down the box and hands it to Will. "I just thought it was a way of decorating a church aisle." She turns back and starts adding costs to a receipt. "Well that, and finding something for the bride's five-year-old niece to do."

"Did you get married in a church?" I ask Nora. I know she was married once when she was younger. I think she got divorced soon after the wedding. She has mentioned that it was the shortest marriage on record in Stevens County.

"St. John's Cathedral on a Saturday in June, five o'clock in the evening. The bridesmaids wore pink satin tea-length dresses and I had a designer gown flown in from Paris. We had a five-course dinner at the Beaumont Club on the river with a four-piece string ensemble as entertainment. There were pink and white roses in every bouquet, in each windowsill arranged beside white candles, and draped across the altar." She blows out a breath. "It was a very elaborate event."

I am surprised. I had no idea Nora would have had such a big wedding. She turns to see me staring at her.

"What?" she asks.

I shrug and get back to the yellow bouquets I am making for Henry and Lou Ann. "I just hadn't expected all that," I answer.

"My father was one of the richest men in Spokane," she explains "My mother needed my wedding to prove she was worthy of being his wife. I would have been happy just to go to the courthouse, but that was not to be." She opens the register and places the slip of paper underneath the cash drawer. "And in three days, before we even returned from our honeymoon, it was clear that a lot more time and energy had been spent on the wedding than on the relationship. We filed for divorce when we got home and my mother didn't speak to me again. She died a couple of years later from a botched plastic surgery and I became a drunk."

I glance down at Will, who is still standing there, holding the cardboard box Nora had placed in his arms a few minutes ago. He is watching her, his big brown eyes filled with a sorrow too old for a little boy.

Nora sees him, too, and she reaches down and squeezes him on the shoulder. "It was a nice wedding, though," she says, as a way to lighten the mood, I suppose. "And I had two flower girls throwing petals down the aisle." She slides a piece of his hair out of his eyes. "I walked all the way from the front of that church to that altar with my father escorting me, feeling like I was the most beautiful girl in the world. Even if I didn't stay married, that feeling was worth every nickel my mother spent." She winks at Will. "Plus, I got some great presents, and I kept every one of them."

Will smiles. He and Nora have gotten close since they have been working together. "I like presents," he says, "but I don't think I'll ever get married."

Nora thumps him on the head lightly. "You'll get married," she announces. "And you'll wear a new suit with a white orchid on your lapel and there will be rose petals all around you and there will be corny music playing and everybody will be watching and you'll think your bride is the prettiest girl you've ever seen when she is walking toward you down that aisle. And you'll be nervous and your hands will sweat and your stomach will do flips, but when she gets beside you and when you turn and face the minister to say your vows and hear that you're married, joined to this one you love forever, you'll think to yourself, *This is the best day of my life*."

Will studies the older woman for only a second. "Yuck," he says, and heads out of the room with the box.

I laugh and finish up the bouquets.

THIRTY-FIVE

WE did good today," I tell Clem as I unlock the door and walk into my house. I got all the arrangements finished for Saturday's and Sunday's weddings, got Bernie's mother's bouquet put together, and got a good start on pieces for the church homecoming and graduation party. I should get everything completed and ready to go by the end of the day tomorrow. Saturday I will close the shop to go to Henry and Lou Ann's wedding and then I'll have to get things ready for the next blissful event scheduled for Sunday at six o'clock at St. Bede's.

Jenny pushed ahead her wedding when she got the report from her doctor that the cancer was gone. She had met with the healer six times, and after the sixth session she scheduled a body scan at the hospital. She was sure she was free of disease and decided that when her prognosis was confirmed, she was getting married. She saw no reason to wait until the fall. She claimed that she and Justin were in love and she didn't want to waste another second putting her life on hold while she fought cancer. The scan was clear and she called me on her way back from Spokane. She waited until she knew for sure that the priest and I were free before she phoned her mother, telling her that everything was planned and all she needed to do was get an airplane ticket and come for the event. It appears as if the ten-year-old girl who stood up to bullies is now standing up to cancer and her mother. And I don't know which is scarier.

The flowers are the same, pink gerberas, everything I have in stock plus whatever Cooper had in his truck and whatever I could get from the other florists: standards and minis, Bella Vistas, flamingoes, loveliness. Every blush daisy in northeastern Washington will be on display at this wedding. And once I told the story to Cooper and the other florists, it turns out that Jenny and Justin don't have to pay a dime for any of the flowers. All the daisies are free.

I feed Clementine, get myself a glass of wine, and sit down on the sofa, propping my foot in front of me on the coffee table. I'm tired and I realize I haven't sat down all day. I didn't even eat lunch. I worked ten hours straight, pulling yellow stems for Saturday and pink ones for Sunday, mixing lavender and red roses for Bernie's mother and organizing what I could for the party and the homecoming. I close my eyes and see only flashes of color.

Still, I feel good about the work I accomplished today. I feel good that my foot is well enough that I can do what I enjoy doing. In spite of how exhausted I am, I know it was a productive day and I am very happy about these two weddings.

I think about Henry, how he ran across the street to take me to his backyard as soon as he knew I was out of the hospital and back at work. I remember how proud he was that the wedding would take place behind his shop, how he pushed me around in my wheelchair, showing me all the different elements of his yard and gardens. I remember the soft way he spoke of Lou Ann, the tender way he opened the small box to show me the wedding rings.

"I-it's m-m-my mother's," he said, showing me the diamond

that he had not yet given to his fiancée. He had it in his pocket and he pulled it out when he proposed, but he asked for it back because he wanted to get it sized to fit her and because he wanted to add something to the setting, hoping to make it even more special for his bride.

It was made of white gold and the stone in the center was a simple princess-cut diamond, but he had the jeweler place small diamonds on both sides, creating something unique.

"What is that shape?" I asked him, noticing that the side stones were fashioned in some artistic creation that I couldn't make out.

"B-b-bees," he answered.

I looked up. I did not understand the symbolism.

"F-f-for royalty," he explained, his cheeks turning red.

I had been moved by the romance in Henry's gift, told him it was the most beautiful ring I had ever seen, and as I think about Lou Ann's engagement gift I think of Jenny's too.

Justin had confessed to me weeks after Jenny announced the wedding that he didn't have enough money for the ring he wanted to buy her. With all the lost wages, all the money spent on gas and hotel bills to take her and stay with her at the hospital, they had ended up pawning the ring he had originally bought. He had been planning to buy a new one once he got back on his feet and could afford one. She had surprised him more than anyone else when she decided upon a new wedding date, and he had almost said no because he knew he didn't have money to buy a ring. Later, he happened to mention his concern to Dan during the final session Jenny had with the healer when they were waiting together.

Dan went home that afternoon, sorted through his jewelry, and found a tie clip he had been given by NASA, a gold bar with four small diamonds, marking the four missions he took to the moon. He took it as well as his own wedding band to the same jeweler Henry had seen and had him make an engagement ring for Jenny as well as wedding bands for the young couple. He presented them to Justin earlier this week, and he told me later, his eyes a little misty, how the boy had sobbed and hugged him so tightly he thought he had cracked a rib.

Just like the rings, I understand that both of these weddings are pretty special events.

I reach up and rub my foot. Clementine has finished her supper and joined me on the sofa. I take a sip of my wine and fall back.

You should invite that animal doctor to come with you to the weddings. I suddenly hear the suggestion ringing in my ear.

Carl had stopped by the shop to pick up a few green plants for a tennis tournament party at the club. He was borrowing a couple of ferns, a ficus, and a begonia rex. "He's quite the dreamboat."

I had felt Nora's eyes burning a hole in my back, and when I turned around she just raised her eyebrows and shrugged. It was her classic *I told you so* look.

Carl had gone on to explain that John had stopped by the club to ask about membership, that he had played golf in college and thought he might like to get back to the sport. He had asked only about the rate for a single member.

"He mentioned Henry's wedding," Carl said as he loaded the last plant in his car. "I think you should call and ask him to go with you. He's still new here," he went on to say. "You'd just be doing him a favor, just helping him get to know folks."

At the time I had waved away the suggestion. I had so much to do I didn't have time to think about taking a date to the wedding. I still had mums to arrange and daisies to trim; I figured I would be lucky just to make it to the wedding on time, do what I could with the last of my bouquets, and then slip on a dress and head across the street for the ceremony. I certainly wouldn't be able to arrange meeting a date and driving together.

"No, it is still a silly notion," I tell myself now.

But then I realize that I'm almost finished with all my tasks, that I would have time to come home, get ready, and ride with someone else. I would have time for Henry's wedding to be a date.

And why not? I ask myself. Why don't I ask Dr. John Cash to join me? What have I got to lose? Jenny beat cancer by standing up to it. Henry risked everything to tell the woman he loved that he loved her. Dan says not allowing himself to fall in love again is his greatest regret, and Nora tells me at least once a week that I have been alone too long. So why not? Why don't I just pick up that phone and call him? It's just like Carl said. I'm simply a longtime Creekside resident who would be happy to introduce a newcomer around to others, help him get settled. It's not a date as much as it is just going to an event together.

"I'm going to do it," I say to Clementine, who looks up and doesn't appear at all convinced that I'm about to make the call.

"I will too," I say. And I slide off the sofa and walk over and get my phone. I punch in the number in my contact list, the number he gave me after Clementine got hurt so that I could check on my dog while I was in the hospital.

I wait while the phone rings, proud of my confidence, my lack of fear, my steady hand. And then I hear the voice and all of that resolve and courage is instantly gone.

"Hello," I hear, and I do not at all recognize the woman's voice on the other end.

I hang up immediately.

·THIRTY-SIX·

"A RE you ready?" Dan is standing in the doorway of the shop. He is wearing a navy sports coat and tan slacks. I can tell he's lost weight and his color is a little ashen. I wonder if the cancer has spread, whether he should be out and about. But then he smiles and I decide this is not the time to question such a thing. "You look fabulous," he adds, and I grin in return.

I am wearing a dress Nora gave me. It is light blue, sleeveless, and I have to say it fits me very well. She claimed she had bought it along with another one for a friend in Colville but that it turned out they were too small and she thought I might like them. She said exactly those words as she handed me the Nordstrom's bag, but I remember how she looked when I told her a couple of days before then that I was wearing the pink dress from 1991 to both of the events this weekend. She closed her eyes and held her hand across her chest like she was fighting a lung infection.

Apparently, one cannot be seen in the same attire at two events scheduled one day apart, and apparently, Nora sneaked into my house and stole my old dress because after I explained what I would be wearing and after she showed up at the shop with these two dresses she claims she bought for this mystery friend, I have not been able to find it. She says she has no idea what happened to the dress, but I can tell she's lying because she won't look me in the eye when she lies, and she can't look me in the eye when I ask her friend's name in Colville and she won't look me in the eye when I ask her if she took my pink dress. She just waves away the question like it's an insect buzzing around her head.

"You are a rhapsody of beauty in blue," Dan says, and I glance down at the dress and smile. He does have a way with his words.

He opens the door to lead us out, and suddenly I remember something.

"Wait!" And I hurry over to the refrigerator and take out the boutonniere I made for him. It includes green dendrobium orchids, hot pink roses, and green ivy. I hurry back and pin it to his lapel. I stand back and admire it. "Perfect," I say.

He glances down at the small bouquet. "Ah, Ruby, you bring me great joy."

I smile. I turn back to Clementine, who is resting behind the counter. "We'll be back in a jiff," I tell her, then grab the keys and lock the door, and together we walk out of the shop.

"Thank you for asking me to go with you," I say to Dan as we cross the street.

Ever the gentleman, he holds my arm and keeps a slow and steady gait. He understands I am still a little handicapped in heels.

"Honestly, I thought you probably already had a date," he replies.

I shake my head, recalling the voice answering John Cash's phone. "Nope," I respond. "No dates for the florist."

We enter the yard through the gate next to the barbershop and immediately find Nora and Jimmy and move over to the two seats next to them.

I give Nora a little kiss on the cheek. I can see how she is admiring my dress.

"You said his yard was beautiful, but I had no idea!" Nora comments as I lean over and give Jimmy the same greeting as I gave her.

I watch as she looks around, measuring Henry's little paradise. "I always thought he was cooking meth back here behind that big fence."

Jimmy shakes his head.

"Well, I did," she insists. "And don't tell me that thought didn't cross your mind once or twice."

I turn to Dan and smile. "You remember Nora," I say, by way of introduction, and also to change the subject.

She lights up. "Hello, Captain Miller," and she holds out her hand, which he takes.

"Pleasure," he notes, and then nods to Jimmy. "Good afternoon."

"Afternoon," comes the response.

"Who's officiating?" Nora wants to know.

We take our seats. And I glance around to see if he is here.

"Dr. Buckley," I answer, calling out the name of the former veterinarian. I can't help myself, but I also look to see if his replacement is also somewhere close by. I don't see either of them.

"He's here," Nora reports, and I'm not sure which man she's talking about. And she looks at me and can see I am confused. "Buckley," she adds. "Up there," and she motions with her chin to the area in front of us.

"Right," I say, seeing the former veterinarian.

"The other one, too."

And I feel her watching me. I do not respond.

"He's with someone." And I see that she is more disappointed than I am. I did not tell her about my courage, my resolve, my phone call and quick hang up.

I simply nod, denying the urge to glance around.

She's about to say something else when the music starts and the best man, Lou Ann's boss at the library, Clyde Bowlin, and Henry join Wade at the front. They stand near the pond, a wedding arch wrapped in yellow and white blooms with two big baskets of yellow dahlias and irises situated at either side of it. When the wedding song is played, we all stand.

Lou Ann is prettier than I have ever seen her. Usually dressed very conservatively in corduroy skirts and sensible shoes, she has never been one to call attention to herself, but today she is radiant. She has on makeup, pink lipstick, and her hair is down, shoulder-length and curled. She's not wearing her glasses or a sweater set and she is smiling, something else I don't recall from my brief encounters with her when I check out my books. Her dress is simple, a long white gown with a yellow silk ribbon tied around her waist, matching the bouquets, the baskets of flowers, the maid of honor's dress, and the yellow tie that Henry is wearing, along with the single yellow gladiolus boutonniere in his lapel that is surrounded by variegated pittosporum in an ivory satin ribbon.

She is being escorted by her brother, a civil engineer from Seattle. Henry had explained that both of her parents were dead but she was very close to her younger brother. Henry had met him once. He'd asked for a haircut, and Henry had liked him right away.

We remain standing for the greeting and a prayer, and then we take our seats.

I listen as Dr. Buckley speaks of commitments and promises, but I am watching the clouds move across the sky. It is a bright day, lovely, a warm afternoon in early summer. It is my favorite sort of day and I remember as a child that when school was over for the season, Daisy and I would wake up to sunshine pouring through our window and she would always say the silliest thing. She would sit up and shake me until I answered. "Wake up, Ruby!" And she would keep punching me until I finally opened my eyes. When I did, she would be hovering over me, her breath warm against my face. "Looks like good light," and I would roll over, yanking the covers away from her and pulling the pillow over my head.

I always wondered but never asked where she got such a funny line. It always sounded like something an old person would say, not a child, not your sister waking you up when it was far too early. "Looks like good light." And it became a joke for us as we got older.

"How's your day?" she would call and ask when I was in college, and later, in law school, and she was still staying at our grandparents', still struggling to find her way.

"Looks like good light," I would answer, and then we'd both laugh and talk about how we were, the boy she was dating, the way we missed each other and when I was coming home.

"Looks like good light," I whisper to myself now, thinking of Daisy sitting beside me, watching the same clouds, the same bright sun, the same exchange of vows.

"Look at each other and make sure you never forget this moment. Soon you will make promises that will change everything. For today you shall say to the world—This is my husband. This is my wife."

I recognize the last two lines from Dr. Buckley's message come from the author Robert Fulghum. They are taken from a piece he wrote titled "Union." A lot of brides ask me about it and want to know if I have a copy when they talk to me about their weddings. I started keeping a file of such things when I became a florist because I discovered that along with bouquets and boutonnieres, there are a lot of questions about the ceremony itself and what might be read or shared. I keep this one along with several other poems and readings that might be of interest. It turns out the file, now taking up the space of one cabinet drawer, has been used quite a bit.

Nora told me once that for someone who has never known what it is to love, I sure have a lot to say about it. I smiled when she said it because it sounded exactly like something my sister would say. And of course, they would both be right.

Henry stumbles a bit while saying his vows, but no one seems to notice. Dr. Buckley simply waits until he finishes, and Henry sounds less like a man who stutters and more like a nervous groom in love. His disability is hardly noticed at all.

They finish with the words, the exchange of rings, and the lighting of a candle, and I watch as Lou Ann lifts her fingers to Henry's mouth, clearly so in love with this man, leans in, and kisses him.

I am filled to the brim and I am utterly empty and I wonder how it is that a person can be both things in exactly the same moment.

·THIRTY-SEVEN·

"O NE down, one to go," I say as Clementine takes her place under the table at the shop. I've just returned from the church, making sure everything is in place and just right before the wedding this evening. I decided to come by and clean up a little this afternoon. After all the craziness of these last few days, it looks like a tornado hit the place and I'd rather take care of this today than start the new week off with a mess. Besides, I like a day with no distractions so that I can focus on my work. And just as soon as I have this thought, I hear a knock on the front door. Clementine gets there before I do. I peek through the window and see that it's my date for the evening's event.

"Will," I say, unlocking the door and letting the boy in. "What on earth happened to you?"

His eye is swollen and red. He's fallen or been in a fight or some accident that landed what appears to be a fist to the face.

"Clarence Trembley called me a freak." He shuffles in, pets Clementine, and waits while I close and lock the door. When I'm done, he moves around the counter and takes a seat on the stool placed against the back wall.

"Well, let me see if I've got something to help with the swelling." I head to the back room and search in the freezer unit of the small refrigerator where we keep our lunches. There's a gel pack in there that I used on my ankle, and I take it out and return to Will. "Here, put this on your eye. Hopefully, it doesn't smell like my feet."

He does as I tell him and leans against the wall behind him. "I hit him back," he confesses.

I pull the chair around and sit across from him. Clementine takes her place between us. "Well, I guess he had it coming," I say, noticing the grass stains on the boy's pants, the rip in his T-shirt. I try to remember if I know Clarence Trembley, but I don't recognize the name. "When did this happen?" I wonder if he's come straight from the fight. Maybe I should call his grandmother.

"Just now," he answers, without moving. "We were at church. I told Grandma I was coming over here."

"Well, Sunday school must have changed since I was a regular. Last I remember, they were teaching nonviolence as a means to settle differences. Of course, there is that story of Jesus getting mad and turning over all the tables in the fellowship hall." I wait to see if he thinks I'm funny.

He doesn't.

"So what happened with you and Clarence Trembley?" I ask.

There is no response.

"Why did he call you a freak?"

Will sits up, lifts the gel pack off his eye. It's an honest-to-goodness shiner and I wonder if a pack of frozen peas would do a better job of reducing the swelling. I always heard that's best for black eyes, but it doesn't really matter because I don't keep frozen peas.

"He said that because my mama used drugs, I was born addicted, too, that I'm a drug addict and a freak."

I haven't heard if Will's mother was using drugs when she was pregnant, but knowing some of her history and knowing my own story of an addicted mother, I figure it's pretty unlikely that she stayed clean and sober for nine months. Still, I haven't seen any of the usual signs in Will of a child born with an addiction.

I think about the boy and his fight and recall that when we moved in with our grandparents, both Daisy and I were given extensive psychological testing when we started school. Somewhere along the way someone had diagnosed us both with fetal alcohol syndrome. We were lucky because we didn't have the disease. Neither of us was hyperactive or demonstrated fine or gross motor developmental delays, although I was described as uncoordinated by my physical education teacher when I was in junior high. Still, we never seemed to suffer from our mother's addiction. And when I think about Will and our time together in the last six months, I realize that I've never seen him display impaired language development or problems with memory or poor judgment. He showed me his report card from this past year at school, and while he won't likely be selected for advanced placement in his classes, he's doing quite well overall. And even if he does have developmental problems as a result of his mother's addiction, Clarence Trembley isn't the one who ought to be passing out information about a diagnosis.

"You're not a freak," I say, and he stares at me. "Although you're looking a little weird with that massive blob for an eye. What's that monster with one big eye named, Cyclod?"

I see the faintest possibility of a smile. He thinks it's funny when I get names wrong. Once I called an Aucasaurus, his favorite dinosaur, an Unclesaurus, and he cracked up, laughed about it for weeks.

"Cyclops," he says, playing along. "But his eye was in the middle of his forehead."

"Oh." Will certainly knows his monsters and dinosaurs.

"Well, even with only one good eye, you're not a freak. You are a smart, funny, caring boy, and Clarence Trembley is a jerk."

He puts the gel pack on his eye and leans back. "Can I still go with you to the wedding?"

"Of course," I answer. "Are you going to change clothes?" I ask. He shrugs.

"Yeah, it's fine with me if you want to wear what you have on; we just need to clean off some of those grass stains. Do you have another T-shirt?"

He nods.

I get up from the chair and decide I will start with straightening up the paperwork. Nora does a great job keeping up with the bills and receipts, but I like things in a certain order. She hasn't figured that out yet. I pull out the books and begin organizing. I think I'll pay the bills first.

"Is Jenny going to die?"

The question surprises me. I turn around and he's no longer leaning against the wall, but rather sitting up and watching me closely.

"I guess we're all going to die," I answer, knowing that's not really what he's looking for. "But no, I don't think she's going to die anytime soon."

He nods.

"What makes you ask that?"

"I heard Grandma talking on the phone. She was talking to Miss Duncan from the church and she said she thought they moved up the date of the wedding because Jenny is dying. She said she thought it was a desperate act." He puts the pack on his eye, leans back. "What's a desperate act?"

"It's doing something because you feel overwhelmed or really anxious." I study him. "Like hitting a boy who calls you a freak."

I know he's rolling his eyes, but I can't see them because they're both covered with the gel pack.

"Do you think she's desperate?" he asks.

I shake my head. "No more than the rest of us." With his lack of response, I'm guessing he wants more, so I go on. "Jenny is better, much better, and she decided she didn't want to wait to get married. She loves Justin. Justin loves her and she doesn't feel sick now and she wants to start their new life together." I turn back to the receipts on the counter. "That's not desperate; that's knowing what you want and going for it."

"Why would Grandma talk about her like that?"

I sort through the week's records, separate them, and order them chronologically. "I don't know, Will; maybe you should ask her."

There is silence and I turn back around, but he's not looking because he still has his eyes covered. "You like Jenny a lot, don't you?"

I know that he visited her when she was in the hospital, that he kept some of the old flowers that I threw out and took them to her. When I saw what he was doing, I had first thought he was taking them to his mother's grave, but then Jenny let the cat out of the bag. She told me he brought her so many bouquets that Justin got a little jealous. We had both been touched by the boy's concern and his obvious crush. I had not, however, mentioned to him that I knew about his floral gifts to the bride-to-be.

He shrugs, his face still shielded. "She's pretty, I guess."

"She is," I say in agreement. "She's also kind and sweet and she's beating the cancer."

He leans up and the pack drops off his face into his lap. He reaches for it, holds it there. "Sometimes I worry that everybody I love will die."

I am shocked by the honesty, the truthfulness, the ache of familiarity. I only nod. I see no reason to comment.

He leans down and gives Clementine a rub on her neck, and I

suddenly realize how hard it was for him when she was hurt. He stayed away from us for almost a week, and at the time I had not understood why he disappeared. I thought his grandmother had told him not to bother us, that it was a matter of polite parenting. I assumed he wanted to come but was kept away. But now, hearing what I just heard, seeing how he thinks, it all makes sense. He stayed away because he thought Clementine was going to die and he didn't want to love her when she did. He thought somehow that loving others made them go away. He thought that just as it had happened with his mother if he loved someone again, she would die.

And yet he came back. After a week, he showed up at my door with a plate of cookies for me and a dog biscuit for Clementine. He came back to us both. And now I see what a brave little boy he is, loving a dog that almost died, falling for a girl with cancer, sticking it out with me.

Sometimes adults surprise me with their generosity of spirit, their tender acts of kindness, but really it's the children who touch me the most. They seem to unfold the easiest. They're the ones who love with abandon, the ones who keep putting their hearts out there to be broken. They're the ones who teach the rest of us what it is to love.

"Have you had lunch?" I ask, and he shakes his head. "I haven't either. Let's get some Chinese food. I'll call Juanita. We can go for a walk out by the creek, then I'll drive you over to get another shirt for the wedding."

He smiles and I put away the stack of bills, realizing that I can get to this tomorrow.

Thirty-Eight

Well, she's lost about ten pounds, but that didn't hurt her."
Dr. Cash is finishing up his exam of Clementine. She's
completed the course of antibiotics and there are no more welts or
swelling. She's mostly back to herself, albeit a smaller version.

"I still don't know what got into her, chasing that thing." I am
standing beside her as she sits on the table.

"Maybe she thought it was a cat," he suggests.

"Maybe," I say. That's about as good an explanation as any, I
suppose. Clem does love to chase the cats.

"And what about you?"

I sense him looking at me, and for some odd reason I blush.
"Oh, I'm fine," I answer.

"No, I mean what were you doing chasing the porcupine? I
never did figure out how you got all those quills in you."

I shake my head. "Honestly, I don't remember. I think I tripped
and fell on the thing, and then I carried this one all the way to the
truck, so I don't know. Either they came out when I landed on it or

I got them from her." I motion toward Clem, who turns away. She's still embarrassed about the whole thing.

"What did they feel like?" he asks, and I can see Clem glance at me, happy she is no longer the center of attention, happy to have someone explain what it is to be punctured by hundreds of tiny needles.

I shrug. "I don't know. I didn't feel anything at first. Then, after a day, my whole body hurt."

He nods, gives a sympathetic smile. He opens Clem's mouth to examine her throat and I see that he's wearing his wedding ring. I hadn't noticed this before, even though I had seen him at the weekend weddings with a woman who was both a little clingy and quite beautiful. I had thought she was a new lover. I see now she was his wife.

"The swelling is gone in her throat and tongue too. It doesn't appear to be inflamed anymore. I'd say she's back to normal." He removes his hands from Clem's snout and leans in to touch her nose to nose. It's sweet. He takes the medical chart that is behind my dog and starts to write some notes. Clementine, happy to hear the news that she is fine, settles down on the table.

"They were both nice weddings," he says. "This past weekend," he adds, explaining, as if I weren't paying attention.

"Yes," I respond.

"The flowers were beautiful," he adds.

I nod, even though I realize he can't see me because he has his head down.

Clementine is watching me. I give her my *What?* look, and she just sighs and turns away.

"I didn't know Dr. Buckley was ordained. He officiates with great professionalism."

"Yeah, I guess we're the only town in Washington where the veterinarian is licensed to wed. I heard he used to run a special where he'd neuter your dog and marry you at a twenty percent discount."

Clementine shakes her head. I know it was lame.

"Maybe I should get ordained too," he says, and looks up with a smile, and man, he is beautiful. "I'm a sucker for weddings."

"Yeah, I've heard marriage can be a good thing." And I can't help myself, but I glance down at his left hand and he knows exactly what I'm looking at.

He stretches out his fingers. "My ex-wife called a couple of months ago. She wants to try again," he says, explaining the ring, his date over the weekend.

Suddenly, I want to finish up this appointment as quickly as possible. I just nod and shift my weight from side to side. Could I look any more awkward?

"I'm sorry. You don't need to hear any of this."

I shake my head, trying to dismiss his need for an apology. "It's quite all right," I say. "I hope things will work out for you."

I keep waiting for him to finish up and take Clementine off the table. I would do it myself, but she hates it when I try to lift her. I was surprised that she let me carry her after the porcupine attack, but now that I think about it, she didn't have a lot of say about that. Besides, I think she was in shock and couldn't really stop me.

"I thought we deserved another shot."

I'm thinking, *Okay, okay . . . call Dr. Buckley and talk to him. He's ordained; he was married. Why are you telling me this?*

"It's just . . ."

And suddenly, my prayers are answered. My cell phone rings.

"Oh, excuse me," I say, and pull my phone out of my coat pocket. I glance at the number before I answer.

"Hey, Nora." I am very cheerful.

"What's wrong with you?" she asks.

"I don't know what you mean," I say.

"You sound weird. Are you being carjacked?"

"No, no, no . . ." I realize I do sound a bit too enthusiastic and try to tone it down just a bit. "What do you need?"

There's a pause on the other end. She's trying to decide if there's something wrong and if I'm talking in some code. I know her far too well.

"I was going to see if you wanted me to wait until you got back or if it was all right to go ahead and close up."

I left the shop a couple of hours ago to make deliveries and didn't mention this appointment. I knew if I did, she'd make me go home and change clothes. She thought I was only going to the nursing home to drop off a few single roses in bud vases for the monthly birthdays; take a plant, a small dish garden variety with dieffenbachia, dracaena sanderiana, variegated ivy, palm, and green philodendron to James Harvey, who was in the hospital recovering from gall bladder surgery; and a large vase of blue hydrangea, crème roses, graceful white oriental lilies, a white disbud mum, purple statice, and lavender limonium to Trina Earl, sent by her sister in Dallas, who just wanted her to know she was thinking of her. I told Jimmy I would make the deliveries because I needed to run a few personal errands. I hadn't told either of them what time I would be finished.

"Yes, yes, go ahead and lock up. I'm on my way back but you don't need to wait. I'll be there in just a few minutes." My voice is pitched a little too high. Even Clementine seems bothered by my tone. She is staring at me with concern.

I smile and make a goofy gesture, pretending that I am just so very busy, all for the benefit of Dr. Cash.

"Okay, then, I'll hurry on down there."

"If I'm going to lock up, you don't have to hurry on down here."

"That's right. I'll be right there."

"Are you on crack?"

"No, no, not today. Okay, then I'll see you tomorrow. Bye-bye now."

"If you're being carjacked, start counting. I'll hang up and call 911."

There's a pause.

"Are you going to start counting?" she asks.

"Nope. I am just fine and dandy and I will see you tomorrow." And I hang up before she can ask me anything else.

"Everything okay?" Dr. Cash wants to know.

"Just fine. But I guess we need to be heading out of here. You must be wanting to get home too." And I wish I had chosen something else to say. This offered him a perfect opportunity to tell me more about his wife, who is probably waiting there for him. And frankly, I don't want to hear any of that.

I pick up Clementine, who grunts, and set her on the floor before Dr. Cash has a chance to respond or help. I click on her leash and give him a big smile.

He seems surprised. "Uh, okay." And he reaches down, gives Clementine a good pat on the head. "You stay away from those spiky cats."

I open the door and we walk out. The lobby is empty as I realize that I must be his last appointment of the day.

"Shall I pay you now?" I ask, even as I am still walking. "Or you can just use my card. I'm sure it's on file." I'm almost at the front door.

"I'll just bill you," he replies, stopping at the reception desk, and he says something else but I am already in the parking lot, waving good-bye.

"Just get in the van and don't say a word," I tell Clementine, who looks at me like I am the craziest human in all of the Pacific Northwest.

THIRTY-NINE

W<small>ELL</small>, good for him; any marriage is worth a second try."

I came over to Dan's house because he wanted to show me something. I haven't seen him since Jenny's wedding, where he took the role of her father, escorting her to the altar to stand next to Justin. He gave the blessing of the community since she refused to be "given away" and because she thinks of Creekside as her family now. She asked him to represent this little town, offer the blessing of the people, and walk her down the aisle.

"I guess," I say.

We are in his den. He's fixed us martinis and even made Clementine a special chicken broth cocktail that she's drinking from a margarita glass. There's classical music playing on his stereo. Mozart, Symphony no. 41. It's from 1788. I know this because he showed me the CD when I came in.

It's nice being with Dan. I feel comfortable and at ease. Either the astronaut has become a very good friend or he makes a strong drink. Whatever the case, I'm relaxed. I just told him about Dr. Cash and my visit with him a few days ago.

"Were you hoping for something to happen between the two of you?"

"Maybe," I answer.

"That's good," he responds.

"That's not good," I reply. "He's back with his wife. How can that be good?"

He smiles at me, takes a drink from his martini, and then puts down his glass. "Come with me." And he guides me to a sliding glass door, opens it, and leads me out to the deck.

There's a large telescope pointed upward and it has gotten dark enough now that the stars are filling up the sky.

"If you look, you will see the planet Jupiter."

I place my eye against the eyepiece and see many stars, but there is one brighter and more prominent than the others. I am sure this is the planet.

"Did you find it?"

And I nod.

"I don't think you're able to see it tonight, but sometimes with the right telescope, you can make out a small oval ring on its surface. It's called the Great Red Spot."

I look and look but I don't see an oval ring.

"It's actually a storm and it's been there for more than three hundred years. Nobody knows how it goes on for so long."

"But if I can't even see it, it must be really small," I say.

"It's actually big enough to contain two planets the size of Earth."

"Wow!"

"The planet's quite beautiful, don't you agree?"

"Absolutely."

"Jupiter has been called the wandering star since prehistoric times. I guess the early astronomers had a hard time locating it."

"She just had somewhere else she wanted to be," I say, and I glance over at Dan, who is smiling.

"Maybe that's what it was," he replies.

I look again at the sky and I see so many lights, so many stars, I can now understand how Dan was changed once he was in space. Just to see what I see from a deck in Washington State is beyond words. I move away from the telescope and take Dan's hand. "Thank you," I say.

He nods in understanding and we return to the den and our drinks and the music. We are quiet for a while and then my curiosity gets the better of me.

"Why do you think it's good that I was hopeful that something might happen between Dr. Cash and me?"

"It's good because you're letting your guard down a little."

"I don't have a guard." I sit down and take a big sip of my drink.

"Okay," he responds.

I see what he's doing.

"You think I have a guard?"

"Did you know that I met you and your sister when you were little?" he asks.

I shake my head. This is news to me.

"I came to Creekside to accept some civic award and I spoke to your elementary school."

I try to remember, but I don't recall the event.

"I shook your hand before the ceremony began. You introduced your sister to me and then you took your seats with your designated classes." He pauses and I keep trying to remember the event that he seems to recall so clearly.

"Your mother came in the auditorium just as I was finishing my speech." He hesitates again. "I think she had been drinking."

And suddenly, it all came back. The humiliation, the attempt to hide, the desperate way I searched for Daisy sitting on the other side of the gymnasium, the principal taking my mother by the arm, leading her out, all the kids looking at me, staring at me, laughing at me. No wonder I didn't remember an astronaut's speech. No wonder I don't remember the astronaut; I repressed that entire afternoon, most of that entire school year, in fact. We had moved in with our grandparents and out of the blue our mother showed up at school and wanted to see her little girls. It was a terrible day.

"How did you find out it was my mother?"

"I asked around. I was going to speak to you and your sister later, but you left the school and the principal couldn't find you."

"Yeah, well, it was kind of a bad day and we wanted to get home." I remember grabbing Daisy when the bell rang and running all the way to the farm. I didn't want anybody to have the chance to tease or bully us. I wanted to get out of there as fast as I could.

"I recalled your names when I came back and bought the property out here. The real estate agent showed me your grandparents' farm first because it was for sale. She mentioned you being in law school and your sister's death and when she said your names, I remembered you from that day at the elementary school. She said you both had lived here until you finished school, but you had moved away and you didn't want the property. She said your grandparents died and then later your sister. You came, but only for brief periods. You asked her to put the farm on the market only a few months after the death of your sister. Her name was Daisy, right?"

I nodded, remembering all of that, noting all of it was true. Granddaddy went first, suffering from diabetes, the doctors removing one limb after another, him begging to die. And then Grandmother had a heart attack and I found out from the farmer's wife who lived beside them. Daisy ended up living there on and off, paying the property taxes from the little bit of money they left us, but not really taking care of the place. And finally, after Daisy died I just sent an e-mail to Kathy Shepherd telling her to sell it and get whatever she could. It was the farmer next door who ended up buying it, the sale helping me open up the shop.

"When you came back and I met you again, I remembered that little girl from the elementary school. I remember seeing you holding your sister's hand and running out of the auditorium. The truth is I've known you a long time and I have always hoped that you would find a way to survive all the things you were handed in this life."

I hold up my martini glass. "And so I did," I say in response.

"And so you did," he agrees.

I clear my throat. I don't know why but I am starting to cry.

"But in order to do so you had to make a few adjustments."

I nod.

I remember getting into bed after Daisy died, the simple easy way I pulled back the covers, slipped inside, and planned never to get out, how I lay there for days and days, waiting to die. And how I never did. How the flowers got me up, how beauty lifted me from that place and brought me back to life. But I was never the same after that. And I see now that the astronaut is right. In binding up my shattered heart in order to get out of the bed and on with my life, I had become bound to my grief, restricted by my losses.

"It has served you well," he noted. "Your guard. I doubt you could have done all you have done without it."

I nod, listening to him describe my life, reveal the intimate details, speak of the harbored secrets. And I think of my grief, my sorrow, as the Great Red Spot on Jupiter, a storm that has been brewing for three hundred years. I cannot imagine my life without it.

"You have helped along a lot of loves, celebrated births, honored lives, marked occasions, found ways to encourage forgiveness. You have done a great service to this little town."

I clear my throat again, take a drink.

"And yet, when I hear you made a little space to think of love for yourself, a tiny little opening for someone else to come in, it gives me pause." He waits. "It gives me hope."

"That I might lower my guard?"

"Yes, that you might lower your guard," he answers.

I think about John Cash, the decision to ask him to the wedding, the shame I carried around with me, the awkward way I felt in his presence. I think I prefer having my guard up to feeling all that I have felt in the last few days, but I don't say these things to Dan. I don't want to hear some grand bit of wisdom like *It's better to have loved and lost than never to have loved at all*. I think I've heard all I can bear of that stuff tonight.

"So, let's talk about you," I say, changing the subject. "What is going on with you?"

He puts down his glass and nods, not at all hesitant to move the conversation in that direction. "I have started to die," he says.

This is not at all what I expected to hear.

"I know, it sounds odd," he adds. "But I can tell by the things that are happening in my body. I have less desire to eat or drink, to engage in common activities. I dream brilliant dreams and I have to pull myself awake. I think of people I have not thought about in years, remember things, want to be forgiven."

He shakes his head in wonder or disbelief. I can only guess.

"It is magnificent."

This man mystifies me.

"I am finally returning to stardust, back to the beginning of time, back to the exquisite matter from which we first came, and I am so lucky that I know what is going on, that I am conscious to this experience." He closes his eyes and takes in a deep breath. "Magnificent," he says again.

"How do you plan to go?" I ask, wondering if he will become a hospice patient, hire a caregiver, or if he'll check himself into the hospital when he knows he is near the end.

"I haven't quite decided that, but I will. Sometime soon, I will."

The music crescendos and we stop to listen. I watch him close his eyes, and I decide to close mine too. And it is beautiful and rich and full. When it stops, I look over and Dan is weeping. And I understand now that this is what he wanted me to see. Not the planet Jupiter, not the stars on a bright clear night, not a storm that never diminishes.

He wanted me to observe this, know this, understand this. He wanted me to see a heart fully open. And he is right. It is magnificent.

I turn away as the symphony's fourth movement, Molto allegro, begins, and I close my eyes, and breathe.

·FORTY·

It is not a funeral I was expecting to arrange. I had to call the florist in Deer Park and ask for white carnations, an extra couple of spathiphyllums, and even a large standing wire wreath. I have been so busy I hadn't realized I had used my last one at Jackson Field's funeral last month. With the surgery and all the weddings, the high school graduation, and summer socials, I miscalculated my inventory. I sold most of my plants, forgot to order the basics, carnations and greenery, and I let my wreath supplies dwindle. I lost track of what I have on hand and I am not prepared for this event.

Like everyone here, I am sometimes surprised by the deaths in Creekside. There are automobile wrecks and heart attacks, massive strokes and even suicides that no one expects. Those are always the hardest funerals to arrange. Family members stumble over the flowers they want. They can't recall what the dead person loved, what kind of spray to place across the casket. And the people who call in their orders are even more helpless. "Just send something nice," is what I hear a lot. And because I usually know the deceased and because I want my flowers to bring a certain measure of peace and dignity to the service, I do my best. Even with short notice, I try to arrange bouquets and baskets and select plants that speak of the care and sympathy that people want to express. Still, not having any warning, not expecting a funeral to occur, makes it difficult for a florist to plan.

Often, however, even when everyone else might be shocked by death, I have some idea of who is sick and who is dying. There are orders placed for deliveries to be made to the hospitals, and while those orders are placed, there are sometimes questions about what arrangements are acceptable in certain units. These questions offer a number of clues regarding the condition and prognosis of a patient. Can you have flowers on the oncology floor? Do they allow plants in intensive care? And even if there are no revealing questions, sometimes the customer, the family member from out of town calling in the order or the loved one on their way to the hospital who stops by, gives me a full report.

It seems that they want to talk about the surgery or the disease or how helpless they feel. They tell the story about the doctor's visit and the results of the medical tests or the car wreck or the way life was disrupted, recalling the simplest details to me, a stranger or at best an acquaintance, because each time they tell the story they hope they will better understand. And over the years and through the illnesses and deaths I have learned to listen without rushing them or pinning them down to a cost or delivery date because I know what they are doing and just like I need a table to arrange my flowers, I know they need space to arrange their sorrow. I consider it to be simply part of my job.

Not always, but often, when I have heard the hospital floor where a patient is located, how long they have been hospitalized, when I hear the stories of despair and sadness from their loved ones, I have some idea of their condition. And based upon the news so freely given, the reports when the orders are made, I sometimes know when to start working on flowers for a funeral. I don't say so to anyone, for to do so would be presumptuous and callous; but sometimes I know. And I prepare. I order a few necessary supplies, a bunch of fresh flowers, a couple of extra cyclamens and dieffenbachia so I'm a bit more prepared, a little more ready. But not this time. Not for this funeral. I had no warning, no premonition, no rambling report from a loved one. This death was completely unexpected.

Juanita Norris was taking out the laundry to the clothesline that stretched across her back lawn. She washes sheets and towels on Monday, preferring to start the week with clean linen. She had made no complaints of chest pains or dizziness, headaches or shortness of breath to her husband or grandson as she prepared their morning meals and sat at the breakfast table alongside them both. She was talking about repairing the quilt on Will's bed, asking her husband if he had seen her box of thread and making plans to make preserves, the fruit trees filled with ripe pears. She had cleaned the table, humming while she washed the dishes, and made sure Will's shirt was clean and that his new pair of shorts was big enough. She had teased him that he was growing faster than she could dress him, and the two of them had laughed and hugged each other before he left for the day.

Claude drove his grandson to town, dropping him off at the library, where he was turning in *The Boys from Brooklyn* and hoping to get a copy of *Under the Black Ensign*, by L. Ron Hubbard, a book that was recommended by Captain Miller and one that had required a special request made to the librarian. He planned to stay there until lunchtime, reading or playing on the computer, when he would meet his grandfather at the deli and then work the afternoon with me at the shop.

It was Clifton, the mailman, delivering the day's mail, who

spotted Juanita down beneath the clothesline, the white sheet billowing around her, a corner grasped in her hand. He called 911 and she was taken to the hospital but was never revived, the cause of death most likely a stroke or massive heart attack. Clifton found Claude at the hardware store and the two of them rode together to the emergency room, where they were met by Dr. Herbert Long and the grave news that Juanita was dead. Will was walking to the deli when he saw his grandfather's truck turn in his direction. He said that he knew something was wrong just by how slowly he was driving. He said it was just like before, just like the awful time before, and he wonders if bad news has a way of stopping time.

Claude took him to the hospital, where he said his good-byes, and then he asked to come to the shop. He needed to work, he told his grandfather, and for whatever reason, Claude agreed.

That was four hours ago. I have called the florist in Deer Park, already taken a couple of orders, and started working on a spray.

"Can we use the tulips?" he asks, knowing what is in the cooler, knowing what I have on hand.

"Of course," I answer. "Do you want pink or yellow?"

He stands in front of me, his thin shoulders slumped. "Pink," he says softly. "She likes pink. And do you have any of those gold daisies? The ones called faith? She'd like those. She always talked about needing faith."

I nod. Will has learned a lot since he's been in the shop.

It's just the two of us at the shop with Clementine. Nora and Jimmy don't work on Mondays since it's usually slow and because it gives them a two-day weekend, and sometimes in the summer they like to take off on Sundays and drive to Priest Lake or up to the Canadian border. I think they drove to Idaho yesterday, but I'm not sure since I haven't spoken to either of them. When Will came in to tell me the news, I wanted to call Nora and tell her, but I don't feel right about telling his story now that he's sticking around. I told him I'd take him home or out to the cemetery or anywhere he wanted to go, but he said he liked it here and asked if he could just do his afternoon chores. I couldn't really see any reason to deny him, but now it is close to five o'clock and I'm not sure what to do.

He looks up at the clock and walks over and picks up Clementine's leash and my dog quickly follows him. They stand at the door.

"Do you think she found Mama?" he asks, and I immediately understand. I had wondered the same thing when Daisy died. I had wondered if the dead somehow greet each other, if there is a way they know the time someone dies and they gather at just the right spot to welcome them or see them, if they are somehow designated as the guide to the new world.

"Yes, I do," I say.

He turns and looks at me.

"So, she wasn't by herself?"

I shake my head.

"I think she would have liked it if Mama was there. I think it wouldn't have been so lonesome that way."

I nod and watch as he clasps the leash to Clementine's collar, heading out into the evening sun.

·Forty-One·

SOMETIMES you have only one moment to get it right and the thing is, you don't always know the moment when it arrives. There's no ticking clock or game show host waiting for your answer; there's no audience watching, hedging bets on what you'll do; in real life the moment suddenly presents itself and either you make the right choice or you blow it. Apparently, the moment came and I blew it.

Since Nora and Jimmy still aren't home yet and Carl has to work at a golf tournament, I find myself at Dan's. I left Will and drove up the hill and I am sitting in his driveway trying to decide if I should be bothering him on a Monday evening, trying to decide if I really want to say this thing out loud, speak of my shame to someone I admire, admit the choice I have made. And I am just about to back out and drive home when my cell phone rings. I answer it.

"Are you coming in or are you just going to sit out there?"

"I have Clementine," I say.

"Yes," he replies, and I take that as permission to bring my dog along.

He opens the door just as I make my way up the steps. Clementine goes in ahead of me. She thinks this is a huge waste of time.

"I'm sorry," I begin.

"For what?" he asks, moving aside so that I can enter.

"For taking your time."

I look at him closely and I can see that he has lost more weight and that his color has grayed a slightly deeper shade.

"Ruby, time with a friend is never taken, only shared." And he closes the door. "Wine? Soda? Tea?"

"Nothing," I reply, and I wait for him to take a seat and then I take one across from him on the sofa. Clementine has already found a place by the sliding glass doors.

"I'm having a wheat germ smoothie," he announces, holding up his glass. It's filled with a thick green substance and I shake my head. It doesn't look like anything I'm interested in.

"No thank you," I say.

"Juanita Norris died," he says, letting me know he is caught up. I nod.

"And the boy thought you would ask him to live with you?"

I had told him part of the situation when I called him before coming over. I nod.

"And you said no?"

I shake my head. "It wasn't quite like that."

He takes a swallow of his smoothie, waiting for me to fill him in.

"I was driving him home, and when we pulled up to his house I said that I thought his grandfather would be glad to see him. I said he was probably making them dinner and would be glad that he didn't have to eat alone."

Dan nods.

I go on. "And he said that he didn't think his grandfather really wanted him to stay, that it was Juanita who took care of him. He said that he had heard a conversation between his grandparents and that Claude had suggested he should go into foster care."

"That's a harsh thing to hear."

I nod. "I know."

There's a pause.

"And that's when he asked you if you would be his guardian?"

I shake my head. "He wasn't that forthright."

Dan waits.

"He said something like he wasn't sure what would happen to him, where he might end up." And I stop because I realize that this was the moment I missed, this was the test I failed.

So does Dan. "And you did not make an offer."

I look at him and shake my head. "I told him that I was sure Claude wouldn't want him to leave now and that with all the people in Creekside who loved him, there would be a place for him to stay."

I watch as Dan turns away.

"I just never thought about having a child," I explain. "I love Will, I do. I think we've got a lot in common. I just never thought about it."

He nods. There is a polite smile.

"I know Jenny and Justin will take him, or Henry and Lou Ann, they've gotten attached to him, too. And it's not even like Claude has said he didn't want to keep him. Shoot, I bet even Nora would adopt him. They love each other."

He raises his eyebrows but still doesn't speak.

"Claude said that stuff before Juanita died. I'm sure he wants to keep Will now." I fidget in my chair. I glance over and watch as Clementine eyes me suspiciously.

"It takes a lot to raise a child," Dan finally says, easing my guilt.

"Right," I agree, a little too quickly.

"It's a lot of responsibility for a single person."

"I know," I say, the relief more obvious than I want to show.

"You have to do what you can," he advises. "Only you know what that is."

"I don't have a place for him to sleep," I say. "There's only one bathroom in my house. There's hardly enough room for just my stuff. How would that work? What happens when he's a teenager? I don't know anything about raising a teenager." I slide down in my seat. Clementine turns away, disgusted with me.

"I'm sure you're making the right decision," Dan adds.

"Yes," I answer. "I'm sure it's the right thing." I fold my arms across my chest. "And I'm happy to help out. I didn't say that. If Jenny or Henry takes him and needs a weekend off, I'm happy to let him sleep over. He can keep his job and he can still walk Clem every day. That doesn't have to change."

Dan nods. There's the polite smile again. He takes the last swallow of his smoothie. "Then it seems like you didn't really make a mistake after all."

I blink, remembering that I had told him that I needed to talk because I had made a mistake. That was why I had come over, to talk about a mistake I had made. If it was a mistake, then I would need to fix it. If this is not a mistake, then there's nothing to fix.

"You just told the truth."

Suddenly, there's something more than relief I feel. I glance away.

"That's right, isn't it?" he asks. "You didn't make a mistake. You don't really want to be Will's guardian. And in his way, he asked and you told him." He pauses. "That's what happened, right?"

So it wasn't a moment that I missed. It wasn't a failed choice I made. I had simply told Will the truth of how I felt. If the moment presented itself again I would likely choose the same thing all over again. This realization, however, does not make me feel any better.

"Ruby, do you know how flowers bloom?"

"What?"

"Flowers. Do you know, scientifically, how they bloom?"

I stare at Dan. It's not a question I have ever really considered. He sits up in his chair and I see him flinch. I had not noticed before, but I think he must be in pain.

I shrug. "The inside petals push the outside petals out?"

He shakes his head. "The exact opposite," he says. "Blooming happens because plants build up instabilities."

I don't even bother to ask because I'm sure he's got more to say about this.

"A team at Harvard studied Asiatic lilies."

I nod. Only Captain Dan Miller would know about studies at Harvard on flowers.

"It turns out that the instabilities that shape roots and blossoms often come about when certain cells become longer than others. The rapid growth causes strain, which bends the soft tissues. Now, what hasn't been discovered is exactly which cells do the tugging, but what has been found out is that the outer borders of petals and sepals ruffle during blooming, while inner margins remain smooth. Those wavy surfaces give clues that cells might be growing faster at the edges, like adding slack to a rope. That extra growth could, possibly, coax the petal to go from curving in inside the flower to curving out. It's only growing at the edge, you see, on the margin, the outside." He's staring right into my eyes, trying to help me understand. "The blooming happens on the outside before it happens in the middle."

I am still nodding even though I have no idea what he is trying to say.

"Sometimes we think there is supposed to be this great spiritual awakening that happens before we make a change in our lives. We expect some 'aha' moment, some beautiful enlightening experience to shape us into the people we want to be, but sometimes it just happens from the circumstances in our lives that present themselves. We become who we are meant to be because of the things along our edges that pull us into existence."

"I don't understand," I say.

And he smiles and nods as if he has said all he intends to say. "I'm tired," he announces. "I think I need to lie down."

"Oh, okay." And I stand up from my seat just as he does the same and we take each other by the hands. "I'm sorry I bothered you," I add, and I am. I worry that I have exasperated him.

He tightens his grasp. "You are never a bother, Ruby. I am glad you chose me."

And I feel my face redden because he is right. I did choose him. I called his number. I told him the story. I came to his house. He is my friend. I chose him.

"Can I do anything for you?" I ask, wondering how he is getting his medications, how he is taking care of himself.

"I am only glad you came. I didn't know how much I wanted to see you until you arrived. I hope you will come again soon."

And he gives me a little kiss on the cheek and walks around me to the back of the house, leaving me to find my own way out.

·FORTY-TWO·

I DON'T see Will again until the funeral three days later. He is dressed in starched khaki pants and a light blue dress shirt. He is even wearing a tie, a clip-on that looks like one from his grandfather's closet. For a little boy he appears terribly old. He nods at me when he comes into the church with Claude. At least he doesn't seem mad. And I am glad for that.

It turns out I was right. As soon as they heard about Juanita's death, Jenny and Justin called Claude and they do in fact want to adopt Will. Everyone thinks they'll make a lovely family and I am sure the newlyweds will be excellent parents. It's easy to see that they care about the boy and it's good for him to have two caregivers, two young parents, a father and a mother.

Jenny's hair has grown back and even though it's still short, it's thick and curly and she's eating more and has gained weight. She stopped in the shop yesterday, telling me their plans, telling me and Nora how she and Justin want to move into the little house next to the Catholic church, the old parsonage that has been vacant for years, raise Will and have a couple of other children. She was so full of life that I envy her cheerfulness. She and Justin are sitting with Will, their arms wrapped tightly around him. Already, they are bonding.

I am sitting with Nora. Jimmy is a pallbearer, situated up front with the family, and the church is packed with everyone from Creekside. Juanita was well known and well liked. I glance around at all my customers, thinking of them and their floral preferences. Yellow roses and belladonnas, calla lilies and sunflowers, I know them all. And when we catch each other's glances, there are smiles and nods. We are a tight community.

The altar is filled with arrangements. I know Juanita would have asked that money be given to charity rather than purchasing all the flowers, but Claude didn't think to list the instruction in the obituary and since it wasn't listed, I got the calls. I only hope Will likes what has been made and that he is pleased with the pink tulips and the gold gerberas that cover the casket and fill the vases and baskets that line the altar.

"Dear family and friends." The minister starts the service and I begin to drift, remembering Daisy's funeral, remembering how broken and alone I felt, how resolved I was to death, to endings, to a life muted and colorless. I sit in the crowded church and suddenly I am back to where I think I must have started.

"For everything there is a season," he reads from Ecclesiastes. "And a time for every matter under heaven. A time to be born, and a time to die; a time to plant, and a time to pluck up what is planted . . ." And on and on he goes while I peel away the years, remembering how it was to become who I am today.

"You're too serious," Daisy would tell me when we were teenagers and I was studying for a test or writing a paper. "Let's go out."

"I can't go out," I would say night after night, watching her sneak out the bedroom window, laughing as she fell into the backseat of some boy's car, then later feeling her crawl into the bed beside me, her breath hot on my neck as she curled around me.

"You awake?" she always asked.

"No."

"You sleepy?"

"No."

And she would tell me about the boy and the date, the things she did, the places they went.

"One day you won't come back," I would say, dreading how it would feel when I would sleep alone.

"No, one day you won't come back. You'll go off to college and leave me here."

And she was right. That's what I did and I guess, thinking about it now, that was why she sneaked out every night, leaving me alone. She was learning how to make it on her own, learning how to make it in Creekside without me. And she was helping me learn how to make it without her too, helping me understand what it feels like to sleep alone.

Only I didn't learn. I always thought she'd come back. Just before dawn, just before the light broke across the sky, I always thought she'd sneak through that bedroom window, crawl into bed, and come back.

I glance over in Will's direction. I can hardly see him, pressed between Jenny and Justin. I wonder how he's feeling. I wonder if he finds comfort in thinking Juanita is with his mom or if he just feels abandoned, left alone once again. I wonder how we are ever able to fit all the sorrow and loss into one heart, one lifetime.

"She was a compassionate and caring woman whose life was built around the service of others." The pastor was a friend of Juanita's, and it's easy to see that he is moved by this loss.

The preacher who did Daisy's service did not know her. He was recommended by the funeral home director, a retired military chaplain who had to keep looking down at his notes to recall my sister's name. A few friends were horrified at his mistakes, the way he spoke of her as if she had been sad and suffering, but I was in such a state of shock it hardly even mattered. No one could have said anything that would have comforted me anyway. I simply went through the motions, one foot in front of the other. I breathed in. I breathed out.

"You okay?"

I realize that I am sitting alone in the church. Everyone else has left, including Nora, including Jenny and Justin and Will. I do not even know what time it is.

I turn around and the pastor has taken a seat in the pew behind me.

I nod.

"How long have I been in here?" I ask, checking my watch.

"The service was over about an hour ago. We all went to the cemetery. When I got back I saw that your van was still in the parking lot. I've been in my office a while and I'm getting ready to leave, but I wanted to make sure you were okay."

"Oh."

"Are you?"

"What?"

"Okay?"

I nod.

"You're Ruby Jewell, right? The florist. I know that Madeline does most of our orders. I guess we haven't really ever met."

"You're Reverend Frederic," I say. "We met at the Guilfords' wedding and the Shepherds' anniversary party. I fixed an arrangement for your wife when she was in the hospital."

He nods. "Yes, yes, that's right. I'm sorry. Since I live over in Valley and only come a couple of days a week, I feel like I don't always know the people in this community."

He is still sitting behind me, and after glancing only once in his direction, I am facing forward.

"Juanita was a special person," he says, and I remember how he got a bit choked up in his eulogy.

"I didn't know her very well," I confess. "I'm more of a friend with her grandson."

"Will." He calls out the boy's name. "Sweet kid."

There's a pause.

"He does some work for you, doesn't he?"

I nod.

"And he was with you when you had an accident?"

I recall the porcupine, the broken ankle, the way Will begged not to leave me.

"He made his grandmother bring him to church to pray."

This was something I hadn't heard before.

"Madeline came and unlocked the door for them. She said they stayed here all night. And I think you and Clementine were on the prayer list for a month. I'm not sure that any of the church people ever realized they were praying for a dog, but it probably wouldn't have mattered anyway; they love Will and would have prayed for the porcupine if he asked."

I manage a smile.

"Did you know that he comes in early on Sundays and freshens up the floral arrangements? I see him in here every week, pinching off a few of the leaves, adding a little water. He likes to tell me the names of the flowers in the vases. I think he knows them all."

More surprises. He never told me he even notices the flowers in the sanctuary on Sunday mornings.

"It seems like you've taught him a lot in the short time he's been with you. Funny what kids pick up, isn't it?"

"Yeah, I guess it is."

"You never know what you're teaching somebody. And I suppose you don't always know when you're learning, either. Funny how that works, too, I guess."

And I think about what Will has taught me, how he showed me the clump of bighead clover near the cemetery and the few delicate stems of gayfeather near the creek across the street from the shop. I think about how he made me close my eyes and guess the wildflowers by how they smelled and how he thought deer fern was a crisper green than the dagger. I think about how he makes me feel hopeful.

"Well, anyway, you can stay here as long as you want. Just pull the front door closed when you leave so it locks."

I feel him stand behind me. He places his hand on my shoulder. "We appreciate all you do for this town, Ruby," he says and squeezes. "You have your own ministry, you know, bringing beauty into our lives." He lets go. "Sometimes I think it's the only thing that will save us."

And I turn to say good-bye, but he has already gone.

·Forty-Three·

"S HE wants a nice bouquet and a couple of boutonnieres for Justin and Will." Nora is giving me the morning messages.

I was at the club in a meeting with the ladies' tennis team. They are very specific about the flowers they want for their banquet. They're branching out this year and are requesting tropical: heliconia, birds of paradise, ginger. Apparently, a tennis player from Colville said Creekside copied their banquet design ideas year before last, going with pink and purple dahlias, so this year they want to steer clear of any resemblances. They're going with fern curls and anthuriums, single stems with just a few strands of ti leaves. With the other tropicals they've ordered, this banquet certainly won't look like any others, but they're going to have to pay. Tropicals are the most expensive flowers I sell.

"I thought it was just a paper being signed at the courthouse," I say, knowing that the formal request made by Jenny and Justin to adopt Will was pushed quickly through the system and has been approved. They are moving into their new house later this week. Will stopped by yesterday to tell me.

"Well, it is, but Jenny thinks there ought to be a ceremony. She wants flowers." Nora slides the receipt behind the others. "She's invited the priest to go and offer a blessing, and then she wants to have a little reception at the church. She wants you to decorate."

I feel my chest tighten.

"And Vivian called and wants to meet about the wedding."

"I just met with her last week. She's sticking with the sunflowers and blue irises."

Nora shakes her head. "I think she's changed her mind. She likes oriental lilies. She was surfing the net and saw a floral design she liked. She's thinking she'd like to have an Asian theme."

I blow out a breath. "I've already made the order."

Nora shrugs.

"And Stan wants to know if you can deliver flowers to the clinic in Moses Lake. His sister is getting her nose fixed."

"That's almost two hours away!"

"Hey, I'm just passing along the messages here. Don't shoot the mailman."

I walk around the counter to the design table behind her.

"I'm just so tired of bending over backward for the people in this town. I do everything for them—plan their weddings, manage their calendars, handle their funerals—and do you know I haven't raised my prices in ten years?"

I throw my notebook and keys on the table. Clementine gets up and leaves the room.

"Gas has gone up and all of my expenses have increased and I'm hardly making enough to cover costs. And now they want me to cancel orders I've already made and then drive clear to Moses Lake for a twenty-five-dollar vase of mums for somebody having plastic surgery?"

I go over to the refrigerator and take out a soda, slamming the door when I'm done. When I turn around, Nora is staring at me.

"What?" I ask, knowing that she clearly wants to say something.

She holds up her hands in a gesture of surrender. "I've not got anything to say," she replies, but she keeps staring like she does.

I wait.

She doesn't disappoint. She does have something to say.

"Have you been reading your *Oprah* magazine I subscribed for you?"

I don't answer. I have no idea where she's going with this. I shake my head.

"Well, you need to start taking a look at her columns."

I wait.

"You want to tell me what Oprah would have to say to me?"

She pauses. "Well, who am I to speak for the queen? But I think she would probably say that you need to make some changes or start a gratitude journal or put the oxygen mask on yourself before others because you are clearly not living your best life."

I look around for something to throw at her, but she immediately sees what I'm contemplating and she hurries around the counter, making it to the front door and out of my range.

"I'm going to Walmart," she announces. "We're out of the double-faced satin pink ribbon and I know Jenny will want that on her bouquet." And she is gone before I can reply or pick up anything and hurl it.

I sigh and watch her leave, and then I walk over and pick up the messages that Nora was reading and glance at them. I look up when I hear the bell on the front door signal that someone is coming in.

"You're still in danger of getting hit in the head," I say, thinking Nora has returned for something.

It isn't Nora.

"Wow. I didn't realize florists had a violent streak." John Cash has entered the shop.

I put down the messages and smooth down the front of my sweatshirt, lifting myself for a proper greeting. "Well, of course, you knew that," I say, trying to regain my composure. "You know what happened to the porcupine."

"Ah, right," he says, smiling. He glances around me. "And speaking of . . . where's the pooch?"

I turn to look where Clementine is usually resting and remember her recent departure. "She also knows the harm I can do."

And just like that, she appears from the back room, walks around the counter, ignoring me, and heads straight to the veterinarian. He promptly gives her a good scratch and tender greeting. "Hello, Miss Clem," he says, and she looks at me smugly.

I roll my eyes.

"She's gaining some of her weight back," he reports.

And I give that same smug look back at her. She is very sensitive about her weight and I know it.

"Yeah, she's a little portly."

She turns around, offering me her backside.

"No, not portly. I think she's perfectly fit." And he's rubbing her belly now.

She turns around to face me and she's one up.

He turns his attention to me, and Clementine returns to her spot beneath the table.

"So, how are you?" he asks. Being polite, I suppose.

"Good. And you?"

He nods. "I'm okay." And he slides his hands in his pockets just slowly enough that I am able to see his fingers, his unadorned fingers. The wedding ring is gone.

"I need a new plant," he announces.

"What happened to the old one?" I ask.

He shrugs. "Oh well, that is a good story."

I wait. I like good stories.

He clears his throat. "Maria," and he pauses. "That's my ex-wife," he explains.

I nod.

"She left a couple of days ago and it seems she took a few of my things."

"She stole your bamboo?" I ask, thinking that is pretty low, even for an ex-wife. "It's for peace and good luck. How can you steal something that's supposed to bring good luck? It seems like that would alter your karma."

He shakes his head. "She's never really cared much about karma."

"Oh," I reply. "So, you want something different?"

"Because that first good luck wasn't all that good?"

I hadn't said that, but I guess that's what I was thinking.

"Well, it *was* stolen."

He laughs ever so slightly.

I walk around the counter over to the plant stand near the window. I pick up a hot pink kalanchoe. "How about a calendiva?" I pinch off a dead leaf and hold it up.

He studies it and then notices the hanging plant above my head. "What's that one?"

I put down the plant in my hands. "*Senecio herreanus*," I answer. "This one is bananas."

"That sounds about right for my life right now."

And I reach up and take it from the hook in the window. I walk around him and stand behind the counter. I take a towel and wipe off the bottom of the planter, turn it around and make sure it is tidy and in good shape. After clearing out a few dead leaves, I am convinced it is ready to go. "Put it in a place that isn't too sunny; this succulent prefers a little shade. And keep it well drained."

He is nodding his head. He reaches in his back pocket and pulls out his wallet.

"Nah, here." I hand him the hanging plant. "This one is a makeup gift for the one that was stolen. Maybe it will bring you better luck than the bamboo."

He smiles and reaches for it. Our fingers touch as I hand him the plant and I feel a bit of a charge run through me. I quickly pull away.

"I guess I'll see you at Will's party," he says, and I know I look surprised.

I had forgotten there was a party.

"When he's adopted," he explains. "Jenny invited me."

I nod. I guess once I decorate, I'm invited too.

"You know, I sort of thought you'd adopt him," he says.

I don't respond.

"You too seem to go together."

I am at a loss for words.

"Okay, well, I'll see you soon. Thanks again for the bananas."

I nod. I find my voice. "You're welcome," I say.

And he turns and heads out the door.

·FORTY-FOUR·

I CANNOT arrange the flowers. I have taken every stem from the buckets in the cooler and it's like they wilt in my hands. I use wire; I try the foam; the flowers refuse to stand. They refuse to blend, refuse to deliver. I am like an artist who can't paint. I have lost my way.

I try light orange roses, orange spray roses, and Matsumoto asters. I make an attempt with yellow daisy spray chrysanthemums, red miniature carnations, orange carnations and alstroemeria; I even accent with bupleurum, but it's as if the flowers have gone on strike. Everything I bind, every bouquet I arrange is flat and dreary and lifeless. I may have to call Edna in Deer Park and consign the work to her.

Nora and Jimmy left early. They were so tired of hearing me complain and fight with the flowers that they both took the afternoon off without pay. Nora isn't even teasing me or giving me herbal tea. She hasn't mentioned Oprah once. She even knows that John Cash is single again, but she's not pushing this time. It's as if she's been silenced by what is happening, as if she knows there is no remedy for what is lost.

"Just go home," she said before she left, before she ushered Jimmy out the back door. "Quit trying, just go home."

And I could see the pity in her eyes; it had been there all morning as I fumbled and stumbled over the orders, the Sunday morning sanctuary flowers, a get-well bouquet, and Kathy Shepherd's order for a basket of tulips. I managed the basket although it lacks whimsy and fire, but she took the vase away from me when I started breaking the stems of the alstroemeria, the slender tendrils cracking like little bones.

"Here, give them to me," she insisted, and she finished the bouquet for Clara Robinson, an order placed from her son in California to be delivered later today at the hospital. "And Jimmy and I will drop it off on our way to the meeting," she added.

"Let's just give the Lutherans a plant for Sunday. Use one of the cyclamen; you've got hot pink and white. They'll be fine with one of those."

I let her take that too. That only leaves the flowers for tonight. I still have to create the arrangements for Will.

The new family has an appointment in Judge Hennesay's chambers at four o'clock, and then there will be a party to follow. Jenny wanted the same flowers she had at her wedding, pink gerberas, with a few bunches of purple asters to aid in the banishing of the sorrows of the past. She wanted pink and purple tulips in tall clear vases scattered on the tables in the parish hall and long-stemmed pink roses to be handed out when people left. I knew she and Justin didn't have the money to afford such a lavish celebration, so I had told her earlier this week that I would donate all the flowers. I hadn't realized she wanted so many.

"It's okay if you don't have arrangements on all the tables," Nora called from the road to say. "I know this is costly. Just make a couple of centerpieces for the serving tables and use bud vases on the rest."

But cost was not the problem. I would give all of my inventory to Jenny and Justin. I don't care about the money.

I am bending down, leaning on my elbows over the design table. I hear Cooper come in the back. He is not due today and I wonder why he is here. He greets Clementine and then comes through the door and sees me.

"Well, great rose of Sharon, what on earth is wrong with you?"

I don't even look up. I just shake my head.

"Are you going to throw up?" he asks. "You been sniffing angel trumpet?"

I shake my head again, knowing he's referring to the deadly plant that makes people do wacky things without even being aware of their actions. I do not answer.

He walks in and jumps up, taking a seat on the counter. "No Colombian devil's breath, no oleander, no western water hemlock?" He names all the poisonous plants.

I just keep shaking my head.

"Well, then what's the word?"

He studies the arrangement set in front of me. "You practicing blindfolded?"

I glance down at the bouquet, the whisper daisies pressed against the flamingo minis, the ivy loose and shabby, overrunning the vase, the pink long-stemmed rose raised high above them all, sticking out like a too-tall girl. It's a train wreck.

"All day," I say. "It's been like this all day."

He jumps down and walks in my direction. He raises his hand and checks my forehead.

"I'm not sick, I told you." And I pull away.

"Then what's wrong?" He yanks the rose out of the vase, grabs a pair of scissors, snips off the end and puts it back, then pulls apart the daisies and thins the greenery. Even without the other flowers, the arrangement already looks one hundred times better.

I shake my head and walk to the stool against the back wall. I sit down and watch as he pulls another pink rose and a stem of gypsophila out of the bucket, a lavender iris and a few white spray roses, and finishes the arrangement. He cups the flowers in his hands and leans down to smell, and then he lifts up and turns to me.

"How many more you got?"

"Just daisies and roses," I answer. "I just need to do a few stems of pink gerberas in bud vases and then the white bucket to hold all the pink roses. That's all," I say. "That's all I have left."

He walks out of the room and comes back with the box of small vases and sets them out on the table. He pulls out the daisies and fills them, one by one, while I watch. Then he goes into the cooler and returns with two black buckets and he finds all of the pink buds and gathers them together. He takes them back and returns with the white bucket, which he wipes and cleans and fills with flowers. It takes him all of about fifteen minutes to complete what was taking me all day.

"Now, do you want me to take these to the church?"

And I study him, wondering how he knew what needed to be done, wondering how he knew where the flowers were going.

"Will's party," he replies, as if he has heard the questions rattling around in my brain. "I was invited, too." He twirls the bucket in his hand and checks to make sure the blooms are all healthy. He pulls off a couple of petals where the edges have started to brown. "Last week when I made the delivery, he told me about the party and asked me to come."

I nod. I wasn't here when that happened, but it doesn't surprise me. Cooper and Will are friends. Cooper lets him climb up in the truck and collect the flowers I have ordered. Most of what the boy has learned has actually come from my wholesale guy, not from me.

"This is a good thing, right?" he asks.

I glance away.

"From what you've told me and what Will says, those two are great."

I still do not speak. Of course, he is right. Jenny and Justin will make splendid parents. Will is very lucky to have them.

"I'll just take these to the van," he notes, heading out the back.

And I just sit and drop my face into my hands.

·FORTY-FIVE·

I'M going to take a walk," I say, getting out of the van and heading in the direction of the cemetery. Clementine joins me when Cooper opens the back.

"Do you have a layout design in mind for these?"

I hear the question but I don't answer. I just keep walking. Cooper can put the flowers where he wants them. It's not that hard to put vases on tables. He'll be fine.

I walk up Flowery Trail. This street name always makes me smile, but not today. I don't even think of it. I don't notice the traffic. I just make sure Clem is far enough off the road, but that's about the only sensible thing I can manage. I don't know what's wrong with me. I should be happy for Will. I should be happy for Jenny and Justin and Will.

Jenny will make a wonderful mother. She will play computer games with Will and bake him cookies. She will help him with his math homework and make sure his room is clean and tidy and that his clothes fit. She will ride a bicycle with him and buy him a dog. She will be like a big sister, a really cool babysitter. She will adore him.

And Justin is a great guy. He will teach Will how to repair a flat and drive a stick shift. He can take him to monster truck shows and hockey games at the arena in Spokane. They'll have the father-son talk and Will can learn how to work with his hands, how to fix things and paint. Soon they'll have a couple of babies and Will can be a big brother and teach someone else the things he's learned from Justin. It's perfect. It's absolutely perfect.

But I am still a mess.

I get to the grave and sit down. I cross my legs and lift my face to the sun. Clementine sits beside me. She doesn't wander as much since the fight.

"I don't know why I can't be happy," I say to my dead sister. "I have my own business. I have a house, friends. I finally figured out how to order movies on the television." I look at the headstone. *DAISY JEWELL*, it reads, bold and frozen in the rock.

"He's good with them," I add. "He's better off with them." And I stretch my arms behind me and lean back. I think about Daisy and me and the one emergency foster home where we were taken after Mama hit me with the belt buckle and everything came apart. It was a large house, ranch style, three levels with a basement that was made into a game room. We shared a bedroom where there were two single beds, thin headboards painted white. There were pink bedspreads and pillows with ruffles and two desks with writing paper and crayons, both of them set against the wall, making the room look like a college dormitory.

There were three other children in the house: a teenager, a shy, clumsy boy who had a room to himself downstairs, and two toddlers who shared the nursery, which was on the other side of the parents' bedroom. We were there for three days before Grandmother finally found us, Daddy calling her from the road, telling her what had happened and how he couldn't take it anymore. Once she found us, however, we were still not allowed to go. There was apparently some discussion among social workers and the foster parents about whether we should be allowed to leave with family. I've since learned that the common thought at that time was that if one parent abused drugs or hit her children, the other parent was considered just as negligent and the grandparents were also thought to be unfit. There appears to be a different philosophy today, but back then, removing the child from the family was the ideal solution.

While Daisy and I waited for the papers to be filed and the issues to be sorted out, we worked out an escape. We drew plans and even stole money from the teenage boy, and on our second night at the foster home, after finishing our chores, eating our supper, and enduring the family Bible study, we went to our room and made our preparations to leave. We had apples and crackers we had taken from the pantry and we filled our pillowcases with a change of clothes and bars of soap. We counted our coins, stuffed our pockets with socks and underwear, and waited until everyone was asleep. That was when we planned to sneak out.

"Do you have a flashlight?" Daisy asked.

"I stole one from the garage," I answered, feeling the lump under my head, the pillowcase filled with the supplies. "But I don't think it has batteries."

"Then how do we see?"

"I'll try to buy us some when we get to a store."

"What store?"

"The Family Dollar," I answered. "It's right there on the corner." We had stopped there before we arrived; the social worker had needed to make a call before she drove over and left us at the house.

"Do you think we'll find a nice person to take us?" Daisy asked.

We were in our beds, under the covers, pretending to be asleep in case the foster mother peeked in to check on us.

"Maybe," I answered. And I thought of the two of us standing on the side of the interstate, the lights of cars speeding past. We had planned to walk to the highway and then hitchhike to Grandmother's.

"If we waited until morning we might have a better chance of getting a ride."

And I suddenly realized that Daisy was having second thoughts.

"If we wait until morning, we can't sneak out," I reminded her. The foster mother had a tendency to hover. I guess she had experienced runaways before.

Daisy didn't respond.

"Are you scared?"

She didn't answer, but I could imagine her nodding.

"Come over here," I said, and she jumped from her bed and crawled in beside me, bringing her pillowcase, stuffed with clothes and snacks and soap.

"We don't have to go," I said, wrapping my arms around her. "It's not that bad here." I thought of the chocolate cookies we had that afternoon, the gentle way the father smiled, the toddlers crawling into my lap as we watched TV.

"I thought you said we should."

"I don't know, Daisy. I don't know what to do."

And she grabbed my arms, pulling me tighter around her.

"It's okay if we stay," she said.

"You sure?" I asked.

"It's not so bad. And we're together, right? That's what matters most, isn't it?"

And it wasn't long before I heard her breathing deepen and grow steady and felt her grip loosen. We didn't run away that night; we just fell asleep together.

"But we were kids," I say to Daisy now, knowing the memory was from her. "Of course we believed that back then we were just kids. All we knew was having each other. Being a parent is different. There are different things you have to know, have to take care of. He's a boy. He's almost a teenager," I argue.

I hear nothing from my dead sister. She has said her piece.

I watch the sun as it hides behind the clouds, shows itself, and then disappears again. It is like a child playing.

"It's too late now anyway," I say, peering at the time on my watch, realizing that the papers have been signed, the deed done, the party started.

Clementine raises her head and looks over to the other side of the cemetery. She jumps up and races to the grave we have visited before.

·Forty-Six·

Hey, what are you doing here?" I followed Clem to Will, who was putting a pink rose at his mother's site and one at the new grave dug beside it. I assume he got them from the church and from the bucket of flowers to be handed out as people leave.

He shrugs. "I just missed them."

I nod.

He sits down in front of his mother's grave and I make a place beside him.

"Everybody at the church?"

"Yeah," he answers. "I told Jenny I'd be right back."

"How did the meeting with the judge go?"

He shrugs again. "Okay, I guess."

"Did you like him?"

"He had hair growing out of his nose."

"Like Mr. Jackson?" I ask, remembering Will telling me about the guidance counselor at his school.

"Yeah. It was kind of gross."

I nod.

"Cooper said you were probably out here."

"Well, he was right." I pick a few rocks from under me and smooth down the place where I am sitting.

"He also said that you were acting weird all day."

I smile. "Coop exaggerates," I tell him.

"He said you were trying to add bark to the orchids."

"What's wrong with that?" I hadn't exactly remembered doing that, but it wasn't that unlikely, the way I was feeling.

Will turns to me as if I have just said something most outrageous. "You don't add bark to them. It dries out the plant. You use sphagnum moss for orchids."

I punch him in the arm. "You're too young to know that much about orchid care."

"I only know what you've taught me," he answers.

I study the boy. He is beautiful with those long lashes, those big brown eyes. He can see I'm admiring him, and he blushes and turns away.

"So, how's it been with Jenny?"

"She's cool," he replies. "She and Justin have Xbox and Blu-Ray."

"What's that?"

He gives me that look again, and I grin.

Now he hits me in the arm.

"I know what they are, it's those cartoon channels on cable." And I rub my arm because he packs a punch with that little fist.

He rolls his eyes. "Clementine doesn't go sniff around the fence anymore?"

I glance over at the dog resting in front of us beside the headstone.

"No, I think she's decided that she's smelled enough from that corner of the universe."

Will picks up a stick and tosses it near the fence.

Clementine yawns.

"It ain't happening," I say.

"When did you come get the flowers?" he asks, referring to the arrangements that had been placed at his grandmother's grave after the service.

I turn to the grave beside us and see that there are still a few bouquets left, the ones with heartier blooms. Most of the others had wilted and died sometime during the day. Sometimes I collect them so that the family doesn't have to bother with them.

"Yesterday," I answer. "I figured it would be okay with you and Claude to pick them up."

He nods. "There were a lot of them."

"Yep," I say. "Juanita had a lot of friends."

"She told me that friends are the family members we get to choose."

"That makes sense," I agree.

"What about family members?" he asks.

And I don't follow him. "What about them?"

"Do you think we choose them, too?"

"You mean like before we get here?"

"Yeah, do you think we're given to a certain person because we need them or they need us?"

I study him. "Who have you been talking to?" I ask. The question sounds like it is way above his head.

"It's just something I heard," he answers.

"From where?"

"From Captain Miller."

"You talked to Captain Miller about choosing your parents?" I didn't even know that Will had spent much time with Dan.

"He came over after Grandma died. He brought me some books about space, a couple of his model airplanes."

I nod. That sounds like Dan. "And he told you we're assigned our parents?"

Will shrugs. "I asked him what it was like in outer space; you know, if it was like heaven and there were angels and stuff."

I'm paying attention.

"And he told me about how he figured some things out when he was there, how he felt like he was a part of everything and in everything, and that everything and everybody is connected."

"Yep, he told me the same thing," I say. "It's a little freaky, I think."

"Anyway, I asked him if he thought there was some big plan of the universe, like they say in church."

"Okay."

"And he said he thought there was, and especially when it came to the people in our lives. He said that we find the people we need and that they stay with us until we don't need them anymore. And then they go to another planet and they find someone else."

"Hmm. And what do you think?" I ask the boy.

"I like it better than just thinking they die and leave us."

I close my eyes and think about it. I must say I like it better, too.

We don't speak for a few minutes. There is a little noise from the road, a dog barking in the distance. Clementine hears that one too. She rises up.

"So, it's official?" I ask.

Will turns to me. His face is a question mark.

"You and Jenny and Justin? You got adopted."

And he looks away without answering.

"They're real nice," he says, and I suddenly feel strangely lightheaded, as if I may faint or fall. I feel unstable and I reach down to hold on to the ground.

"What?" I ask.

"I'm going to stay with them," he adds. "You know, for a while."

"But you didn't get adopted?"

He shakes his head, and it's as if my chest is going to burst.

I close my eyes and feel his slender hand on top of mine.

I take a breath, the air filling my lungs, my cells thick with oxygen, and I am suddenly and completely conscious while the thin edge around me loosens and falls open.

FORTY-SEVEN

T HERE'LL be lilies."

Nora has just told me her news. She'd burst through the front door like a police officer making an arrest. She glows.

"Of course we'll have lilies," she replies. "Those pretty pink ones that have the little lip of green."

"Callas," I say, knowing exactly the one she means.

"Yes, pink and yellow calla lilies." She claps her hands. "Divine."

I also decide to order a few stems of the white orientals, adding a little touch of class.

"And I want you and Will to walk me down the aisle. Carl will do my hair and makeup. And I will buy a new dress."

"Nordstrom's?" I smile.

"Of course."

"I'm not sure I can handle another shopping trip to Nordstrom's."

She laughs.

"Will it be an outside venue?" I ask.

At the moment I'm still working on Vivian's wedding. She's changed her mind again, shifted themes from Asian to French country to seaside, even postponed it by a couple of weeks, and I told her that I refuse to place an order with Cooper until she is absolutely certain of what she wants.

I wish now I had never played with that fire. Vivian is more complicated than I imagined. I'm not sure Conrad knows what he's gotten himself in for.

"Outside, inside, I don't care; I'm too old to be worrying about all those silly details." She fans herself and moves behind the counter. She opens the register and takes out twenty dollars. "I didn't get a chance to pick up the wire you needed," she explains, and closes the drawer.

"Does Jimmy have a preference?" I ask. I'm arranging the same orchids that were used to seduce Vivian. She suddenly remembered what an effect they had on her, and today she thinks she wants to use those for her bouquet. I'm putting a few small bouquets together so she can get an idea of how they would look. It's only two weeks until the new date of the blessed event and I know that if she wants orchids, she needs to decide now. It always takes a little longer to get those from the buyer.

"Jimmy doesn't care one way or the other. He just wants me happy." She clutches the money to her chest. "He's such a good man; I don't know why it took me so long to notice." Suddenly she understands what I'm doing. "Why are you messing with the orchids? I thought Vivian was going Asian."

"She said she thought she was too big to go with an Asian theme, that she kept looking at all the websites and pictures and that all the brides were tiny little women and she finally decided that she was too tall for the patterns and décor."

Nora shakes her head. "You know, they seem like normal, well-balanced women and then they get an engagement ring and they just fall off their rockers."

"Well, be careful what you say . . . you may turn into a bride-zilla, too!"

She waves away the comment. "All I care about is the cake. I want a big, frosted, fattening chocolate cake." She holds out her arms to demonstrate how large a cake she means. It's big.

I look at her and smile and I suddenly remember the last time she acted like this. It was when Will and I arrived at the church and broke the news, and she opened her arms wide and ran clear across the parish hall, picked us both up and swung us around. I'm pretty sure she's had weekly appointments with the chiropractor since then, but I think even knowing what she knows now about picking up people, she'd do the same thing again. Like everyone close to us, she is still overcome.

Even Justin and Jenny seemed pleased, claiming that they would never have wanted to force themselves on Will if he had wanted something different. And the adoption party stayed true to its original purpose; it just changed celebrants. Will moved in with me that night and until we find a bigger place, I bought a sleeper sofa and his bed is in the living room. Since he doesn't have his own room yet, I did splurge and buy him one of those game boxes and already every night I feel I am failing as a parent when I hear him still playing after midnight. But it is summer and he sleeps late and so far, three weeks and counting, I haven't screwed things up too badly and I also know that I have not felt this complete, this happy in a very long time.

"I can't believe you're getting married," I say, stopping what I'm doing and taking in Nora's glow.

She appears surprised. "Of course you can," she replies. "You called it long before I did."

And I have to laugh. I do recall the comment I made about the two of them, the comment I still feel sorry about. "So, how did he propose?"

"He didn't propose," she answers.

I raise an eyebrow.

"Well, if I had waited around for him to propose we'd be decorating for your wedding long before mine."

"You then? You proposed to him."

She holds out her hand, a big diamond flashing on her ring finger. "Bought my own ring too." She studies it. "We used his Visa, of course."

"Of course," I respond.

"I just was so happy about you and Will and all the love in this town and Jenny's good health and I started thinking how time is flying past and if you love somebody you ought to get on with it. And that's what I'm doing."

"And that was your proposal to Jimmy, let's get on with it?"

"Something like that," she responds, and then moves around me, taking a seat on the stool. She puts the twenty dollars in her purse.

"Will there be a honeymoon?" I tie two single-stem cymbidium with a full bunch of Hawaiian dendrobiums. I hold it up and show Nora. She wrinkles her forehead. She doesn't approve.

"Too many," she says.

And so I take away the green and purple orchids and try the cymbidium with a couple of stems of phale. It looks a lot better.

She nods her approval.

"Jimmy is still on probation and isn't supposed to leave the state, so we may just go over to the coast for a few days."

"That'll be nice for fall."

"Fall?" She sounds surprised.

"Isn't that what you're thinking?" I ask, glancing over at the calendar and seeing that it is already mid-July. I figure every wedding needs a couple of months to plan.

"We're planning next weekend," she announces.

"Next weekend?" I put down the flowers and turn to her, my mouth falling open. "You can't be ready by next weekend."

"What's there to be ready for?" she asks. "We get a license from the courthouse. We ask the doggie doc to meet us somewhere. I have an arm full of calla lilies, a chocolate cake from the Mennonites, and my three best friends. What else is there?"

"Music, invitations, birdseed, those little mints with your names printed on them . . ."

She waves her hand in front of her face. "I'm sticking to John Lennon on this one."

I wait.

"All you need is love." She smiles.

"And lilies," I add.

"Okay, I'll go with you and Lennon. All you need is love and lilies."

·FORTY-EIGHT·

How much longer are you going to be in there?" Will is standing at the bathroom door.

I have just settled into a nice lavender bubble bath. I sit up. "Maybe an hour," I answer.

"An hour?" I hear his little-boy sigh. "I have to pee."

I stand up and pull the shower curtain closed. "I asked you before I started and you said you didn't need the bathroom." I sit back down. "Okay, you can come in."

I hear the door open. "Well, that was before I drank all the orange juice." He turns on the light, immediately changing the mood of the candlelit room.

"You drank another carton of juice?" I am sure I am buying as many groceries as the octomom.

"I thought you wanted me to drink juice instead of sodas." I hear him lift the seat on the commode.

"Well, yeah, but not a carton of it a day."

I turn on the hot water so I don't have to listen. When I think there's been enough time for him to complete what he came in to do, I turn it off.

He finishes and zips up his pants.

"Wash your hands," I say.

And he does.

"Did you flush?"

And he does that too.

"Did you put the seat down?"

I hear it fall.

"Is that a vanilla candle?"

"I believe it is."

And I hear him pick up the candle and then put it down. "Smells good." There is a pause and I think he must be on his way out. "Ruby . . ." He isn't.

"Yeah?"

"I'm starting fifth grade next month."

"Yes," I reply, not sure why he's telling me news I already know. "We have all the right papers filed and we met your homeroom teacher last Wednesday night. Mr. Evans, I believe, is his name. Seems nice enough."

I wait for a response. There is none. I fold the washcloth and place it over my eyes. I breathe in the scent of lavender.

"I've never been in fifth grade."

"Well, as I recall, it's not that much different from fourth grade," I say, trying to reassure him.

"It's a little different," he says.

"Okay," I respond.

"We change classes in the morning and after lunch. I'll have three teachers instead of one."

"But that can be a good thing because if you don't like one, you don't have to stay with her all day."

I suddenly remember Mrs. Willie from fifth-grade science. She was very strict and smelled like formaldehyde. I was always glad when the bell rang and I could go to English.

"Suppose I get a locker that I can't reach."

I hear him drop the top on the commode and sit down. It looks like my luxurious soaking solitude is gone.

"Then you'll tell your homeroom teacher and they'll give you one you can reach."

He seems to be thinking about that. He's quiet for a few seconds.

"I can pick an instrument and play in the band."

"Do you want to play in the band?"

"Nah."

"Okay."

"I can choose a sport and stay after school and practice."

"Do you want to play a sport?"

He must be considering the idea; he's quiet.

"Maybe baseball."

And I realize that I should have asked him that earlier. Maybe he would have played this summer. Don't boys play baseball in the summer? There are so many things to learn.

"Then we'll sign you up for baseball."

He's quiet again.

"Mama always took me shopping before school started," he explains. "For school and my birthday." I remember the date of his birthday and decide that a shopping trip makes a lot of sense. "Well, we can go Sunday, if you want," I say. "You want to go to Spokane or to Colville?"

"Spokane, I guess," he replies.

"What kinds of things do you buy?" I have no idea of what a ten-year-old boy needs for school. Does he buy jeans? Sneakers? Should we wait and see what other boys are wearing?

"I need a new backpack and I wanted some of those shoes like Justin wears."

"Converse," I tell him. "I had a pair in college. Maybe I'll buy a pair for me too."

He doesn't respond.

"Or is that too weird? Having a . . ." Suddenly, I don't know the word.

"Mom?" he asks, and I feel strangely warm.

I finish. "Is that weird having a mom wearing the same shoes as you?"

He must be thinking about it and I actually feel a little nervous that he will change the thing he just said, the very simple but important thing.

"Nah, that's okay. Just not the same color," he adds. "I'm getting black."

"Then I'll go with white or maybe pink." I feel my cheeks redden. I am blushing at being called a mom.

I hear the door come open and I'm guessing Clementine has joined us as well. Apparently, there's a party in my bathroom. She sticks her head in through the curtain and I wave. She leaves the side of the tub and I hear her plop down next to the toilet. I'm thinking we definitely have to get a bigger house, one with two bathrooms.

"Oh, you had a phone call right after you came in here," he says.

He tells me this and I recall thinking I had heard it ring but had forgotten to ask him about it.

"Who was it?" I expect to hear from Nora and Jimmy. They left for Seattle a couple of days ago and I've been wondering how the honeymoon is going.

"Captain Miller," he answers.

And I realize that I haven't talked to Dan in a few days. The last time I saw him was at the library. He was dropping off some of his books and CDs to donate. He looked gaunt but refused to complain about how he was feeling. I plan to take him some soup and bread this weekend.

"He said he had some more science books for me and a couple of CDs for you and that he'd leave them at the back door of the shop this evening."

I wonder why he would do that and not just drop them off here at the house.

"Is that all he said?"

"He said it was a clear sky tonight and just after sunset Jupiter would be extra bright. He told me to tell you to make sure we both went out to see it. He said about seven o'clock and he made me repeat what he was saying. I guess it's kind of important. He wants us to go outside and look at the planet Jupiter at seven."

I glance at my watch. It's ten minutes before seven. "Well, I guess we better get moving." I stand up. "Can you hand me the towel on the floor?" I ask.

And his little hand reaches in. I take it.

"Thanks for the talk, Will," I say, not minding at all the short soak and crowded room.

·Forty-Nine·

I DON'T see it," he says.

We are standing outside, facing west, the direction I think I had seen the planet before when I saw it for the first time from Dan's deck.

"Well, he said it was sometimes called the wandering planet because it was not always where the stargazers gazed." I look up and around. I don't see a shining planet, either.

"Maybe it's too early," Will responds. "It's still pretty light out."

I think the same thing since it isn't quite dark yet and there are only a few stars out. "But he was pretty specific, right? He said seven o'clock."

Will nods.

I find this a very odd phone call and wonder why Dan would have asked us both to come outside this evening. I think that maybe I should call him for better instructions.

"Let's get a couple of chairs," I tell him, deciding not to call. "This might take a while."

Will goes around to the rear of the house and brings us two camping chairs. I open them and we sit down. Will takes the binoculars and studies the sky.

"You like Captain Miller, don't you?" he asks.

"I do, very much. He's smart and kind and he's very nice to me. You like him too, don't you?"

I think about Will and Dan, seeing them together at Nora and Jimmy's wedding, the way he congratulated us when I announced the adoption.

"Yeah, he's cool. He showed me how to make a telescope." Will stops and thinks. "Wait, I should get it!" And he runs inside.

In a few minutes he returns, carrying a small black tube that I don't remember seeing in his things. He points it to the sky.

"Look, you can see really good!"

And I take the apparatus, gaze through it, and have to agree. There is a clearer image of the sky.

"When did he help you make this?" I ask, handing him back the scope.

Will shrugs. "About a month after I got here," he answers. "He came by the house every Sunday."

And I think about how long Dan had been visiting Will and how he never mentioned it to anyone. He had found out about the boy and his mom's death and made a point of giving him a little attention. And once again, I am surprised by the astronaut's choices.

"He bought a lens from the eye doctor." And he shows it to me. "And it's just a cardboard tube for the eyepiece. Grandma gave him the one from the paper towels."

I nod, following along.

"Then this is the diaphragm"—he points to a narrow black card—"and it's made from a thick piece of paper, like poster board." He shows me the center. "See the hole?"

"I do," I answer.

"You make a bunch of little cuts around the edge of the disk to make a set of tabs. Then you wet the tabs and place the tube cap on one end of the tube and bend the tabs around the outside."

"This is way over my head," I say.

"It's not so hard," Will explains. "And then you finish by gluing the tabs together and when the glue is dry, you take the cap off and cut in the cap a hole that is smaller in diameter than the outside diameter of the principal tube."

I shake my head. "He taught you all that?" I ask, bewildered.

Will nods. "Yep, and he told me about the planets and the stars and how they are spheres of plasma held together by gravity." He gazes through his telescope.

"You going to be an astronaut, too?" I ask.

He shrugs. It is for him, a perfectly logical question.

"I don't know, maybe," he answers. And he goes back to gazing up at the sky.

"Captain Miller is sick," I tell Will, not sure why I feel it is necessary to break this news to the boy.

"I know," he answers. "He has cancer."

"He told you about that, too?" I ask, although I'm not all that surprised. Dan values truth-telling.

Will nods. "He said it was spreading throughout his body and that he wouldn't get better from it."

"Like Jenny did?" I add.

"Yeah, like her."

"What else did he say?"

"Just that he had lived a really full and happy life and that he wasn't afraid of what would happen next."

I think about Dan, about our long talks, the dinner at his house where he showed me the planet for the first time. "Did he show you Jupiter?"

Will nods.

"Its mass is two point five times that of all the other planets in our solar system combined."

He's starting to sound like an encyclopedia now.

"Did he tell you about the Great Red Spot?"

"He showed it to me," he answers, and I see that I don't really have anything on him. "He has a really nice telescope."

"He does," I agree.

"He was really glad you adopted me," Will adds.

I nod.

"He was the one who said that maybe I should wait a little while before going with Jenny and Justin."

Another surprise. I hadn't really been told the reasons why Will chose not to sign the papers, but I hadn't really expected to hear that the suggestion came from Dan.

"Really?"

Will nods.

"He just told me that sometimes grown-ups need a little longer than kids to know what is in their hearts. And that I should give it some more time."

"And you knew he was talking about me?"

There is the slightest grin on the boy's face.

"You did?" I ask.

He shrugs.

So Dan had orchestrated this whole thing. He knew I would adopt Will. I shake my head. I will have a few things to say to him when I see him.

And as if on cue, it appears. The sound of a piston twin engine, the Cessna 337, Dan's plane. I hear it long before I see it and I know what it means before he even drops down, dips his wings, a greeting in our direction, and heads west.

"There it is!" Will shouts, and he has found the planet Jupiter, just making its appearance, just starting to shine.

"Yes," I reply. "There it is."

And I see now that Dan has finally chosen how he wants to leave the Earth, how he plans to make his transition, how to return to his stardust. He finished all of his tasks, tied up all of the loose ends, and he got in his plane to fly away.

"You know, a lot of people think that planets are stars," Will says, not realizing what I have seen, not realizing what is taking place before our eyes. "But they aren't," he adds. "Stars have their own light," he explains. "Planets don't."

I watch the plane move farther and farther into the horizon and I picture his smile and wave. And I hold up my hand as well and then place it across my heart.

"Their own light," I reply. "That would be exactly right," I say, even though I am sure Will does not understand. "He has his own light."

·Fifty·

T HE arrangement was really nice," Will says as I cover him
with a blanket. It's still summer but the nights are cooling
off. I'm tucking him in his sofa bed and I sit down beside him and
the mattress droops. It can't be very comfortable and I know we
have to figure out somewhere else for him to sleep.

"Thank you," I respond, knowing that he's talking about the
flowers I selected for the memorial service and picnic that a few of
us had for Dan at a small cove over at Holland's Lake. I arranged the
blooms while I listened to one of the CDs Dan gave me, choosing
blue hydrangea, orange roses, light pink Asiatic lilies, pink alstroemeria, hot pink gerberas, and purple daisies with a bit of rich green
salal. Every bloom I arranged, every stem I selected, I thought of
him, his kindness, his adventuresome spirit, his wide-open heart.

The gathering had been Will's idea. Nora and Jimmy and I
were discussing whether we should plan a funeral for Dan when
Will made the suggestion of meeting outside, placing flowers in
the lake, and then eating a meal together.

Most of the people in town were invited, but some of them refused because officially Dan has not been declared dead. As far as what the authorities are saying, he is still only missing. There can't be a declaration of death until a certain amount of time passes. And there are some who don't believe that he's dead, some who think he'll come back. But I know he won't. I know he's found his way to exit this world and he's gone. So those of us at the shop and a few from around Creekside gathered at the lake at sunset to say our good-byes and, in his honor, to eat fine food and drink some very expensive wine.

"I was glad that Nora started," he tells me. "I thought we might be standing out there until dark, waiting for somebody to say something."

I nod.

"I didn't know she understood physics like that."

"I know. I never heard that Captain Miller taught her the theory of relativity."

"Yeah, it was funny hearing her say that energy and mass are equivalent and transmutable."

"I know, right?" I shake my head.

Nora had explained to us that Dan was the smartest man she knew, and she stunned us all by reciting the general and specific relative theories and then explaining how the speed of light in a vacuum is the same for all observers, regardless of their relative motion or of the motion of the source of the light. Of course, she also told us how Dan had shown her how to work the clock on her DVD and how to record *Real Housewives of Orange County*. That made us laugh, which eased a little of the tension. And she had finished her remembrance by saying that Dan loved this world and all that was beyond it. Like everything Nora says, her words were both odd and lovely.

"I was surprised that Jenny announced that Dan had bought their house," I say, remembering how the young woman wept when she shared that news. Dan had told her that he thought of her as a daughter and that walking her down the aisle on her wedding day was the happiest day of his life. And Jenny wanted us all to know that he bought the little parsonage from the Catholic church and gave it to her and Justin and then told them not to tell anyone. His desire for anonymity was one more example of his goodness.

Will nods.

"You were thoughtful to give her a daisy and Justin a tulip."

He smiles and I remember how he walked over and handed them each a flower.

"Who were all those people Mr. Carl was talking about?"

"They're designers," I answer. "Carl was remembering all the designer clothes and shoes Dan wore."

"Oh." He pauses. "I guess everybody has different ways of thinking of people, huh?"

"Yeah, I guess."

I lie down beside him and we're quiet for a bit as we both remember the others who spoke, the things people said.

I think of how Henry cleared his throat and how Lou Ann took him by the hand. "Ca-Ca-Captain Miller a-a-always came ear-early for his h-h-haircut. He li-liked t-to c-c-come in the morn-ing," he had said, his face red, his eyes puffy from crying.

"He t-told m-me once that l-l-love c-c-could not wait. I g-g-gave L-Lou Ann th-th-that first bouquet th-the n-next day."

When he finished, Lou Ann leaned over and gave her husband a kiss and then walked over and took two flowers from Will's basket and returned to stand next to Henry.

"Dr. John said some nice stuff," Will notes, and I turn on my side to face him and remember how I hadn't even known John was there before he spoke.

"I like what he said about the animals and God, about how Cap-tain Miller had told him that God made the animals first because he knew they could be good teachers for people if we would just pay attention. I liked how Captain Miller had thanked him for taking care of the teachers."

I remember how both Will and I looked over at Clementine when John had said this and how I had reached in the basket, taken a flower, and given it to him.

"Are you going to marry him?"

I sit up. "What? Where did that come from?" I ask.

"He gives you that googly-eye look like Justin gives Jenny. And you always turn red when he's around." He shrugs. "I just figure you'll get married sometime."

"Well, I don't think that's happening," I respond, and lie back down.

We're quiet for a while.

"I didn't think you were going to take a turn," he notes, and I nod, thinking about how hard it was to read what I had written, how clumsy and awkward I felt, taking out the paper, unfolding it, how my hands shook and my voice faltered.

"It was good though. Captain Miller would have liked it."

I smile. I remember how Will leaned into me, the way he kept looking at me and looking at me, the way he nudged me to say it was my time. Reluctantly, I had finally read the words I had spent all night trying to write.

"Captain Daniel Miller knew me for a long time before I knew him. And he never told me about that until just recently."

I kept staring down at the page even though I was reading something that wasn't there. "Like Nora, I also thought he was the smartest man I knew. But I never learned the theory of relativity like she did," I improvised.

"To me, he was smart in things of the heart." And then I went back to my script.

"He taught me to tell the truth and not to be afraid and he was my very good friend." And it was then that I felt Will's arm slip around my waist. "And even though he wants us to believe that he is still with us in stardust and morning light, I will miss him very much." And I had stopped then, even though I had found a beautiful quotation about unfolding and living fully. That was as much as I could bear to say.

"You were pretty great with that poem," I tell him, recalling how he shared the passage he had found in one of the books Dan gave him, an inscription that had been penned by Sir Walter Raleigh.

"When at heart you should be sad." He had memorized it.

"Pondering the joys we had, listen and keep very still. If the lowing from the hill or the toiling of a bell do not serve to break the spell, listen: you may be allowed to hear my laughter from a cloud."

Will and I are quiet for a few minutes, thinking about the words of the poem, thinking about the evening and how we stood silent for a few minutes as the sun lowered in the western sky, how Justin and Jenny went first, walking to the shore, arm in arm, dropping their flowers in the water. When they returned to the gathering, Nora and Jimmy took their turn. Then the others, and finally I felt Will pull me along and I walked beside him and dropped the orange rose he had given me, watching as it bobbled and swayed, moving away from where we were standing.

We ate before it got dark, gathering around the picnic table, sharing the food we had brought and the other memories we kept, the vase of flowers, a model of a space shuttle, a photograph of Dan next to his airplane, our impromptu altar.

"I don't know what made me look in that book," Will says, talking about the poem and how he happened to find it before the service, how he copied it on a piece of paper, believing that Dan had left it for him to read, how he learned it line by line. "I just opened it up and there it was."

"Sounds like it was just meant to be," I say, thinking how I never used to believe in that kind of serendipity, how I was never easy with things I couldn't explain, the mysteries of life.

"Do you think he just flew away?" he asks, and I roll over and lift up my arm and he slides beneath it. "Do you think he's okay, wherever he is?"

I hold Will and imagine Dan moving farther and farther into the horizon. I don't know if he crashed into a mountain or fell into the ocean. I don't know at what moment he died or where he was when he took his last breath. But I do know that he got what he wanted, that he closed his eyes and let go and was able to say, like that old man in Houston, that janitor who taught Dan gratitude, that everything was good with his heart. I don't know a lot about anything else, but I do know that.

"I think he's fine," I say to Will, and I gather him in, pulling him close. "I think he's perfectly and completely fine."

FIFTY-ONE

Kathy says it's important." Nora is on the phone. She's at the shop early this morning, checking on stock and cleaning up after the weekend.

It was the end-of-summer crafts fair in Creekside and we had set up a booth selling gladioli and stems of red roses and bunches of September flowers. We participate every year, and every year it takes a few days to clean up the mess we leave in the shop on Sunday.

"Well, I'm sure it's important," I respond. "She thinks all of her orders are important, but it's Will's first day of school. I can't get there until after I drop him off."

"I don't think it's an order," she tells me, but I don't care. "I think she has something for you."

"Then she can just leave it with you."

"Nope, she says she wants to see your face when she puts it in your hands."

I have no idea what Kathy Shepherd wants to give me, but right now all I care about is making sure Will is prepared and ready for this important day.

"We're a bit busy this morning," I explain.

"How is the little man?" Nora knows we've been anticipating this day for weeks. She even went shopping with us when we went to buy school supplies, insisting on buying everything for him, filling the shopping cart with things he'll never use, like colored pencils and a Spanish dictionary.

I hear him in the bathroom, talking to Clem, telling her that he'll be at the shop by three thirty to take her for her walk.

"He's a little nervous, but he's good," I report.

There is a pause. I am trying to make up the sofa, glancing at the clock, wondering how long he's going to be before I can get in and brush my teeth.

"How are you?"

And when she asks, I stop what I am doing and have to catch my breath. The question throws me.

"Not what you thought, huh?"

I clear my throat. "He needs a desk and I don't know where we're going to add another piece of furniture to this room." I'm diverting.

"You're not going to be one of those mothers who parks in front of the school where everybody can see you and then makes the boy give you a hug, are you?"

I know she's trying to lighten the mood.

"I plan to walk with him to the front door." I smile.

"Are you taking photographs?"

"I have a camera and a video recorder," I answer.

"He's going to need therapy, you know that, right?"

"He wouldn't be my son if he didn't," I respond.

He comes out of the bathroom, walks into the room, and looks at me.

I drop the phone to my chin. "It's Aunt Nora," I tell him. "She and Jimmy want to come with us."

He rolls his eyes and I grin.

"Tell him I love him," Nora instructs me.

"Here, you tell him," and I pass the phone to Will.

I watch him as he listens. He's gotten so tall and I stare at him and I can't believe he's here, that he's with me, that he's mine.

"Yes, ma'am," he says, a slight blush to his cheeks. "Yes, ma'am," he says again to whatever she's telling him.

"I will," he acknowledges, and nods. "I love you, too." And he pulls the phone away from his ear, ends the call, and hands it to me.

"She's proud of me," he tells me.

"For getting up and going to school?" I ask.

He shrugs. "I guess."

He helps me fold in the bed, puts the pillows back on the sofa, and then sits down to put on his shoes.

"You feeling okay?" I ask, knowing that I am more nervous than he.

"Yeah," he answers.

"I mean, I know you were worried earlier about fifth grade." I am standing over him, hovering, but I can't help myself.

"I'm not worried now," he replies.

"You want another bowl of cereal?" I ask, thinking that maybe one wasn't enough. "Do you have your lunch?"

He pats his backpack, which is on the floor beside him. "It's in here," he says. "I don't want any more cereal."

I wait.

"Are you going like that?" he asks, and I look down and realize I'm still in my pajamas.

I glance at the clock. I have twenty minutes to get him to school. "Geez!" I say, and hurry to my room to throw on my clothes.

When I get back to the living room, Kathy Shepherd is sitting with him on the sofa.

"Hey," I say, and wonder how I didn't hear her come in and how I am going to get her out.

"Hello, Ruby," she says.

Her makeup is perfect and she's wearing a suit, a navy blue one with navy pumps, three-inch heels. Her posture is perfect and I feel myself lengthen as I watch her size me up.

I am wearing my old jeans and a stained sweatshirt, but I do have on my new red Converse high-tops. At least I have something going for me. I look over at Will and he glances at my shoes and smiles.

"What can I do for you, Kathy?" I ask, hoping she isn't planning to talk, hoping she can see what is happening here.

"It's a big day," she replies, turning to Will.

"Fifth grade," I note. "And it starts in about fifteen minutes."

She stands. "I'm sorry, I know you're in a rush but I just couldn't hold on to this any longer." And she reaches in her designer purse that Carl would recognize by the season and year and pulls out an envelope and hands it to me.

I look at it and then at her. "What is it?" I ask.

"Well, since you know that they found Captain Miller's plane, and they've decided there's no way he could have survived the crash, he has officially been declared dead."

I don't know what to say. This is news we had all heard last week when his Cessna was discovered about two hundred miles off the coast, and this is news that I don't think is a great way for Will to start school. I hold the envelope but keep watching her. I'm not sure how to move this conversation along.

"You should open that," she informs me.

I glance at Will, who has stood and put on his backpack.

I open the envelope, thick with papers, and pull them out. "It's a deed," I say, reading along.

"Yes," she replies. "To your and Will's property," she adds.

"What?" I keep reading, and I see that it is the deed for Dan's place on the golf course. He has left me his house.

"He apparently made more real estate deals this year than I did."

I look at her, stunned.

"He did all the paperwork in the spring, signed it over to you, but he told me not to share the news until after his death." She places her hand across her heart. "Of course, I didn't think it would be this soon. I just thought he was making his plans for . . . you know, later."

I nod. I turn to Will and back to Kathy. I am shaking my head.

"And then when he flew away, I wasn't sure what to do, so I asked Bernie and he told me that there had to be a death certificate first, and so . . ." She shrugs. "Now there is one and this is yours."

"We have a new house," I say to Will.

He is as surprised as I am.

"You have a beautiful house," Kathy agrees. "And I will be happy to help you get rid of this one."

I watch her as she glances around, noticing the flaws and particulars of this little house, watching as she works the numbers. "Of course, if you're happy here and you'd rather put Captain Miller's on the market and keep this one, I can handle that sale too."

I look at Will and then at all of his clothes stacked against the wall, his sheets rolled and thrown into the corner. I think about our one bathroom and how we don't have enough shelves for all our books and music, how the mattress on the sofa bed is about four inches thick, and I turn back to Kathy.

"We'll be out of here before the calendulas arrive," I say, grinning.

I see Kathy's confusion.

"Calendulas," Will chimes in. "The flower of the month," he explains. "She's saying we'll be in our new house by October."

·Fifty-Two·

W ELL, let's try the daisy tea," I tell him.

Justin has come over to the shop because Jenny is sick again. It's been a number of weeks that she's been nauseated, vomiting everything she eats. She's dizzy and very fatigued. I've already sent her violets and nasturtiums to ease her symptoms, but nothing seems to help and she's reluctant to go back to the doctor. Neither she nor Justin can stand to hear bad news.

I go over to my shelf of petals and seeds and take out a pack of daisy leaves. "Just put these in a strainer and pour boiling water over them. Let it steep a few minutes," I explain. "That's how they work best."

He looks at me and nods. He has tears in his eyes. "Maybe we should call that healer," he says.

"I think you should," I agree. "Do you know how to reach him?"

He nods. "He gave us his number in New Mexico before he left, but Jenny doesn't want to call him because she's worried she's done something wrong to bring the cancer back. She doesn't want to disappoint him."

"She didn't do anything wrong to bring the cancer back," I say, and he nods.

"I know," he replies. "But it's hard to convince her."

"Do you want me to call him?" I ask.

"I don't know, maybe," he says, and I decide to let it alone.

"Let's make her a bouquet too," I say cheerfully, thinking that maybe some pink gerberas will lift her spirits. "I'll put some more violets with them, to help with the dizziness."

I walk back to the cooler and grab what I have. I take the brightest standards, the boldest minis, and I find a few stems of deep rich purple violets, and as I fill my arms with flowers I realize I am as desperate as Justin. I cannot fix Jenny. I cannot put enough stems in a vase to wipe away the worries, the sorrow, the fear. I walk back to the design table and face him.

"She's been really good for so long," he says, as if he's been waiting for me to return so that he can say the things he needs to say.

I nod.

"It was a miracle she got better before," he adds.

"Then maybe there will be another miracle," I tell him. I place the flowers on the table and begin to arrange them. A stem of pink, a bunch of purple.

"But how many do you get?" he asks, and the question stumps me.

"I don't know."

"Isn't it selfish to ask for another one?"

I feel the heat in my fingers as I pull and place the flowers. All of my energy is pouring into the vase.

"Everyone asks for more than one," I say. "It's not selfish, it's just human."

I think about all that I have wished for, all I have wanted and needed, all of my prayers. I think about Daisy and Mama and Clementine and Will. I think about all the people lining up at my door hoping for a miracle, buying flowers, wanting to express what it is they cannot pray for. "We all ask for more than one," I say again.

He is silent as he watches me arrange the flowers.

"Is Will doing okay?" He changes the subject.

I smile. I am glad to talk about my son. "He's is doing very well. He's playing indoor soccer and is thinking about signing up for baseball in the spring. He likes his math teacher a lot and has decided that science is his favorite subject. In fact, he has already won a prize in the school's science fair." I stop what I'm doing and glance over at Justin. "He built the entire solar system and not one of those with painted Styrofoam balls."

Justin nods. He's seen the kind I'm talking about. I'm sure that everyone has.

"He used some computer program that I don't understand and used photographs and 3-D technology. I can already tell that I won't be able to help him with his homework by next semester."

"Yeah, he's a smart boy," Justin notes.

I add a few sprigs of bear grass, a strand of eucalyptus, and spin the vase around to make sure it's just right. I stop what I am doing and glance up. I look at Justin and it hits me.

"I don't think I ever thanked you for letting me adopt him," I say.

He drops his face, and suddenly I understand.

"It was harder on you and Jenny than you let on," I say, realizing now what I hadn't before.

He shrugs. "We could see he wanted to be with you."

"But you were both excited about having him."

He doesn't respond.

"I'm sorry, Justin." I reach over and touch his hand.

"We figured he'd be our first child and then we'd have a couple more."

I leave my hand there, on top of his, such a simple thing.

"We both wanted a house full of kids."

I think about what he's saying, the telling of a dream.

"She wanted two girls and two boys and I just wanted whoever came." He pulls his hand away from mine and runs his fingers through his hair, a nervous gesture. He glances over at the clock and then at the arrangement. "We both thought Will would help us get ready, you know, make a great older brother."

I nod. He's right; Will would make a terrific sibling. I look down at the flowers and the pink gerbera. The large standard is staring at me; it's as if it has something to say. I study its face, the fresh bloom, and suddenly I think of something I had never considered before.

There is an awkward pause and I feel Justin stand up from the stool where he was sitting.

"I guess I need to be going, Ms. Ruby," he says. He notices what I am doing. "Are you okay?"

I stare at the flower, its message quietly coming through.

"Justin, has Jenny seen anybody about her symptoms?" I ask. "Her regular doctor, a nurse practitioner, the pharmacist?"

He shakes his head slowly. "I think we've both been denying what's going on. We dread having to start all those appointments again. We've been hoping she just had a virus and that she'll get better."

"Tell me her symptoms again."

He lets out a long breath; it's a litany he doesn't want to repeat, but once more, for me, he does. "She wakes up sick every morning, feels like she's going to throw up. She's really tired all day, has to take a nap after lunch. She's nauseated, only wants to eat saltine crackers or potato chips. She made me go to the store for the vinegar ones, the saltiest ones they have."

He stops.

"She thinks salty things will make her feel better. It's like she craves them or something."

And his eyes light up. Just like that. The light comes on. He's having the same thought I just had, the one the pink gerbera gave me.

"Justin, I can't speak from any personal experience, but that sounds a lot like being pregnant."

There is a wild look in his eyes. "What should I do?"

"Well, first, breathe."

And he inhales.

"And then, I'd say you go to the drugstore and buy one of those pregnancy tests."

He closes his eyes and shakes his head.

"Breathe out," I tell him.

He exhales, opens his eyes.

He doesn't move.

I wait.

"The pharmacy is that way." I point to the right.

He is still shaking his head but manages to walk around the counter. He opens the door.

"Wait!" I hurry to his side. "Don't forget your jacket."

I walk over to the coat hook where he had hung his light coat. I hand it to him, and he puts it on and turns to leave.

"Oh, wait!"

He turns to me again.

"Don't forget these." I hand him the vase of flowers, but he stares down at them as if he doesn't know what to do with them, as if his hands can't wrap around them.

"Never mind," I tell him, taking back the magic flowers. "You can come get them later, like maybe when there's good news."

He stares at me, still in a state of shock.

"Go!" I say, and I watch him turn and run up the street.

·FIFTY-THREE·

"Poinsettias, poinsettias, poinsettias." Nora is looking over the orders called in over the last few days. She and Jimmy took a short trip to Seattle to celebrate their birthdays. She's come back to a pad full of holiday orders. "How did that plant get to be so popular?"

"Fleur de Bueno Noche," I say. "Flower of the Holy Night, also called the Christmas Stars; it's the celebrated plant of the season."

"Well, at least there's no arranging them, right?"

I smile. "Right. We just order the plants from Cooper and give them out as they come in."

"When is he coming, anyway?" she wants to know.

"He called about an hour ago. He's stopping at Valley to meet the new florist." I turn to Nora. "She's young," I say.

"Then we should expect him tomorrow," she adds, and we both laugh.

"What else you got going on?"

I think about the question. "There's the club Christmas party. Carl wants ilex and hypericum."

"Berries?" she asks. "Carl wants a room full of berries?"

"He's tired of blooms," I tell her and shrug. "It'll be nice."

"There's Jenny's baby shower December twenty-third."

"Pink or blue?" She eyes me as if I might know that too.

Everyone in town seems to think I had something to do with the pregnancy. The way Justin tells it, I knew it before anyone else and that I somehow made it happen.

"I don't know," I answer, but feel myself leaning in the direction of the delphiniums, most of which happen to be blue. I won't tell this for now and will mix in a few pink roses so as not to reveal my premonitions.

"Boy, what a year!" She sighs and takes a seat on the stool. Clementine yawns and I see her feet stretch out from under the table.

I stop making the arrangements for the nursing home holiday party and walk over and pour myself a cup of coffee. It's nice to have a break. I hold up the pot, offering it to Nora, but she waves it away. "It has been, hasn't it?" I shake my head and walk back to the table. "Accidents, adoptions, marriages, pregnancies . . ."

"Deaths," Nora adds, and I stop, remembering Dan and Juanita.

"Yes."

"Moves." She takes off her glasses and wipes them with the sleeve of her sweater. "You out of all your boxes?"

I nod. "Even have the decorations up."

"Well, aren't you the chipper house owner?" She puts her glasses on and places her hands on her knees.

"Just living my best life," I say, and I reach over and give her a big nudge, almost pushing her off her seat.

"I'll write Oprah and let her know," she says, retaining her balance.

"Please do," I reply.

"So has John stopped by?"

"I can't believe it. You actually made it an entire fifteen minutes without asking me about John Cash."

She grins. "Well?"

"He helped put up the tree," I answer.

And she claps.

I roll my eyes. "Why is it so important to you that I have romance?"

She stares at me like I've just said the most ridiculous thing she's ever heard. "You ask me a question like that?"

"Yes, I do."

"Ruby Jewell, you are the queen of romance. You're the Cupid of Creekside. You've been arranging relationships, putting couples together, stirring the pot, making the magic for everyone in this town as long as you've been sticking roses in a vase. Everybody here has been waiting for you to drink the Kool-Aid you've been handing out for twenty years."

I am stunned by her speech. I have never really noticed a disconnect from what I want for others and what I have wanted for myself. "Who says this?"

"Who says this?" she repeats. "Who *doesn't* say this?"

"Well, I don't believe you," I tell her.

"Fine. Let's call somebody and ask them." She walks over to the phone, picks it up, and dials a number.

I go over, take her seat, and watch.

"Madeline, it's Nora. Will you please tell me what you ask about Ruby every time we talk?" She hands me the phone.

"I ask you if Ruby's found love."

There is a pause.

"Nora? Nora? Are you still here?"

I hand her back the phone.

"Thanks, Madeline," and she hangs up and dials another number.

"Stan, it's Nora at the shop. Can you tell me what you said to me about Ruby the last time I saw you at the chiropractor's?" She holds the phone up so I can hear.

"Let's see." I recognize Stan's voice on the line. "I think I said that for somebody so artful at arranging the hearts of others, Ruby doesn't seem to have the same gift for herself."

I feel a little offended.

"Nora, are you there?"

There is a pause as she puts the phone to her ear. "Oh, it's fine, you didn't say anything she doesn't need to hear." And she tells him good-bye and hangs up.

She dials again. "Vivian, it's Nora. What do you think about the fact that Ruby is still single?"

She hands me the phone.

"Oh gosh, Nora, I don't think anything more than anybody else thinks about that."

And I am about to hand her the phone and tell her that she was wrong about that call when Vivian goes on. "Everybody thinks she's too busy worrying about romance for other people and not worried enough about romance for herself."

"Well, that's because it takes some of you so long to figure things out, I don't have time to think about myself," I say, and then hear the line go dead.

I keep the phone this time.

"Okay, so what?" I ask. "So what that people think I don't do enough for myself to have romance? I like spending my time helping love along for others. What's so wrong with that?"

"There's nothing wrong with it," she answers. "It's just that we all think it's time now for you."

I am about to respond by telling her all that I have to do, all the arrangements I have to make, the wristlets for the high school holiday party that need to be created by the weekend, the church socials that require decorations, the nursing home centerpiece, the berries for the club—but before I can start my litany, she asks the question I have refused to ask myself all of my life.

"What are you so afraid of?"

And suddenly, I think about Will and the thing he said to me months ago, the thing he said when we worried that Jenny wasn't going to make it.

"I am afraid that everyone I love will die."

The truth blossoms right in front of me.

And Nora walks to me, stands very close, reaches out, and holds my chin in her hand. She smells of lilac, Charles Joly, the double magenta variety that blooms early.

"Everyone is going to die," she tells me. "You can't stop that from happening whether you love them or not." She studies me. "What made you finally decide to adopt Will?"

I shrug. "I don't know," I answer.

"You opened your heart," she says. "You fought against the fear and you let your heart open. That's how you did it."

I lower my eyes.

"And you can do it again," she says. "Because now you see how good it feels, don't you? Wouldn't you do the same thing all over again even if Will dies today? Wouldn't you be glad that you had whatever time you had with him, your heart completely open, wouldn't you do it all over again?" She lets go of my chin, stepping away, and the smell of lilacs fades.

"I don't know," I repeat to myself. "I don't know if love can really overcome grief."

"Well, I do," she says confidently. She pauses, and I think she has said her piece.

But she has not.

"Do you remember when I was pulling out those porcupine quills from you after the accident?"

I nod slightly. Much of that night still feels like a fog, but I remember Nora leaning over me, yanking the tiny needles from my hands and chest.

"It was horrible and I kept thinking how much I must be hurting you. I almost couldn't do it but I pulled them, spine after spine, telling myself, *Ruby has quills all around her heart. There is a wall of spikes that must come down. I must find a way to get to her heart.*"

She glances away, shaking her head. "It was the only way I could do what was necessary, the only way I could keep doing what I was certain was hurting you. But then I began to think that what I was saying was more than just words to keep me pulling out the quills. I began to think it was true."

She has me now.

"I have known for a long time that you built a wall around yourself. I know what Daisy's death did to you, how it broke you, and how the only way you could survive was by closing yourself off to anything or anybody who scared you. That wall was thick and strong. I know that Dan Miller helped you crack it open and then Will walked in and blasted through it, and now it is time to let yourself love again, let yourself be wide open, risk it all."

I look away and face the front window.

"You just got it taken down," she says. "The wall around your heart, it just got taken down. Don't build it up again. Now is the time to love. Now."

I close my eyes and try to breathe. I try to let her words in. I try to see how it might be.

It is a long time before I open them and when I do, Nora is peering out the window. There is just a second as I try to understand what she is seeing and then she turns back to me and smiles; and it is clear. I take in the breath and release it, and as I do I watch as the winter sky collapses. It is as if all the stars are exploding. Everything bound is suddenly loosed. All around us, descending from heaven like petals of white roses, the first snow of the season is falling.

FIFTY-FOUR

R UBY, I can't believe I forgot again. Happy New Year, Clementine."

The wind chime on the front door sounds. Clementine raises
her head, yawns, and then settles back down; she is sleeping beneath
the table as I come around the corner. I am carrying a short clear
glass vase filled with a bouquet of roses, yellow ones from Lubbock,
a dozen of them surrounded by thin stems of baby's breath with a
few slender reeds of fresh eucalyptus and bear grass.

"They are spectacular," Stan Marcus says, shaking his head.
"Exactly what she likes. You are omnipotent."

"Stan, I am not omnipotent."

"That's right, I keep forgetting. You just have a great database."

I smile. "A computer," I tease him. "It's a computer. Maybe you
should think about getting one."

"Not as long as I have Marcy," he answers.

"And yellow pads," I add.

"Exactly."

"How many years?" I ask.

"Forty-seven," he answers. And then he grins. "You?"

"Not yet one," I say, putting the vase on the counter and holding up my left hand, still marveling at the ring that was placed there.

"It was a beautiful wedding," he tells me, and I am still smiling.

"It was, wasn't it?" And I cannot help myself; I lean back against the design table and sigh and remember the day last spring when we gathered once more for love in Henry's backyard, Nora running around trying to get people in their seats, Carl trying to make sure my dress is just right, Will and Clem walking me down the aisle, John and Dr. Buckley waiting for me. The yard wild and full of color, my hair and arms adorned with the mountain flowers Will had picked, the soft way everything bloomed.

"We'd been waiting for that day a long time."

And I am jolted back to the present moment.

"Yes, so I heard," I say.

"Will doing all right?"

"He's had a great holiday, learned to ski," I answer. "This is his last day before school starts. I think he and John may hit the slopes one more time."

"That's fabulous," Stan remarks.

"It is for him, not so much for me," I answer, recalling how worried I got every time I watched him standing at the top of the mountain, getting ready to come down.

"And your holidays?" I ask.

"Well, they were a little sad since this is the first Christmas without Mama, but they were okay," he says.

I watch the tears fill his eyes and remember the funeral late last summer. He had ordered a spray of red and pink roses, and a wreath to match, and he had asked for a small service to be held at the Lutheran church. There were a few green plants called in, bromeliads and a waterfall phale, a bouquet of tulips from his cousin in Oregon.

"Did you see the sky last night?" he asks, clearing his throat and changing the subject.

And I think about John and Will and me standing on the deck, Dan's super telescope pointed west, the stars blazing, the meteor shower dancing all around us, the larger planets bright and shining. "We did," I answer, and I start ringing up the sale.

"It was something else," Stan comments. "It was like fireworks, you know those ones with the white clusters of starbursts?"

"I do," I reply, thinking about how the sky lit up, Will yelling at us to make sure we didn't miss anything, the kiss John and I shared. Suddenly, I think of something else.

"Hey, did you know that Mozart's Symphony number forty-one is also called the Jupiter Symphony?"

I suddenly remember the night John told me that, Dan's music playing on the stereo, the same music that Dan played for me when I went to his house to see the planet for the first time. I had been so surprised about the nickname of the piece that I hadn't even noticed when John pulled out the small ring box from the front pocket of his jacket and knelt before me.

"What's wrong?" I had asked, thinking at first that he had fallen.

"Nothing's wrong," he told me, opening the box and looking up at me, so hopeful, so worried, so unbelievably perfect.

"I did not know that," Stan answers, not understanding why I would ask. "But I will keep that in mind the next time I am listening to classical music."

"Do you need a card?" I ask, returning to the things at hand.

"I have taken care of that," he says, and smiles.

"Yes, that's right," I say.

Stan still keeps a stack of greeting cards at his office. He reaches in his back pocket and takes out his wallet and hands me his credit card.

I take the same Visa I have taken for years, run it through the machine, and hand him his receipt.

He signs it and hands back the copy, picking up his credit card from the counter and putting it in his wallet again.

"So, see you in a couple of weeks?" I ask.

"January thirtieth," he says, remembering the exact date of her birthday. "She'll be sixty-seven," he reminds me.

"And she doesn't look a day over forty," I reply.

He grins, knowing that I am saying the thing he always does.

"I am a lucky man." And he takes the vase of flowers and heads to the door.

"We're all lucky," I say, and I see him as he throws up his hand to wave good-bye.

I watch him walk across the street to his office.

"It's true, isn't it?" I turn to Clementine, who doesn't bother to open her eyes, and I see the way her hair has changed from yellow to white around her face. I hadn't noticed before how much she's aged, and I reach down and give her a rub.

"You and I are the lucky ones, aren't we?" I ask her.

She opens her eyes and yawns.

"I'm glad you like Will and John," I tell her, thinking of how we sometimes all crawl into the bed, Will, John, and me under the covers, Clem at our feet, how we watch a movie, and eat popcorn, how easy things are with us all, how uncomplicated it all unfolded once I stopped being afraid, how gently I was pulled at my edges until everything loosened and fell open.

"The boys are great," I say to Clementine. "But of course we all know everything good started with you."

She stretches her legs, enjoying the praise. I scratch her back, her neck, and give her a gentle pat on her stomach. I stay that way for a few minutes, just spending a little time with my dog, loving her, thanking her.

When I stand up, John is at the counter and Will is at his side.

"How did you come in without ringing the chime?" I ask them, moving toward them.

John takes me by the hands. "We thought we'd surprise you," he says, and smiles.

"Well, that you did," I reply, leaning up to kiss him and to kiss my son. I pull away and stare at them both, noticing how my lungs fill and my heart expands. I breathe out a long, full breath.

"That you most certainly did."

·EPILOGUE·

WHEN she comes to me, she is not crazy or dead. She is young and beautiful and very much alive. She wears flowers in her hair, daisies, of course, white ones, "day's eyes," I tell her, the phrase from Old English, what they used to call the flowers because they opened to the sun and folded in on themselves at night. And she laughs at me, like she did when we were children.

"You know too much," she says, and to hear her again, to see her like this is more than I can bear.

"You are so perfect," I tell her, and she smiles and lets me look at her, just look at her, the way I have wanted for so long.

"You will be perfect, too," she says, and reaches for me.

I glance behind me and I see my son. He himself is old, but he is happy and he sits beside me with children around him, a wife at his side. He has flowers in his lap, yellow bells and goldeneyes, tiny trumpets and pink mountain heather, blooms he found on his hike to the lake.

Even after all he learned from Cooper and the summer classes he took at the community college on floral design, even after seeing acres of tulips in Seattle and vast stretches of roses in Portland, even after traveling to England and Japan to see some of the most beautiful gardens in the world, Will has always preferred the wild-flowers, always choosing to add fireweed and bitterroot, primrose and spotted knapweed to bouquets, anything he could find on his explorations in the mountains or along the desert floors; these are the blooms he is most passionate about.

Of course, John and I always thought Will would choose sci-ence for his field of study, that he might become a teacher or pro-fessor, maybe even follow Dan's dream and become an astronaut or astronomer. In the end, however, even though he stuck to science, he found that he loved botany and followed his heart to become a plant enthusiast, researching the medicinal qualities of flowers for years, traipsing around the world, studying seeds and blooms until he tired of the travel and then eventually returned to Creekside, taking over the shop.

He married Jenny and Justin's oldest daughter, Claire, the brainy one who worked with John, who went to college and studied the science of veterinary medicine and returned to her hometown to work with her mentor, the girl who had loved Will from the very beginning of her life.

And though it took years to unfold, years for it all to come together, it was like the two of them took over our lives, perfectly, symmetrically, magically, letting my husband and me enjoy each other and the little town we both loved.

I had a very good life.

I reach for my son and he takes my hands and I nod at him and smile, the way we sometimes do when the words are no longer necessary. And I see him understand what I am telling him and though I can tell it is not easy, he nods too, letting me know it is okay to go.

I lean back against my pillow and close my eyes and everything blooms. Daisy and John and Nora and Jimmy, everyone I love who has left me is present, a pack of friendly dogs who were my companions over the years, Clementine, of course, leading. Even Dan is here, not just in the form of stardust or planet matter; he is exactly as I remember him.

As I hold out my hands to join them, I feel it again, that gentle easy way I have learned of unfolding, the simple way I am pulled and released. It was slow to come to me, taking years to finally happen, but once I was shown, once I finally was shown, it happened again and again and again. Will and then John, Claire, and Jessie and Danny, my grandchildren.

"We become who we are meant to be because of the things along our edges that pull us into existence."

I recall the words Dan spoke to me before I knew to adopt Will, the way he explained to me the thing I should have known, the one lesson I should have been able to teach, how flowers bloom, how hearts open. But I hadn't known it until a boy stood outside my shop window, his sorrow even weightier than my own. Even though I had seen the flowers open and bloom, open and bloom, open and bloom, season after season, I did not fully understand the art of such a thing until there was Will.

I open my eyes and let go a breath and the next one I take in is sweet and fragrant, a garden of color and beauty, and not of this world.

I open myself for the final time.

I have, completely and at last, bloomed.

ACKNOWLEDGMENTS

This story is about learning to open your heart to love, and as I write these words I understand that my own heart is open only because of divine grace and the love and guidance of many wonderful teachers. I wish to acknowledge my loving parents, who set me on the right path, and my siblings, Sharon and Kerry, my earliest companions, for walking with me and showing me the way. I am grateful for exquisite friends, my beloveds, those of you who laugh with me, cry with me, wander and dance with me. How do you thank the ones who know and love you best?

Regarding this particular story, I owe a great deal of gratitude to the community of Chewelah, Washington, to the UCC church, and to the talented group known as the Creekside Writers. I am also grateful for the opportunity to have met astronaut Edgar Mitchell when a six-hour delay at the Albuquerque Airport turned into a holy conversation.

To Jackie Cantor and the warm, gracious team at Berkley Books, you have welcomed me and this story with such kindness and enthusiasm, I feel like I am in the company of cherished friends. Thank you, Jackie, for the sweet, easy way you have brought this story to light.

And finally, to my husband, Bob Branard, there is more of you here than just your name on this book's cover. You are the story. You are the beauty that saves me day after day. You are why I bloom. Thank you for this joyful and splendid life we share. I love you.

READERS GUIDE

THE ART
OF ARRANGING FLOWERS

BY

LYNNE BRANARD

DISCUSSION QUESTIONS

1. Regarding missing a flower delivery, Lucy says "that's just a mistake that cannot be forgiven." Why do flowers symbolize something so paramount that missing a delivery would be a disaster? What crucial roles do flowers play in relationships—both romantic and nonromantic—between people?

2. Ruby makes it clear that she has never been in a serious romantic relationship, though we hear undeniably erotic descriptions of plants as "stems of short, curved, tender blades," and "white with little narrow lips of purple." Do you think Ruby expresses her sensuality through her trade? Do you think her passion for flowers is a stand-in for other longings?

3. Nora and Jimmy are both alcoholics, and their relationship is rooted in the recovery process. How do Ruby and Dan forge a similar (platonic) bond, and what fuels that bond?

4. Jimmy tells Ruby that she has a reputation for "fixing hearts." And much later, Nora echoes that the whole town has expressed that sentiment. In "fixing" others' hearts, how might Ruby have neglected her own? Can empathy overextend into self-neglect?

5. Dan says that "When I was in space and saw the stars . . . I felt as if I were seeing something of myself . . . I felt as if I were somehow connected to these great beings." Have you ever felt that kind of ineffable connection that Dan describes? Was it with a person, or a place, or a thing—like Dan's stars?

6. Will says, "Sometimes I worry that everybody I love will die." Many of the characters are either at death's door or have suffered the tragic loss of a loved one. How do they find ways not to live in the constant fear that Will expresses?

7. What is the symbolic significance of Clementine's encounter with the porcupine and Ruby's interference—and subsequent injury? How is that a watershed moment in Ruby's life?

8. Ruby's and Will's lives are both wrought with tragedy. In the prologue, Ruby quotes Hemingway's famous assertion that we become "strong in the broken places." How is this both true and false? How do Will and Ruby reflect the truth in this, and where do they find their strength, or solace?

9. The title points to how serious and sacred a flower arrangement can in fact be. Do you think Ruby's flower arrangements function as characters in the novel? If so, at what crucial moments do they bring other characters together, and in what significant events do they play a part?

10. Barring the prologue and epilogue, the story begins and ends on Stan and Viola Marcus's anniversary. Ruby always has the same exchange with Stan: She remembers his anniversary, and he leaves her shop after stating that he is "the lucky one." Why did the

author choose to bookend the novel in this way? How is Stan's relationship with his wife emblematic of what marriage means?

11. Were you surprised that Ruby changed her mind and decided to adopt Will? Did you think it was a wise or unwise choice? How might the story have been vastly different if Jenny and Justin had adopted Will?

12. Why do you think the author chose to include an epilogue on the day of Ruby's death? What role does death play in the book that makes it a fitting ending?

13. During the conversation with Dan about whether or not Ruby will adopt Will, Dan explains the mechanics of how flowers bloom. "It turns out that the instabilities that shape roots and blossoms often come about when certain cells become longer than others. The rapid growth causes strain, which bends the soft tissues. . . ." What is he really telling Ruby? How does the "biology of blooming" manifest itself in her life?

14. Ruby is near paralyzed by her sister Daisy's death, until she finds herself "pulled out of bed" at the sight of the flora just outside the window. How does the art of arranging flowers take the place of Daisy in Ruby's life? How might Ruby's life have been different if her sister had not died?

15. The Greeks had four words for love: *eros*, *agape*, *philia*, and *storge* (in short: romantic love, spiritual love, friendship, and familial love). How do we see these different types of love manifested in Creekside?

DAMAGED